Octavius Frothingham

The Safest Creed and Twelve Other Recent Discourses of Reason

Octavius Frothingham

The Safest Creed and Twelve Other Recent Discourses of Reason

Reprint of the original, first published in 1874.

1st Edition 2024 | ISBN: 978-3-36884-687-9

Verlag (Publisher): Outlook Verlag GmbH, Zeilweg 44, 60439 Frankfurt, Deutschland
Vertretungsberechtigt (Authorized to represent): E. Roepke, Zeilweg 44, 60439 Frankfurt, Deutschland
Druck (Print): Books on Demand GmbH, In de Tarpen 42, 22848 Norderstedt, Deutschland

THE

SAFEST CREED

AND

TWELVE OTHER RECENT

DISCOURSES OF REASON.

BY

OCTAVIUS B. FROTHINGHAM.

NEW YORK:

ASA K. BUTTS & CO., PUBLISHERS,

36 DEY STREET.

1874.

LANGE, LITTLE & CO.,
PRINTERS, ELECTROTYPERS AND STEREOTYPERS,
108 TO 114 WOOSTER STREET, N. Y.

TABLE OF CONTENTS.

I.

THE SAFEST CREED.

THE great word in the doctrinal part of the New Testament is Salvation. The great word of the Protestant theology is Salvation. Salvation is Safety. Safety is health. "Safe and sound," we say; that is sound which is safe; that is safe which is sound. Health consists in the proper adjustment of the creature to his conditions. Health of body consists in this; it is a perfect understanding between the body and its material surroundings, climate, temperature, food, occupations. The physical constitution is safe when no inherited disease undermines its vitality and exposes it to hidden assault from within the citadel, and when no ill-adjustment of circumstances threatens it with malady.

The safety of the mind consists in a harmonious relation with the intellectual world, which assures to it a healthful, happy activity, undisturbed by tormenting doubt or disabling fear, uncramped by prejudices that limit inquiry, or bigotries that prevent culture. The safety of the heart consists in the fortunate direction and felicitous play of its natural affections. In what does the safety of the soul consist, if not in its sense of security in the world of Providence, its trust in the Eternal?

The safe creed is the desirable one, as all will acknowledge. Salvation under some form is what all demand of their faith. Smile as we will at the absurdity of the statement, to the multitude there is great force in the argument as put by the "evangelical" to the rationalist,

thus: "Whether you be right or not, I, at all events, am
on the safe side. If I am wrong in my belief, no harm
can befall me in consequence ; all that the unbeliever has
is mine. But if *you* are wrong, your soul is in peril.
No penalty is attached to the rejection of your creed;
the rejection of mine brings the penalty of everlasting
damnation."

Salvation is commonly associated with a future state;
if it were not, it would possess no religious significance.
The safety sought is safety after death, not before. The
creed is a policy of insurance against fire hereafter, the
fire being certain, and the validity of the policy being
guaranteed by the Lord of the Universe himself. If this
were so, if these two grand assumptions could be maintained, all debate would be at an end. But this is the
very matter in controversy. If we knew anything about
this hell, its reality, its place, its nature ; if we had reason
to believe that it was a strange, unprecedented, uncon-
jecturable condition, the laws whereof had no relation to
the laws of our terrestrial sphere—a condition in which,
for example, people walked on their heads, ate with their
ears, thought with their stomachs, worshiped with their
collar bones, or by any other arrangement reversed the
rules we are guided by in our present life; if, in a word,
salvation, safety, or health, there, meant something very
different from what we have in mind when we speak of
safety or health—we might listen to the theologian, and
take his prescription. But seeing that nobody knows
anything about hell, not even whether there be such a
place ; seeing that the future after death is all an uncertainty, whereof we have no definite account ; seeing that,
in all our experience, to-day is the child of yesterday and
the parent of to-morrow, and therefore the future, how-

ever long, must be the result of the present, the next life of this life, and the hereafter of the here—it may fairly be assumed that salvation must be the same thing in either state; what is safety in the one will be safety in the other; sanity will everywhere be sanity, and health will everywhere be health. No person can be lost hereafter who is saved now. The healthy soul can have no fear of perdition. This is what Father Taylor had in mind when he made the oft-quoted remark touching Mr. Emerson, " He cannot go to heaven, for he is no Christian; but what would they do with him in hell? He would change the climate; he would turn the tide of emigration that way."

It follows, then, that the present is our only concern. The safest creed is that which gives the best guarantee of mental security under actual circumstances. What this is it may be difficult in detail to say; it would be rash to undertake even in general terms to describe it; for the laws of health are not laid down finally in regard to the body; much less can they be laid down for the mind. We are in the stage of experiment here; all is crude, almost chaotic. The rational method has not, as yet, been applied to the problem; the wisest men are students; the most experienced are seekers. I have no mind to be dogmatic, and am more disposed to consider the general elements of safety and of peril than to declare the rules for entering the one, or avoiding the other. But if safety consists in the natural and harmonious adjustment of the mind to its surroundings, certain positions may be taken with a good deal of confidence.

There is small risk in declaring, for instance, that no creed is safe that has insecure foundations; for the removal of the foundations will endanger the creed, though it be of the noblest and most beautiful. St. Peter's itself would fall were its supports to give way; neither the grandeur of its dome, nor the loveliness of its decorations, nor the richness of its shrines, would save it. The mightiest mind crumbles under the influence of inherited disease.

Now the creed of Christendom does rest on insecure foundations.

One of these is PROPHECY. From first to last, believers have been disposed to rest their faith on this argument, that the Old Testament prefigures the New, that the prophets foretold the Christ. Instances are brought to prove that ages before Jesus appeared, his coming, his character, even the main incidents of his career, particularly his miraculous birth and his tragic death, were predicted; it is asserted that no effort of human reason would have availed to lift this heavy curtain of the future, that it must have been miraculously withdrawn; and it is claimed that the correspondence between the prophecy and the result is perfect, and, this being the case, nothing remains but to accept the system thus authenticated.

But nothing is more certain than that this proof of prophecy has given way, utterly. Scholarship has undermined it; criticism has thrown it down. Discredit has been brought upon every process of the argument. The correspondence between the event and the prediction is denied; the very fact of the prediction is called in question. When tried by historical and literary tests, the whole claim fails to justify itself. This fact has not been extensively divulged as yet; the news has not been widely spread; the intelligence is confined to the comparatively small company of the investigators, and those interested in the investigation. But to these it is familiar knowledge; and they are beginning to communicate it by conversation and writing. Before very long the tidings will be generally made known; and then what is likely to happen? The faith of many will be shaken. Belief will be succeeded by unbelief, confidence by suspicion, trust by despair. The disease of suspicion will seize on the common mind; reason will not be listened to; the heart will refuse to be comforted; souls will feel that they have lost their hold on the eternal wisdom. Such has been the history of multitudes already, and such is destined to be the history of multitudes more.

Another proof is MIRACLE; and this is one of the strongest. But this, like the other, has fallen, though the noise of the ruin has not yet startled the inattentive ear. Not only has each separate miracle been analyzed and resolved into natural elements, the principle that lies at the ground of all miraculous belief, the principle of suspended law, is, by the foremost thinkers and writers of the age, repudiated. The distinction between the Bible miracles and other legends has been obliterated; all stories of miracle have been brought under one general classification; the causes of the growth of legends have been investigated; the conditions of belief in prodigies have been examined; the natural history, so to speak, of marvel has been studied so carefully that for every specimen a place has been found, and a name invented. And the result of it all is that the argument from miracle is pronounced worthless.

The discovery has proved most disastrous to those who made miracle—miracles in general, or special miracles in particular—the corner-stone of their belief. Some have dropped into atheism and materialism. Consider, for example, the melancholy case of those who

1*

build their belief in an infinite mind on the fact of miracle. There are some who do this. There are some who declare that their only escape from the creed of Fatalism is through the persuasion that Elijah called down fire from heaven, or that Jesus came into the world differently from other mortals, or that at his command Lazarus came forth alive from the grave in which he had lain four days, or that he himself on the third day from his crucifixion rose from the dead and appeared visibly and palpably to his friends. Facts like these, they say, testify to the existence of a God superior to Nature; and if such facts are denied, the existence of a God superior to Nature falls into disrepute; so vanish all the hopes and faiths, the aspirations and the consolations, that accompany the sublime creed of the Theist.

But these facts are denied, and are likely to be called in question more and more widely, and more and more roughly. The set of the human intellect is against them, and will be more and more against them. The thinking people are incredulous, and the thinking people are increasing in numbers daily. Men are feeling, and are living as though they felt, that the world they live in is a world of law. The material universe proclaims law in every part of its domain : the stars in their faithful courses, the sun in its rising and going down, the seasons in their beauteous alternation, the plants in their growth, animals in their development—all attest the rule of law. In their practical existence men assume law; the conduct of life presupposes it; business is grounded on it; enterprise rests on it; all social arrangements take it for granted; calculations, statistics, combinations of all kinds, demand it. The numberless insurance offices rest on law. This practical assumption, which is fixed and

unlimited in secular affairs, has not yet, to any very manifest extent, touched the domain of religious credence ;
but it will reach it soon; it is hastening that way, and
when it sweeps over this field as it already sweeps over
the field of practical existence, they who trusted in miracle will be made desolate. Safety demands the instant
removal of all spiritual treasures from such exposed precincts. The building totters. Happy they who have
nothing they prize there!

The case is still sadder when the heart is touched.
How shall we describe the rashness of people who build
their faith in immortality on the resurrection of Jesus,
hanging all their hopes of a hereafter on a cord of tradition two thousand years long, attached at one end to a
fragment of literature at which a hundred sharp-toothed
critics are nibbling ; snapping all tethers beside, casting
off as useless the stays which the soul offers, rejecting
with scorn the helps which the heart throws out, disdain-
ing to touch the lines stretched by history and philosophy, and suspending the full weight of the future world
on a thread which runs across deserts and beneath oceans,
and is exposed to the incessant friction of mind all along
its course ! Can any but madmen take such risk ? The
cord snaps, and the faith is gone; the ship of the soul
drifts away into the inane ; darkness gathers about the
drifting spirits ; the vessel, freighted with the heart's
most precious treasures of hope, drives away into the
darkness and never is seen more. To confound the supports of a faith with the faith itself, to make the foundations part of the faith, is the height of unwisdom. The
early Christians accounted for the fact that there were
four gospels, and no more, by analogy with two other
facts: one that there were four main divisions of the

earth, the other that the four winds blew from four points of the compass. The argument was satisfactory to them in the condition of their knowledge of geography; but if they had made their geography a constituent part of their faith, what would have become of the gospel records by this time? A Greek proverb says that God hangs the heaviest weights on the smallest wires. But he always makes sure that the wires are strong enough to sustain the weights. It is not quite safe for men to try the experiment. Their wisdom rather consists in a very exact adjustment of wires to weights. A wise saying warns people against trusting all their eggs to one basket. When our ships put to sea, they provide boats in case of shipwreck; they take extra bolts, chains and tackle, against the exigency of disaster to the machinery. If one anchor or cable gives way, the ship need not be lost. Would we expose the mind to risks we carefully guard the person from?

Protestanism grounds its faith on the Scriptures. " The Bible, and the Bible only, is the religion of Protestants." If the Bible were another name for the Rock of Ages, no piece of literature subject to literary laws and literary criticism, but a monument of the divine intelligence, a fragment of intellectual adamant, on which Time can only break his teeth, and the storms of a thousand centuries make no impression, this foundation would be safe, and to build on it would be wise. But we all know that the Bible is nothing of this kind; that it is a book, the product of human intelligence, written in human speech, marked all over with traces of human speculation. We all know that it holds its place in the line of mental development; that it belongs to the literature of a race, to the literature of a single race. We know that the scholarship of the last two hundred years has made havoc with the doctrine of its infallible inspiration, and effectually destroyed its claim to be considered a miraculous volume.

Is it safe, then, to stake the highest moral and spiritual interests of man, the faith in God, the faith in humanity, the faith in the moral law, the faith in providence, the faith in the soul's future, on anything so precarious as a single collection of documents? to stake these vast concerns, we may say, on the interpretation of a chapter or the rendering of a text, on the reading of a commentator, the conjecture of a philologist, the decision of a new grammar or dictionary? a faith that a Gesenius or a Max Müller may undermine, that a Strauss or a Renan may sap; is that a faith for men to put their trust in? That thousands do put their trust in it is all too plain, and the sorrow that comes of it, the unbelief and despair, when the proof they deemed immovable is shaken, testify to the folly of their proceeding. The assaults on the Bible have been taken as assaults on religion, and religion has crumbled when the Bible has given way under attack. The snapping of that single-stranded cord has put in jeopardy the whole celestial freight.

The Romanist exults in the catastrophe. It is just what I predicted, he says, it could not be otherwise. "The Bible is a book; if you allow people to read it for themselves, they will read it variously; in the multitude of interpretations the sense will be lost, controversies will arise, sects will spring up from the controversies; the unity of the faith will be broken, the harmony of the spirit will be destroyed, the authority of the Word will be lost, the assurance of the soul's destiny will be taken away, and skepticism, unbelief, rationalism, materialism, atheism, will come in like a flood. Experience proves the truth of the prophecy. Under Protestantism, Christianity is running out ; religion itself is perishing ; it has come to its last term, the next step will be into utter atheism."

"The only safety," the Romanist goes on to say, "is the Church that never changes ; that is the same yesterday, to-day and forever ; that is, indeed, founded on a rock ; older than the New Testament, resting on apostles and evangelists, Jesus Christ himself being the chief cornerstone, it is unassailable by the forces of the enemy. The gates of hell shall not prevail against it." But have there been no departures from the Church? Does the Church really stand the test of criticism ? Is there no such thing as history ? and does history justify the churchman's claim of divine authority for his institution ? Is the Church purely and demonstrably the work of Divine Providence? Have human wit and witlessness, human will and willfulness, had no part in its creation ? Does its story, from beginning to end, justify its title to rule over the consciences, and prescribe the faith, and lead the hopes of mankind ? Has it never been a story of diplomacy savoring of cunning, of authority asserting itself as despotism and making itself chargeable with bloody crimes, of privilege to teach used for the purpose of fastening on the minds of men dogmas like that of the Immaculate Conception of the Virgin Mary, and the infallibility of the Vicar of Christ ?

The Church has not proved to be a safe refuge. The desertions from it on account of its well-known unseaworthiness, have been by the hundred thousand, and it is a remarkable circumstance that, of those that have abandoned it, a great multitude have lapsed into utter irreligion. Everything goes down with that one bark. Look at the condition of Italy ; look at the condition of Spain; both countries where Romanism has been supreme, both countries in which Romanism has been identified with religion. The type of disbelief in these two lands is of the most stubborn and deadly kind. The religious sentiment seems well-nigh dead there. Atheism, in the dreariest form, abounds ; materialism, of the most literal and prosaic description, is common ; the interest in what we call spiritual, that is, in ideal things, has so far declined as to be regarded with pity and even with ridicule, as the remnant of an outgrown superstition. The world has lost its poetic aspect, life has lost its poetical expression. The sensual element is getting the upper hand; politics are all engrossing, and the tone of politics is low.

The Romanist admits all this, and cries : "See the effect of leaving the Church ! See what comes of abandoning the only ark of safety !" Yes, but the evil happens because the people were taught that the Church was the *only* ark of safety ; and when they left it, as they needs must, it having become impossible for them to remain in it longer as honest people, there was no alternative but drowning. They had no lifeboats, and had never learned to swim or float in the open sea.

No creed is safe that rests on a single foundation, however ancient and imposing. The moment comes when the swiftly flowing river of time loosens the corner-stone, and then the whirling travelers are plunged into an abyss. The safety of rationalism consists in its ability to use all supports and adapt itself to all emergencies ; its hands are free, it is foot-loose ; it has full possession of its powers, and full command of the field for their exercise. It is never without resources, it cannot be re-

duced to extremity; it cannot be driven into a corner.
If one reliance gives way, it has a dozen to fall back on;
if one argument fails, it shifts its position to another. It
has trenches within trenches, lines within lines, walls behind walls. Take away the Old Testament, it has the
New; take away the Bible, it has the sacred writings of
other races; invalidate these, it has the religious sentiment to which all Scriptures give expression; throw
doubt on the religious sentiment, it has recourse to the
facts of human experience, as revealed by the history of
nations, and the result of individual lives; it appeals to
the long line of tradition common to the race of man—
traditions of worship and faith, of moral obedience and
fidelity, of sweetest trust and sublimest anticipation; call
these in question, it takes up the method of science,
and shows how divine things are wrought into the very
texture of the material world; does the scientific man
protest against the use made of his apparatus, rationalism retreats to the stronghold of philosophy from which
it cannot be dislodged.

The rationalist fears nothing. " If his bark sink, 'tis
to another sea," whose waters are more tranquil, whose
gales are less violent, whose shores are not rough with
reefs that menace the mariner with destruction. So far
as ports of refuge are concerned, his is the safest creed.

I contend that it is the safest, too, from its own constitution. It has no articles that are put in jeopardy by
the action of human nature in its normal movements.
It teaches no dogmas that are at variance with the established laws of reason. Its God is not a larger man,
with human limitations and infirmities, subject to emotions as we are, a mechanician, a contriver, a person
conducting the affairs of the universe by methods of di-

plomacy, resorting to expedients, altering and suspending his own laws, repairing his own handiwork, showing partiality in his treatment of his children, granting to some the fullness of light and leaving others in total darkness, electing special tribes and individuals to glory and dooming others to perdition. Rationalism regards God as truly the Infinite and Eternal, and interprets him by the largest constructions that the human mind can put on his works, stripping off whatever is offensive to the finest intelligence and winning thought to the conception of him instead of repelling it, thus making human reason its friend.

It does not deify an individual; it does not vilify the race; it casts no aspersion on the natural faculties, but puts itself as cordially as possible in communication with the wisest, the profoundest, the most sagacious of earth's thinkers. There is no danger, therefore, that the march of mind will sweep it out of the way or leave it behind in the distance. It has not to defend itself against history, science, or philosophy; they are its defenders. The single circumstance of its being unwilling to commit itself to any single statement or definition, its willingness to shape and reshape its formulas in accordance with the growing intelligence of the race, its creedlessness, in other words, is a great safeguard. Its confidence in the spirit of truth is worth a thousand confidences in separate opinions, for the spirit of truth drops its forms as fast as they become useless or obsolete, and leaves on all the bushes by the wayside the cast-off skins of its creeds.

Nearly every dogma of theology—it is safe to say every dogma of the popular theology—stands to-day on the defensive against the prevailing reason of the age. Trinity, Deity of Christ, Atonement, Election, Justification, Hell and Heaven, all are in this painful category. The first principles of revealed religion are challenged. They who hold them are in danger of defeat, and defeat, in hundreds of cases, implies, the loss of everything dear to the religious mind. Surely that is the safest creed which can venture to cast off its armor, and throw its weapons down, and consort peacefully with thoughtful people, and feel secure in the honest sympathy of earnest, liberal men.

But rationalism has a stronger guarantee of safety yet, in that it puts itself in friendliest relations with the human heart. Here, indeed, is a fortress from which it cannot be dislodged. Its idea of the essential rectitude of human nature propitiates the instinctive feelings of all men; its faith in progress commends itself to the earnest approval of all who cherish noble hopes for their kind; its faith in the vital unity of mankind comes home to all philanthropists and reformers, to all industrial and other workers at the social problems that exercise the mind of the generation; its faith in the past authenticates every grand character and sanctifies every glorious memory; its faith in the present is stimulating to every fine purpose; its faith in the future encourages every far-seeing anticipation; its faith in the long future, in the hereafter, enlists the sympathies of those who live in their dreams of affection. Rationalism, in fact, deserves more than any other to be called the religion of the heart, because it legitimates most completely the heart's vital desires.

Can this be claimed for the faith of Christendom? Can it be claimed for the doctrine of human inability? Can it be claimed for the doctrine of regeneration? Can it be claimed for the doctrine of immortality, which limits the boon to Christian believers, and even to the comparatively small class of Christian believers who have experienced the supernatural change which entitles them to the blessedness of the redeemed, the rest being cast into the outer darkness, where the wailing and gnashing of teeth is incessant, where the worm dieth not, and the fire is not quenched?

The popular doctrine of the hereafter cannot be abandoned by those who hold the other points of the "evangelical" creed, for it supposes them all. It is to effect the rescue of the entire human family from hell that the scheme of salvation was devised; and if the hell is abolished, or reduced in compass, or mitigated in character, if it is altered in any respect, the scheme of salvation is unnecessary; the atonement is needless, the incarnation loses its purpose; the Church, as an institution, has no reason for being. Therefore the great preachers of "evangelical" religion cleave to the doctrine in all its original features. They stir up the flames, re-animate the demons, and proclaim the destiny of everlasting fire to the unbelievers. In so doing they are consistent and logical. They cannot do otherwise and maintain their position.

But they have the human heart against them. All deeply feeling men and women struggle, writhe, and, if they do not rebel, bleed. That the heart of man consents to entertain the belief in a hereafter under such conditions, and with such an understanding, is a mystery. Does it? Does not the heart's steady, firm, unanimous protest operate as the most stubborn and formidable foe to the extension of the whole "evangelical" faith? It is hard to overcome the resistance of reason to doctrines that seem inconsistent with the first principles of thought; but to overcome the opposition of the natural affections to doctrines that outrage natural feeling is more than all churches and preachers can do. For my part, I do not hesitate to say, nor should I think that any reasonable man would hesitate to say, that he would be a benefactor of his race who would deliver people from the popular doctrine of the hereafter, even at the expense of denying any hereafter. If immortality is to be a helpless and unmitigated curse to anybody, then annihilation would be a boon to all. So says the heart, instructed in the humanities by the worthiest teachers. The heart of man would prefer to have no future if it is not promised a future which it can load with hope. To the heart, the future means hope; it is the land of hope. We may fashion the form of the hope to suit our own anticipation, desire, or longing, but hope it must be still. A hopeless future is something inconceivable. They who despair of the hereafter make despair a kind of hope; they enjoy a "luxury of woe." But they who live on that luxury probably look no further than annihilation. The luxury of endless burning, either for himself or his friends, it may safely be assumed that no mortal ever dwelt on in fancy.

No creed is safe that places itself in antagonism to the natural human heart. Sooner or later it must go down. The heart will triumph; and it will triumph by either converting the creed or destroying it. In this case, conversion is destruction. To abolish hell is to reconstruct the spiritual universe; and this is the work that is going on.

It is often said of rationalists that they are "all out at sea." It is true, they are, and they rejoice in being so. Out on the wide ocean of truth they are safe. There they have the benefit of all the winds that blow, and room enough; no sunken rocks threaten; no fog-covered reef endangers; above them is the whole canopy of the heavens. The navigator dreads the coast. He keeps off shore in a storm. Few ships are lost in the open sea. The coast line has the perils.

The rationalist dreads definitions, doubles the watch when approaching land, and looks out for breakers. He is on the voyage. His ship is built for the ocean, not for the dock, and out on the ocean he is at home. Arrival is necessary, no ship is always at sea, but arrival is incidental and occasional. He touches port that he may put out to sea again, and be in company with Him, " Whose being is a great deep.".

II.

THE RADICAL BELIEF.

Having the same Spirit of Faith, in which one said, "I believed and therefore spoke," we also believe and therefore speak.—2 Cor. iv, 13.

THESE are words of Paul, the one doubted, suspected, persecuted apostle; the outsider who came inside on grounds against which many protested; the insider who carried outside a faith which many repudiated; the man who announced the gospel of the spirit and preached justification by faith alone, and at the same time declared that he worshiped the God of his fathers, "after the manner called heresy." He believed and therefore spoke. If he had not believed, he would not have spoken, for he would have had nothing to say. All earnest speech is uttered in faith. In faith all good work is done. Unbelief has no gospel, makes no confession, frames no creed, organizes no worship, brings no sacrifice. If men deem it worth their while to preach, will do the amount of studying and thinking that qualifies them for it, are prepared for the many difficulties, discouragements, rebuffs, misunderstandings, misrepresentations, and humiliations that attend it, show themselves ready to submit to the disabilities and sacrifices that so thankless an office entails, it is to be presumed that they have something to say that is very dear to them, and is, in their judgment, very important to their neighbors. If they seem to be deniers, they only seem so in the eyes of those who fail to recognize the affirmation their denial contains.

It is conceded that every affirmation holds a denial in its bosom. Whoever says " Yes," at the same time says " No." To announce a belief is to announce, though silently, an unbelief in something the belief excludes. To make a declaration of faith is to repudiate some opposing declaration which somebody else has put forth. The believer in Moses and the prophets tacitly rejects the traditions of Egypt; the believer in the Christ by that act renounces the anti-Christ; to affirm God is to discard atheism ; to affirm the soul is to put materialism away ; to affirm immortality is to disclaim the doctrine of annihilation. This being conceded, why should it not also be conceded that every denial holds in its bosom an affirmation ? Does not every one who says " No," at the same time say " Yes ? " To declare against a belief, may it not be to announce, though silently, a belief which the discarded article could not hold ? To repudiate a well-known declaration of faith, may it not be to prepare the way for, may it not be to shadow forth, another declaration larger and clearer ? To put aside Moses and the prophets may imply a putting forward of the Christ. To deny the Christ may be an affirmation of Jesus. To place in the background the historical Jesus may be to bring the spiritual Jesus into the foreground. He who says " No " to the Trinity says " Yes " to the Unity. He who disavows hell avows heaven. He pulls down as a preparation for building, and, before he begins to pull down, the plans of the new building lie already finished on his table. Every earnest teacher has his positive aim, and his positive aim is his real aim. He denies in the interest of truth. He destroys in the interest of conservation. He believes and therefore speaks.

I should not urge so simple a thought as this if it were
not of very vital consequence. Until it is seen that denial
implies belief as truly as belief implies denial, no discussion in regard to belief and denial can go on. And in
order that this may be seen, the popular modes of thinking must undergo a change. At present the largest
creeds seem to be the most negative, the broadest beliefs
the most unbelieving, the deepest affirmations the most
abrupt denials. Not he that believes *least* is the infidel,
but he that believes *most*. The most spiritual view of
Christianity is regarded as a rejection of Christianity. To
believe in too much God is held to be equivalent to believing in none. The atheist, according to the vulgar prejudice, is the man who proclaims a living God! A Conservative said lately to a Radical: " You believe so much
that you believe nothing."

We need not go far to seek the explanation of this singular paradox. For a couple of thousand years Christendom
has been in the habit of associating belief with a certain
historical tradition. He only was recognized as a builder
who piled his material on the foundations laid by the
Church, Jesus Christ being the chief corner-stone. To
reject this was to reject everything. To believe anything
else than this, anything aside from this, anything other,
anything more; to believe, however comprehensively,
earnestly, deeply, vitally, was to believe nothing, was, in
fact, utter unbelief. So long as this prejudice lasts—for a
prejudice I must call it—no justice will ever be rendered
to liberal believers. They will always be misapprehended.
Their affirmations will go for nothing. Their belief will
be called skepticism, and infidelity will be the kindest
name given to their faith. As that prejudice declines and
passes away, as it is rapidly doing under the influence of
intelligence, the doubters, provers, deniers come to their

rights, and the beliefs of the unbelievers are recognized as being what they are.

Questions of belief and unbelief continue to intensely interest mankind. They are more fascinating than any questions of practice which seem to be of greater moment. Where these latter attract a few scores of people, the former attract thousands. The chief event of interest in our small circle during the last week was the conference of Unitarian and other Christian churches, and the most attractive feature in the conference was the discussion between the conservative and the radical parties on the common ground of Christian faith. The matter was quite incidental. It was almost irrelevant. The churches came together not to debate theological issues, but to arrange plans for practical work. There were many things to be considered : the occupation of new fields, the organization of societies, the building of churches, the endowment of schools, the maintenance of colleges, the printing of books, the support of missionaries, the reform of social abuses, the removal of social evils, the rescue of the imperiled, the relief of the perishing, the saving of the lost ; but none of these great practical concerns secured the attention, enlisted the feeling, stirred the emotions, as did this apparently unprofitable talking. Crowds flocked to it, precious hours were devoted to it ; the greater number of the delegates and attendants evidently felt that it involved the most momentous issues that were presented. Let us hope that this feeling deserves a better name than curiosity to hear spasmodic eloquence, or delight in witnessing a gladiatorial encounter, or the idle and unprincipled enjoyment of seeing one party or another beaten by a vote. Deeper than all this, though this was most frequently avowed, was, I doubt not, the persuasion that beneath all practice lay belief ; that belief was the basis of noble action of whatever kind; that only as men believed would they speak; that only as men believed would they work; that the question of belief being unanswered, other questions must wait; that the question of belief being answered, other questions would instantly answer themselves.

At all events, whatever the feeling of the participants of the conference, this is the universal persuasion, that life is grounded in faith; that a faithless life must be a foolish one; that a positive faith must declare itself in deeds. The Romanist tries to prove that Protestantism demoralizes, disintegrates, and subverts society. The Protestant argues that Unitarianism necessarily results in anarchy. The Unitarian charges on the liberal doctrine a tendency to unsettle the foundations of morality, and each believer, in turn, while thus discrediting the moral bearings of his neighbor's opinions, claims that the best results will flow from his own. His claim may be unsupported, but he would be stultified if he did not make it.

Of the proceedings of that conference it is not my purpose now to speak. I declined being officially present, though fully entitled to be on every ground, because I knew that the two parties were not and could not be in sympathy, and because, with that knowledge, it seemed better for the party that was in the minority to withdraw. I would not thrust myself in where I was not wanted, and I would not embarrass those who had a work of their own to do in which it was not possible for me to join. There were vital principles enough to serve as a basis for a cordial union in faith and work. Intelligent, educated, experienced men and women, who know, respect, honor, and confide in one another; who agree in all their moral and spiritual ideas; who share with one another the conviction that character, not opinion, insures felicity; who are of one mind as regards the elements of character and

the means of obtaining it; who have the same standards
of private and public virtue, the same views regarding the
constitution and well-being of society, the same convictions touching the laws and conditions of a perfect social
state; men and women who cherish the same moral and
spiritual conceptions of God, the same moral and spiritual
conceptions of Jesus, the same confidence in the ultimate
destination of man, the same trust in Providence, the same
visions of eternity, the same assurance of the divine Fath-
erhood, the same yearning after a brotherhood of men,
certainly ought to be able to assemble peacefully and work
harmoniously, leaving theological questions in entire abey-
ance. But if they will not do this, if they will insist on
making speculative opinions the ground of fellowship,
then should either party do its best to make known what
its speculative opinions are, not shading them away at the
edges, but sharply defining them at the centre, going to
the roots of faith, and not fanning the air with its branches, or tickling the sense with the odor of its blossoms.
Honor requires frankness, and if frankness leads to part-
ing, then let the party be in certainty that thus to part is
wiser than a fair-spoken but ungenuine meeting.

As one of the Radicals I am here this morning to state,
not by any means all the details (that would be an inter-
minable task), but the fundamental principles of the faith
in whose interest and in whose inspiration I speak; for,
after what has been said, our claim to have a faith must be
acknowledged. That this faith is, to a certain extent,
undefinable as yet, and is, to a still greater extent, unde-
fined, is no objection to its reality or its positiveness. A
great deal of time is required to define a faith. The creed
of Christendom has been undergoing definitions for two
thousand years, and the full statement is not made. It is
but a short time since the Pope added a new article, that

of the Virgin's Immaculate Conception, to the faith of the Roman Church. The Protestant theologians in Germany, England, America, are busy modifying, restating, recasting their confessions, giving new interpretations, even to the essentials of belief. Dissatisfied with these, the Unitarians undertake to say once more, and once for all, precisely what Christianity is and precisely what it is not. There is no unanimity of opinion respecting the Christ, his nature, mission, or rule. There is no accord of mind in regard to the Godhead, its inner consciousness, its relation to humanity, its attitude toward the world.

Is it fair, then, to demand of a new faith that it shall state itself fully in its first utterances? May not we have a generation when Christendom has had two thousand years? Must our imperfections condemn us, when its incompleteness is no reproach? Must *our* vagueness be decisive of our falsity, when *its* hesitancy only proves its truth? Because we cannot in half an hour say all we have to say, must it be declared that we have nothing to say whatever? The new faith will get articulated by and by; wait and you will see what it is; at present we will give such hints of it as we can.

I. In the first place, then, we affirm the existence of the RELIGIOUS SENTIMENT in man. We declare that man is a religious being, worshiping from an impulse of his nature, believing from the necessity of his constitution, yearning, hoping, loving, aspiring, because an instinct within him prompts him to do so. While his natural affections attach him to persons; while his moral sentiments vitally connect him with society; his spiritual sentiments of awe, wonder, adoration, gratitude, impel him to cast his thought and feeling abroad toward the invisible, which is also to him the perfect. This motion upward, with its sense of trust, its emotion of prayer, this impulse towards perfection, is inborn in self-conscious men. It was not a creation of the priests, though the priests have taken advantage of it for their purposes. It was not a device of rulers, though rulers, too, have made use of it in order to enslave mankind. It is not the offspring of ignorance, for it outlives it. It is the prophecy and the pledge of a higher, even a spiritual inward and eternal life.

Comte tell us that religion is a feature of the world's childhood. If it is, humanity is still a child, and will be a child for ages to come not to be counted. As mankind advances in intelligence, knowledge, culture, they do not become less religious, but rather more so. Goethe, one of the capacious minds of the world, was a magnificent believer and worshiper, as all who read his writings know. It was he that spoke of the material universe as the " garment" of Deity. Plato was no rudimental man, yet the religious sentiment in him kept full pace with his philosophic march, it even outstripped his swift intelligence. Bacon and Newton were no babes; but they burst into the Infinite only to kneel. Milton and Dante had outgrown the swaddling-clothes of the race; yet in what temples they adored! before what ideal forms they bent their heads! Kant and Fichte, and Hegel and Schleiermacher and Herder, surely had outlived the crudest forms of intelligence; but in what hopes and on what aspirations they lived! The age of science is still the age of faith. As I open the pages of the great explorers and discoverers, even in the world of matter, I find that in proportion to their earnestness is their reverence, their trust, their anticipation. They do not pray, perhaps, but they revere; they do not write confessions, but they avow principles; they call God the unknown and unknowable, but they have the tenderest veneration for his immanent being; they bring no gifts to his altar, but they devote themselves to unfolding his

laws. The last thing that Comte himself did, was to reconstruct religion at the bidding of his heart.

The churchman treats the religious sentiment as if it
was a tiny glimmering spark in the bosom, which he must
tend and feed lest it become extinct, or else a wild flaring
flame, which he must confine within his enclosure that it
may steadily burn. He says to men : "But for me you
would become animals—but for me your souls would die.
Desert my altars, leave my communion, neglect my prayers, abandon my sacraments, withdraw from the protection
of my arms, and your spirits will droop and languish."
We say to the churchman : " Nay, quite otherwise ; it is
to this religious sentiment you patronize that you owe
your own existence; you are not its master, but its servant
and creature : it articulates your creed, voices your choirs,
hallows your altars, springs the arches of your cathedrals,
breathes the power into your apostles, inspires your prophets, sanctifies your saints; your establishments rise and
fall with its tides of feeling. When this creative sentiment is low, your mechanism creaks and groans; when it
is high, you have much ado to prevent it carrying you and
your apparatus away."

The religions of the earth, past and present, are not, in
our judgment, supernaturally and miraculously instituted
for the training and education of the religious sentiment,
but are efforts of the religious sentiment itself to find
God, to express its thoughts of Him, and to pour out to
Him its desires. They attest its power, not its weakness.
There could be no Buddhism or Brahmanism, no Parsee-
ism or Zoroastrism, no Mosaism or Christianism, or Mo-
hammedanism, were there not a spiritual nature to create
them. The saints and saviours vouch for the reality of
the soul. Had man not been a religious being he would
never have prayed; had the religious part of him been

feeble, his prayers would not have fashioned the mountains into temples, constructed oratorios, built organs, or lifted holy men above all the glooms and glories of the earth.

Among rude people, in rude times, the religious sentiment finds very uncouth and ugly expression. Its rites are hideous, and even, it seems to us, degrading. It lurks in frightful caverns; it hallows ill-omened birds and reptiles; it feeds horrid idols with children's blood. It appears as that dreadful thing called Superstition. But all things great and beautiful begin in ugliness. Compare the earliest Christian art with the masterpieces of Raphael; contrast the science of the middle ages with that of our own day. From what rough beginnings philosophy and literature have grown to be the glorious creations they are. Cultivated people have cultivated religions. As humanity matures its faith matures. It thinks more worthily, trusts more sweetly, believes more rationally, worships more purely. Its idols disappear, its temples expand, its forms become light, variable, ethereal, its beliefs spiritual, its charities wide, its hospitality generous. The idea takes the place of the dogma, the principle is substituted for the ordinance, life is set before opinion. As the science, literature, art, philosophy of a people are, such will be the religion; crude and ugly when they are—noble and beautiful when that character belongs to them. As noxious weeds give place to flowers and shrubs and fruit-bearing trees; as poisonous reptiles disappear before higher organizations of form, so do the idolatries and superstitions, the errors and terrors of a brutal age, perish when intellectual light comes in. The religions of mankind are milestones that indicate the progress of the race.

II. The religious sentiment throws out the thought of GOD. The Radical believes in God in the most positive, cordial, and determined manner. Not in the God of any

particular church or confession ; not in the God of the
Romanist, the Protestant, or the technical " Christian " ;
not in any special or individual God ; not, let me say, in *a*
God, but simply and only in God.   He has no thought, he
cannot think of a God who is in time and space, who con-
secrates temples or sanctifies exceptional hours, who lurks
behind altars, nestles in creeds, or inspires officials ; who
created the world in six days, and had to make it over
again, and at last died himself that it might not finally
perish ; who peeps into his earth through holes in a con-
cealing curtain, tears up his own roads and mines his own
bridges in order to visit his own children in the city he
has provided for them ; throws into confusion his own
press-work and breaks up his own forms in order to make
himself more intelligible than he was when every letter
was in place ; who appears to an individual Moses, Sam-
uel, or Isaiah, haunts the dreams of devout men, and rises
upon the vision of pious women ; a God who listens to
private prayers and takes an interest in private fortunes,
and selects tribes or nations for special favors, and vouch-
safes his witness to this or the other generation, and prints
books for his favorite tribe of men.   The God of Abra-
ham, and Isaac, and Jacob the Radical knows not ; he
knows only God.

Of this Being he does not attempt, he does not dare to
attempt a definition ; rather, he tries to break through all
definition, that He may be absolutely without bound or
limitation, pure spirit, pure intelligence, the fullest ideal
of possibility, the fairest dream of the soul.

The more definitions the better, if there must be definition at all ; welcome all there are or can be, rather than
rest in any one.   Let the Trinitarian throw light, if he
can, on the mystery of the divine consciousness ; let the
Unitarian illustrate the harmony of the divine order ; let

the Scientist show God as permanent in the world of matter; let the Transcendentalist show him as indwelling in the world of spirit. Come, Spinoza, and tell us of the God who is the substance of things; come, Hegel, and tell us of the God who unfolds himself in history, and in humanity becomes conscious; come, artist, come, poet, and tell us of God as the Soul of the world; come, Spencer, and tell us of the Unknown and Unknowable; come, Vacherot, and tell us of God the Ideal, the vision of the enlightened intelligence. We want you all; for all together you will not sufficiently declare what the Infinite is; all together you will not succeed in flinging too many lights upon the bosom of the great Deep. We need the multitude of your thoughts to save us from the tyranny of a single creed.

Of the moral attributes of God, the Radical hesitates also to speak. Indeed, he dislikes the word "attributes," as implying faculties distinct from being. He does not say that God is *loving*, but that he is Love. It is not enough to say that He is wise, for He is wisdom; or that He is just, for He is justice; or that He is good, for He is goodness; or that He is merciful, for He is mercy. To this believer's mind, it is inconceivable that God should show favoritism or partiality; that He should hate, loathe, forget, or forsake a living creature; that He should hold any outcast for opinion; that He should hold any outcast for any cause whatsoever; that He should dig a hell big enough to hold an insect, or erect a barrier that would shut out a bird.

The Radical's God is simply a dream of all conceivable perfection, the perfect thought, will, care, providence, in whom none die, but in whom all who live at all, live and move and have their being.

I wish I could use stronger words than these to say what I mean, I wish there were any other form of speech

to convince you how earnestly I mean it. God is; not
has been, or will be; and He is infinitely more than the
best believe or the happiest hope.

III. Next we say that God reveals himself. The Radical
believes in Revelation. Not in incidental or particular
revelations; not in peculiar individual revelation; but in
Revelation. It is a necessity of the Divine Being that
He should reveal himself. He is light, and light must
shine because it is light. He is love, and it is the nature
of love to flow out. God cannot hide, disappear, veil, or
withdraw himself. He spoke creation into existence, and
creation is his articulated word. Nature is not a curtain
dropped before his face, but the visible glory of his face.
The natural universe is not a screen behind which He hides,
but the ether whose waves render Him visible. *Our own
closed eyelids, and they alone, conceal God.*

Revelation is the opening of our eyes. The natural eye
—trained, tutored, and taught—looks directly into God's
countenance, and sees as much of Him as sense can see,
in the transcendent loveliness of earth, sea, sky; revelation
of this breaking in successively with increase of perception
and closeness of study. The intellectual eye opens and
discerns wonders before unsuspected, wonders of law,
system, order, harmony, in whose presence thought stands
enchanted. The moral eye opens, and new realms of deity
appear in the awful forms of truth, obedience, duty, by
which the most ancient heavens are fresh and strong. The
spiritual eye opens last, and lo! the Godhead widens on
man's view; regions of benignity lie all about us; flowers
of tenderness bloom in the bleak spaces of the universe;
tendrils of pity and graciousness twine around the iron
clamps and rods of law; there is a loving radiance in the
sunbeam; there are soft tears in the rain; a sweet purpose
is seen gliding through the domains of nature and life;

footprints of a boundless good will are detected in all the first and latest formations, and God is recognized as Father and Mother, as Saviour and never-forgetting Friend.

It will be seen at once why the highest revelations are made to the very few. There are very few who have the spiritual eye open and clear. Not many enjoy the privilege of moral vision, for they are not cultivated in it. Not many discern much with the eye of intelligence; nay, the multitude perceive nothing distinctly with the eye of sense.

It is as in a picture gallery. A score or so unintelligently admire the pictures; a dozen or two appreciate them; two or three gaze at them with delight, being fully in harmony with the artist's soul; the multitude chat and gossip, or sink down wearily in chairs, yawning and wishing to go home and get to bed. Yet the souls of Titian and Raphael glow in the canvas and offer their wealth to all alike. It is no figure of speech that the pure in heart see God. It is no bigotry to say that none others can. The fiction of shifting screens, openings into heaven, rents in nature's curtain, audible voices in desert or on mountain-tops, hints and communications given to eavesdroppers, is too childish for mention; such fancies belong to the second childhood, of which we all have the same opinion. *The pure in heart see God face to face.* There is no keyhole or crack in the wall, or small preternatural aperture through which any others can get a glimpse of Him. The pure in heart, wherever they are, and whoever, whether Pagan, Christian, Turk, or Jew, whether of the olden time or of to-day, whether men of Jerusalem or men of New York, whether priests or philosophers, prophets or cobblers, ministers or menials, men, matrons, or maids, the pure in heart, and none others, see God.

IV. The Radical believes in CHRISTIANITY as he under-stands it; not as the only religion, by any means, not as the absolute or final religion, not as the best religion for all men, not as the finest expression of the religious senti-ment, but as the most worthy form of it yet manifest. Christianity, as vulgarly interpreted, the Christianity of the Greek church, of the Roman church, of the English church, of the Lutheran and Calvinist churches, of the Arminian and Socinian churches, he rejects utterly as compatible neither with reason, philosophy, science, nor even with the earliest prophecies of their own faith. Their traditions, dogmas, ordinances, forms of worship, theories of human nature, human society, and human life, creeds, definitions, confessions, practices, sentiments, be-liefs, hopes, purposes, anticipations, are, one and all, and for the same reasons, unacceptable, being mainly grotesque and unintelligible representations, which distort or corrupt the ideas they may embody.

To the Radical Christianity is dear as implying purity of moral standard, sweetness of spiritual graces, tender-ness and strength of personal and social aspiration, hope-fulness in regard to human destiny, affectionateness as a faith of the heart. He loves it for its *feeling* towards God and the world, not for its *instruction* respecting God and the world. Greatest of the world's faiths, religion of the most advanced races and of the most modern men, the modern mind must spiritualize and refine Christianity very much before it can accept it, and even then, for many important things—for knowledge, for practical prin-ciples, for working beliefs—must go outside of it wholly.

The Christianity of the Radical is so attenuated as not to be recognized by popular Christendom, but it is not so attenuated as to be to him merely a shadow. It is still a substance, a real thing to his soul. But it is a thing which he naturally appropriates, not a thing by which he allows himself to be appropriated.

V. The Radical believes in JESUS. Not in "the Christ," but in Jesus, as the highest expression of the religious sentiment in human form ; yes, on the whole, the highest manifestation of God. The human form offers the grandest opportunity for the divine manifestation. There is no symbol so perfect as man, the last development of creative power, the most complete exposition of creative wisdom and love. We see God imperfectly till we see Him in the human form ; and in no human form do we see so much of Him as we do in the form of Jesus, as that appears spiritualized to our thoughts.

It is not the Jesus of the creeds that the Radical believes in. It is not the Jesus of the Church. It is not the Jesus of the New Testament, for the New Testament puts words into his mouth which no sweet soul can utter, and thoughts into his mind which no enlightened reason can entertain. We know how the record of his life was made, we know what foreign elements came in, we know how the partisans of his own and after times tried to represent him as favoring their views and originating their schemes. We therefore search and sift, endeavoring to extricate the image from the ooze and rubbish that have accumulated upon it, and retouch its spiritual lineaments, soiled and all but effaced. That a divine soul was here is evident; how divine, his contemporaries did not see. But the spiritual sense of mankind attests him as being one of God's brightest manifestations.

We do not bow the knee to Jesus or sit submissively at his feet; we do not pray to him; he is not our lord and sovereign master. We do not call him Saviour, Redeemer, sole Mediator, and Judge. We do not make him the only foundation or corner-stone of our faith. He is the child of human nature, not its king. The heart does not subject itself to him; it accepts him, authenticates him, places him on his seat of honor, crowns him with his fame. What he is reported to have said inconsistent with its best feeling it refuses to believe that he did say; the ideas that are ascribed to him at variance with its conviction it declines to credit him with. It sees in him the expression of its highest feeling, and is encouraged, cheered, invigorated, consoled by the persuasion that in him its highest feeling has been realized.

But, thinking of Jesus, the Radical's thought flies instantly to his brothers. That *he glorifies them* is the great reflection; that in him their nature is disclosed; that he is the flower of their ugly stem; that in their slime this fair plant had its root. He is the natural man. The Radical, therefore, instead of fixing his gaze on Jesus as a superhuman person, turns it tenderly on the people about him, as being, by this testimony, human. It is no easy thing to do. To see the glory of Jesus is easy enough. To call him divine, whe cannot do as much? The murderer, the ruffian, the traitor will do that. This confession comes lightly from the coarsest mouths. But how many draw the inference? How many say of this drunkard, this thief, his victim of lust and passion, this poor, ill-born creature: He is one of those to whom Jesus was kin? The glory of the Son of Man touches this dust, irradiates and should animate this clay! Be careful, lest your scorn or bitterness prevent its being seen! Be watchful, in order that the sunlight of your hope and the dew of your pity may fall on the places that need it most.

What men are we know, and the knowledge is bitter indeed, agonizing, at times almost maddening. What they may become, what capacities lie in them, what possibilities are theirs, we see in this fair shadowy form of Jesus, and we have faith to believe that in this form all may be glorified. In this name we stand over the tombs of those who are dead in trespasses and sins, and cry: Come forth !

VI. The Radical believes in IMMORTALITY. This is another of the grand declarations of the religious nature of man, and, as such, he listens to the assertions of it that come from all tribes and centuries; the heart's anticipations, the soul's prophecies, the reason's intuitive demonstration—not because Jesus taught it, for Jesus himself received it from the conviction of humanity—not because Jesus demonstrated it by rising from the dead, for had not men believed in immortality they would never have believed that he rose—not because prophets and saints have affirmed it, for prophets and saints are but voices from the believing heart of the world—not because of numerous signs and wonders, apparitions, visions, communications, for these, too, imply a faith that such things may be, and give the persuasion that they are what they seem to be—not for any or all of these superficial reasons, but for a reason deeper than any or all—namely, that the religious nature asseverates, and has always asseverated the truth ; that the more it is enlightened the more positively it asseverates it; that the greatest souls have been most confident of it; that while the critical and practical have denied, the saintly and illuminated have affirmed ; that the loftiest intelligences, like Plato, have given it clearest annunciation ; that grandest souls, like Socrates, have borne most confidently on it their weight; that loveliest hearts, like Jesus, have lived in it as in their home.

The Radical is interested in immortality as a high religious belief. Modern Spiritualists claim ocular and tangible demonstration of the future life ; they are to be congratulated on their conviction. But to this bare fact much remains to be added before the faith can take rank among the *spiritual* convictions of mankind. This alone does not satisfy the soul. The butcher who, pushing up his hat, said: "Once I believed that men and women died like cattle, and there was an end of it; but now, damn it, I think no more of dying than of pulling off my clothes and going to bed," accepted immortality through his fingers, but not through his soul. It was not a religious belief with him; it meant an incident in his biography, not a crowning glory and achievement of his heart. Not from the spiritual nature comes such faith as his.

The Radical believes in immortality meekly, humbly, with a gladness that is tinged with holy fear; as a boon he does not deserve; a gift he dare not think himself justified in snatching; a glory to be prepared and striven for; a vision to be waited on with reverent looks.

On this great belief the Radical does not venture to dogmatize with narrow interpretations. He desires rather that it should be voiced in the most comprehensive manner, by the most variously attuned minds. He loves to have it presented in all possible aspects, that it may respond to all states of feeling; as the craving for continued personal existence after death, as the longing for social intercourse and kindred reunion, as aspiration after unattained goodness, as thirst for supersensual wisdom, as the sigh after more than mortal peace, and, yet further, as the generous desire to live still in and through others, though individuality be extinguished; the inspiring and unselfish passion to bequeath something to humanity, in the way of experience, knowledge, or power, and so to continue a living force in mankind. The belief in immortality takes all these forms according to the minds that entertain it. In all of them it appears as a protest against the power of death to destroy that which is the most precious part of our personality. The nature of man refuses to believe itself wholly perishable, rises in rebellion against the dominion of the grave, and claims the privilege of singing its songs, finishing its education, realizing its dream, perpetuating its influence, or completing its blessedness in other worlds.

VII. The Radical believes in as much of the BIBLE as answers to his cultured reason and his matured conviction, and in no more. He takes what nourishes him, and leaves the rest. He reads it as he reads other books, and judges it. Inspiration is in intelligence, not in print. Scriptural utterances are weighty as the heart authenticates them. When not thus authenticated they pass for naught. The true things in the Bible are not true because they are there, they are there because they are true. The good things in the Bible were good before they were in the Bible, else they would not be good there. The religious nature always brings the Book to judgment. The orthodox abolitionist wrung from the Old Testament the last drop of the virus of slavery before he trusted his conscience to it. The Swedenborgian turns the preposterous or wicked stories into parables in order to make the Word seem divine. The Unitarian compels the Bible to utter his opinions before he vouches for its inspiration. The Universalist empties the ugly meaning from the ugly texts of the New Testament, before he will quote them in proof of his belief.

A refined age rejects the coarseness of the Bible. A knowing age rejects the ignorance of it. A moral age discards its immoralities. A spiritual age changes its raw statements into allegory, or turns away from them altogether.

There are many Bibles. All the soul's writings are Scriptures, wherever and by whomsoever penned. They are intended for spiritual eyes, and only what such can read in them is true. Humanity continually revises its sacred books, comparing them from age to age with the inscriptions on the heart, which come out clear under the purifying action of experience and the illuminating power of culture. Again and again we refer to these, and only what these will ultimately verify will stand.

Such, briefly stated, are the grand articles of the Radical's creed; others there are, of vital importance, which I need not mention, for the plain reason that they are common to all good men. Faith in the general principles of truth and goodness, faith in the moral law, faith in recompense and retribution, in the sacredness of duty, the ministering power of kindness, the graces of humility, patience, meekness, the nobleness of consecration, the joy of sacrifice—these, thank heaven, all worthy men and women share alike. All good men believe in the good life as the acceptable offering, however they may differ as to the means of attaining it. Whatever they may think of the communion of sinners, they all believe in the communion of saints. All good men believe that existence is not worth much unless it be devoted to some generous aims. All are agreed in regard to the qualities that make ends generous; all are persuaded that such ends will never be accomplished except by those who keep themselves rooted and grounded in truth and love.

The Radical believes that the world is to be humanized; that the men and women in it are to be made nobler and better; that society is to be regenerated by the action of the natural laws of reason and goodness. He believes in the highest education of all men and women, in the largest possession of rights, the freest sharing of opportunities, the most cordial participation in privileges, the richest unfolding of powers; in science, philosophy, literature, art, industry, commerce, the most liberal communication between nation with nation and man with man. He believes in developing each and binding all together in human bonds; he believes in the good time coming—the kingdom of God—the heavenly Republic—in which educated reason and experienced conscience shall be the ground of order, peace, and felicity.

III

THE RADICAL'S ROOT.

" Rooted and grounded in Love!"—Ephes. iii. 17.

EVERYTHING that lives has a root. The plant draws sustenance from two worlds, a world of darkness and a world of light, and as much from one as the other. Even the air plants, as we call them, that seem to live entirely on the light and the atmosphere, still derive their nourishment in part from tangible substances. They pine without moisture. Would you make them grow in your hothouse, you must provide something, though it be nothing more than a piece of decaying wood, a lump of charcoal, or a few mossy stones, to which they can attach their tenuous roots. So foolish a thing as the rose of Jericho, which flourishes all over the East—in the Barbary States, in Palestine, and Upper Egypt—lingering by the side of streams, enjoying moist places—a plant that in the dry season pulls its tiny root out of the ground, curls it tightly round its body, and rolls off before the wind until it finds a congenial resting-place, nevertheless has its suckers which it unwinds and drops down when its pleasure serves ; and it always chooses a succulent spot near a stream of water, in a bed of mould, or on a heap of muck. The higher the growth upwards, the deeper the root downwards. Plants that live near the ground need but a feeble hold on the soil. An inch or two of earth suffices. They need not spread at all ; they need only dip. The stem of the crocus and of the violet is very short; a child can pull them up with its fingers; they need no depth of soil. But the great tree that overshadows half an acre, that takes in the sunshine of the whole heavens, and is refreshed by the winds that blow from all the quarters of the globe, reaches down furlong upon furlong; its roots are a subterranean forest stretching out great branches that twine and grasp like anacondas, and appropriate the vitality that ages have deposited. The oak-tree, that is to last perhaps a thousand years, under whose shade generations of children are to play, draws the nurture that sustains it from an area wider than it spreads over in the sky; it lays hold on the very heart of the planet, coils about huge rocks beneath the earth, ties itself in with the knotted roots of other trees, goes plunging and burrowing down towards the centre of the globe in search of things that died centuries before, and are hastening into mould; prowls after the hidden springs of water, finds where the sweetest fountains are, and will even plunge beneath them, pushing its greedy inquiries beyond their ken, levying on other territory that may perchance have treasure of food for it. All the force of man will not start a mountain pine. The tempest of the winter but strips off its leaves; the earthquake that tumbles down the dwellings of a city does not loosen a single one of its fibres; it is an organic thing, a piece of nature; the upper world of light and glory clothes it annually with the splendor of a new creation; the under world, cloudy, dark, and secret, but full of living forces, pours into it the products of all the growth of the planet for a thousand generations.

The analogy holds in regard to human beings. Every individual man and woman has a root; and the grander the growth of human qualities the deeper is the root. The persons who *over*looks his generation you may be sure un-

*der*looks his generation as well.   He whose shadow falls across centuries draws his sustenance from more centuries that have gone before him, and have left no trace save in the wealthy world out of which he sprang.   According to the height of the character is the depth of the source whence it draws supplies.   Here is a man who is ironed to circumstance; in the upper, superficial stratum of things adjacent to him—what we call the conditions of his life— the external apparatus by which his existence is kept in order, furnish the soil he is grounded in.   He depends upon those.   His fibres strike no deeper than his accidents. Is he rich—he blossoms and bears fruit.   Is he poor—he dries up, shrinks away, perishes.   In prosperity he shoots up tall, spreads his branches wide, waves his leafage in the air; adversity strikes him, the foliage is all stripped off, the branches toss idly in the wind, the trunk sways wildly hither and thither, the roots are loosened; if a severer gale than usual strikes him, he is laid prone on the ground.   Is he successful—success feeds him, elates him, makes him happy; his veins are full of sap; his eye is bright; he hold his head high; his hand is open.   Is he unsuccessful—all the geniality is gone; no more light in his eye, no more buoyancy in his step, no more uprightness in his form; his mind has lost its balance; his heart is dead.   Here is a man who, in the season of popularity, is open-minded, bright-hearted, happy, warm in his affections, generous in his impulses; he seems to be ennobled by the regards of his fellow-men.   Is he unpopular—the withdrawal of the sunlight of common favor, the withholding of the praise of ordinary people, take from him the very breath by which he lives, and he blackens and dies.   To be born at the North was once to be a democrat; to be born at the South was to be an apologist for the peculiar institution.   In England, this man believes in monarchy. In Paris, he praises imperialism or republicanism, according to circumstances. In Protestant countries he is a Protestant; in Papal countries, a Papist. In Mecca, he puts off his shoes before entering the sacred precincts, and kisses the black stone. His faith is that of the country he sojourns in; he worships with the multitude, whatever their superstition; he is as he happens to be; like the chameleon, he takes the color of the ground he lies on, some say, of the food he eats; he is a rose of Jericho, always hurrying before the wind, his roots in ·his trunk. If he has roots, nobody knows where they are until, occasionally, for a moment, he finds it convenient to pause and to pump up a little sap into his body from the place where he happens to find himself.

Here is a man with a deeper root, a root in his ancestry. He is a leaf on a family tree. He refers back to his precursors; is proud of their blood in his veins—the red blood, the blue blood, that father, mother, or some more distant ancestor, furnishes. This man is mindful of the stock he springs from, the pit out of which he was digged. He carries himself with a proud consciousness of superior worth, if the stock be noble. A kind of nobility characterizes his look and manner. If it be ignoble, the characteristics none the less appear in him, and none the less is he proud of them; he boasts of their evil prowess, talks haughtily of their wild heroism, exults in their questionable achievements, quotes their strong sayings, tries to carry himself as their descendant and representative. There is a good side to this pride of ancestry, if the ancestry be worthy, but there is a bad side to it even then. The material that a man derives from his ancestry, however rich, does not make him human in the noble sense; it shuts him in with a few qualities; it makes him reserved, exclusive, opinionated, imparts to him the characteristics

of the caste he belongs to.   In fact, the caste spirit itself is
due to this narrow veneration, for it confines men to certain sharply-defined types which clash with each other,
and cause incessant friction and war.   On the whole, root
of ancestry is a bitter one, and the fruit it bears is
bitter.

Let us suppose a man to strike his roots lower down than
this.   He is not, we will say, the creature of his circumstances—he is not the child of his parentage.   He belongs
to his nation; he is an American or German, Frenchman
or Englishman.   His suckers spread out to the limits of
the national domain.   He is not bounded by State lines.
He does not ask whether his neighbor comes from the East
or the West, the North or the South; he is countryman,
and that is enough; he is blood of his blood, and bone of
his bone, a fellow, an equal, and a brother, sacred in his
person and venerable in his rights.   Such a man will be
large, expansive, and generous.   He is the patriot; full of
noble sentiments; a man of comprehensive sympathies and
wide interests.   He can take his brother American by the
hand wherever he meets him, be he rich or poor, fortunate
or unfortunate, attractive or forbidding.   The fact of
belonging to a common country covers a multitude of infirmities.   It cannot be denied that a certain grandeur of
intelligence, a certain faith in ideas, a certain breadth of
allegiance to principles, accompanies this patriotic type.
But neither can it be denied that such a person has his limits.   He believes in American ideas, but in no others; he
praises American principles, but concedes worth to none
beside; you may always know him as a man who exults in
his native land so cordially that the foreigner is a barbarian.   For has he the same feeling to the Englishman?
Does he equally respect the German?   Has he a profound
respect for the Frenchman?   Can he enter sympathetically

into the feelings of the Italian or the Irishman? Not so. He is possibly a bigot in his prejudices, unable to appreciate the intellectual or moral weight of a fellow-man who lives on the other side of the Atlantic or the Pacific sea. In England he has no eye for what may be the advantages of a constitutional monarchy; in Germany he cannot welcome what may be said for the constitution of the empire; in France he fails to understand the peculiar temper of a people that is constantly overturning its own system of government. He can cherish scorn for the stranger, having but one word for stranger and enemy. Noble, wide, grand in many respects, his root, nevertheless, is not so firm that it cannot be shaken by prejudice, passion, and malice. Should the time come when a controversy arises between his own government and another, the right is sure with him to be on one side; his motto is, " Our country, right or wrong," but still, our country.

But now, suppose a man to strike down his roots lower than this—below family, ancestry, class, clan, tribe, country—down into human nature itself; not asking whether one be English, French, German, American, Italian, Irish, but whether he be *human;* suppose a man to really make no distinction between Jew and Greek, barbarian or Scythian, bond or free—to consider simply this one question, whether the individual has the attributes of a human being. Such a man has real roots. He is interested in what concerns his fellows. He strikes down into a principle. He draws sustenance from an idea. His sympathies are world wide. He touches every person at the point where all touch each other. He can surrender himself to a cause. The question with him is, Is it just? Is it right? This is the noblest, the most exhaustive root of all. Deeper than this, deeper than human nature, it is impossible to go. When we see a man striking his roots

3

down into this principle of human nature, we see one who strikes down into the core of things; we see one who is proof against the severest tribulations, sorrows, temptations. No wind can shatter him; no tempest can unseat him; he stands up under calamity, and even comes out stronger from the shock of the elemental war.

I am to speak this morning of the Radical's Root.

What do we mean by a RADICAL? There are three definitions of the term. According to the popular acceptation, the Radical is one who pulls up things by the roots, a destroyer, a revolutionist. This is the definition of the enemy. The genuine Radical rejects it as being no description of himself whatever. The Radical says of himself, "I come not to destroy, but to fulfill." He would pull up nothing by the roots that had roots to support it. He would let even weeds grow in his neighbor's field, if the neighbor preferred them to grain; he has too much respect for things that grow, to disturb them without cause; only the poisonous plants that corrupt the atmosphere and impoverish the land, would he eradicate.

A second definition marks the Radical as one who never can rest until he gets at the root of things. The Radical is represented as a prying, inquisitive, critical, restless person, who is forever burrowing in the ground, can never be satisfied, can never leave any belief or institution alone, can never take a doctrine on trust, must impatiently pull up his corn to see how it grows; a man without intelligent motive, or earnestness of purpose, or serious desire after truth; inheriting a precious vineyard, which has produced luscious grapes for a hundred years, the delicious fruit whereof he has tasted in health and sickness, in clusters and in vintage, since he became a man, he must nevertheless worry and explore and expose the healthy suckers of his vines, that he may ascertain in what precise mixture of soil they are planted; living in a house which has sheltered him and his parents before him, and a line of ancestors before them—a house that in generations has never started, does not show a crack in its walls or a leak in its roof—still he is not content until he has been down in the cellar, tested with the hammer every stone in the substructure, and carried on geological experiments beneath the foundation, at the imminent risk of upsetting the building. This, too, I pronounce a caricature. This, too, is the definition of the antagonist. The Radical is no such person. That there are persons who do this, may be true enough, but they are not necessarily Radicals. It is not the peculiarity of the Radical, that out of mere curiosity, in a spirit of restlessness, from an idle desire to know more than is useful, admissible, or wise, he would unseat anything that has a valid claim to permanence. Whatever has a solid basis he allows to stand.

The Radical is simply one who desires a root, who believes in roots, is sure that nothing is strong without them, and is concerned to know in what sort of soil he is planted. He has no fancy for oaks planted in flower-pots; pine-trees set in porcelain vases are not to him beautiful. Knowing somewhat the uncertainty of the seasons, having had proof of the variableness of climates, he has no wish to be put down in a small area, fenced about on all sides, bricked closely in so that no draught can freshen the air and enliven the soil. He has discovered that in his daily life he must face the tempest and brave the blast, and he would make sure against being stripped by an autumn wind, or sapped by a trickling stream of water, or overturned by a sudden convulsion of nature. He prefers to be able to stand, and, when the storm has passed, still to stand. He calls himself, therefore, what he is, a Radical —a *root-man*, because he believes in a root; the deeper the root, the more he believes in it; and his sincere desire, his only desire, is to know that his root goes down deep enough to hold fast amid the severest stress of weather.

The Radical, therefore, cannot be a sectarian. The sectarian stands planted in a sect, but a sect is a fragment —something cut off from the domain of thought, a small ground-plot, or yard, not an open field. The sectarian is a class or clique man; as the word signifies, a man who is clipped and trimmed down. He is a tree set in a box, not in a meadow. That he has a certain amount of verdure, that he bears a certain quality of fruit, that he has elements of earnestness, of intensity, may be cheerfully granted. Every human being has vitality of some sort; he will grow after a fashion wherever you plant him; if you plant him in a small place, he will make the most of his opportunity, he will ripen to the extent of his limits. But if the limits are cramped, the stature will be stunted. The sectarian is an apple-tree, planted in the cleft of a rock. Chance has put it there; no gardener is responsible for the situation; it makes the best of its handful of earth and thimbleful of moisture; struggles as well as it can to get at the light and air; rejoices, after a sickly fashion, in the sun; holds out its scanty leaf to catch the rain-fall, but after all can get no more sustenance than the conditions allow. The kind wind blows dust into the nook where the poor twisted body is; resolutely the root is let down, and painfully the sustenance there is drawn up, though it be but a mouthful. But you will see only a few wrinkled leaves. On the outermost twig, perhaps, you may discover a single apple, which never ripens, and, when bitten, proves to be sour. The sectarian has a certain amount of force of his own; but the sound he makes as he ripples along, is out of all proportion to the volume of the stream; it is the rattle of a thin current of water flowing over loose pebbles. A very slender rivulet will turn a pretty large mill-wheel if you only make the channel narrow enough. But one can have no more life than his roots supply; the sectarian's mind, therefore, is narrow, dry, thin, and sandy. There is no great impulse, no eager seeking after the new truth. He holds up his little shred of doctrine, and it is not apparent to him that anybody else has any doctrine at all. His heart cannot be genial or diffusive in its charity. It is impossible for him to feel that other men who do not believe as he does, are as good as he is; that they can be sincerely good at all. There is a certain amount of conscience, or of conscientiousness, rather, but it grinds away at the crank of the denominational organization, it turns the creaking wheel of denominational duty, and succeeds in bringing out a certain amount of hard grits which one can, perhaps, make into a dry biscuit. He cannot worship with grandeur of devotion, for his deity is a definition, his God is a dogma. He can only catch a glimpse of the divine love at the bottom of a well as the sun passes over the mouth of it. His soul, therefore, is apt to be arid and barren as his mind; his love of God is love of his denomination, and the love of his denomination is but a species of the love of himself.

The Radical cannot be a sectarian. Can the Radical be a churchman? What is a church, but a more comprehensive and better organized sect, a wider denomination, a more diversified group of believers? There is something grand, truly, in the idea of a church; in every existing church there is much that is noble, majestic, and attractive. A church is an organization, not a machine; it is a growth; it lives through ages of time; it covers a large area of space; it includes people of many conditions, many orders of intellect, many casts of disposition, many tongues, many types of genius, it may be, many different races. It has developed in the course of centuries. There are worlds of experiences in it. Its spiritual soil is strong and succulent, with the joys and sorrows, the thoughts and desires, the aspirations and utterances of generations. Its doctrines are the product of disciplined minds working through many phases of faith. It has sacraments and ceremonies, solemn rites, glorious music, beautiful symbols, poetry, art, architecture. It has great churches, not meeting-houses, that seem to have grown, by the laws of nature, out of the soil. To be rooted in a church is to have roots struck into historic and holy ground; it is to draw moisture from many living springs; it is to appropriate the experience, perhaps, of a nation. The churchman, so he be a true churchman, carries with himself an air of calmness and repose, of dignity and of grace. He seems to be a part of the institution he belongs to ; a piece of this great organism that has lived so long, and comprehended so much, and embraced such various life; something of the spirit of antiquity attaches itself to him. He is conservative ; he has a great trust, a large reverence, an earnestness in thought and feeling that is even impressive and beautiful.

And yet, the churchman, if he be no more than a churchman, is considerably less than human. What does he think of other churches? Of the Roman Church, for instance—of the Greek Church? What respect has he for strange forms of worship ? Does he do more than tolerate extremes that differ from his own ? Does he tolerate such as are hostile? The churchman's mind is slow and opaque ; his heart is rather self-satisfied than sunny ; his conscience rather punctilious than sensitive; his worship is formal; he prays as the church prays—out of a book. He allows the church to think for him, to believe for him, to worship for him, to intercede for him. The church

takes care of him ; pardons his sins ; guarantees his future.
He treads an ecclesiastical path, passes through an ecclesiastical doorway, enters an ecclesiastical heaven. However
pleasantly he talks with other believers, it is over a fence ;
however graciously he looks at them, it is with eyes of
compassion. He cannot help believing that he is in a
safer place than they. You are impressed by him, as by
one who feels sure of his past, his present, and also of his
future, and is good enough to be sorry that his fellow-men
are not as sure of their destiny as he is of his. The ripe-
ness of his belief prevents his being angular, but the interior composure of his mind savors too much of that calm
exclusiveness which enjoys its spiritual privacy, and keeps
intruders out of doors.

The Radical cannot be a churchman. The church is of
comparatively modern origin, traceable to definite beginnings. It is a production of human wit ; a creation of
diplomacy. You can easily go below it, and get at the
secret of it. The Catholic church claims to be older than
the Bible. Is it older than the Hebrew Bible—to mention
no others ? The man who strikes his roots into the Old
Testament, strikes them below the church. The man
whose roots go down into the soil of these antique Scriptures penetrates below all Christendom. The Old Testament, the old Hebrew Bible—what a world it is ! How
wonderful in extent, in comprehensiveness ! What wealth
of antiquity there is in it ! What recesses of wonder
and marvel it contains ! It covers a continent ; it absorbs
the life of a race, and one of the most extraordinary races
that ever lived on the planet. There is in it a universe of
thought, feeling, conviction, purpose ; the experiences of
two thousand years are packed away in its chapters. What
mountain ranges of thought, what sweet valleys of meditation, what noble rivers of psalmody, what delicious

fountains and pure rivulets of praise! What power of conviction, what reaches of exaltation, what breadth of hope, what vistas of anticipation, what thrilling conceptions of Providence, of the world that is, and of the world that is to come! The man who should sink his roots so deeply into the Old Bible that they took up everything there, would be a giant among men. But all depends on the thoroughness of the exploration. Does one root himself in the letter, or in the spirit?—that is the question. He that roots himself in the letter does not go below the surface, hardly pierces the outer crust; knows nothing, perhaps, of the rich world of experience that is stored inside. Now, the Old Testament man as we see him roots himself in the letter. The Puritan rooted himself in the letter. He knew far less than he might of the resources of moral and spiritual sustenance that lay hidden in the spirit below the letter. The soil in which he struck his root was made up in great measure of the *débris* of the Hebrew mind, wild feelings, fanciful speculations, strange superstitions and conceits, that are strewn broadcast over the surface of the history; uncouth beliefs in Providence, rude conceptions of God and man, grotesque notions of the constitution of the world, vagaries respecting the election of certain races of men, and the rejection of others; and the result of all this was a character of austerity and pride, touched here and there with a sweet and rich glow of piety, but having, as the soul of it, more reverence for law than truth, for justice than for love. The Puritan had a grand life in him, but it was rough and severe. He was exclusive, arbitrary, and at times tyrannical. He carried a rod of iron in his hand; his conscience was a rod of iron.

Go down below the letter in which the spirit is hidden, —sink your roots until you strike the New Testament, and you have something infinitely richer. The New Testament is the older, because it is the heart, the soul of the Old Testament. Was not Jesus a Hebrew, and what food did he feed on but that very Bible which we call the Bible of the Hebrews? What was his peculiarity, if not this; that he dropped roots down below the surface of the ancestral mind till they touched a secret core of inspiration in the heart of his race? Everything he had was there, every thought, every feeling, every hope, every anticipation; his trust, his faith in the Heavenly Father, his conception of the paternal Providence, his sentiments of reverence and trust, his patience, his meekness—they are all there. But, with the subtile insight that he possessed, with the exquisite chemistry of his soul, he sent his roots underground; they ran out in every direction until they found those sweetest springs of water, and drew the sustenance thence that made them bud and blossom. When you have penetrated the secret of the Beatitudes, when you have got at the soul of the parables, when you have searched out the hidden thought in the Sermon on the Mount, then, and not before, you have touched the centre of power in the old Hebrew Bible. And when you have done that, you have struck into the richest soil that is offered to the spiritual nature of the Christian. He that will do this will plant himself in the heart of the New Testament—not in the letter, not in the strange, crude, fantastical portions that are heaped upon its surface; he that, going down below all this—below the errors, the mistakes, the superstitions—finds his way into the heart of Jesus himself, will blossom and bloom into a life as exquisitely pure, sweet, and beautiful as is ever seen in Christendom. He will have the divinest qualities, and at the same time the most human; he will be able to submit himself to the Supreme, and to give himself to his

3*

brothers. Trust, patience, meekness, reverence—he will have them all. Simplicity, purity, charity—all these will be his. The Christian Radical roots himself in the heart of Jesus; not in his reported word, not in his incidental thought, but in the heart of his heart. Beyond that, outside of that, he does not go. He explores none of the outlying regions of literature or philosophy. This beautiful Jewish life is enough for him.

And yet, is there nothing more? Is this absolutely all? Is the Hebrew race the only race to be taken into account? Does God give his inspiration to none but those who have lived in Palestine? Did Jesus exhaust humanity? Do we find everything in the New Testament that can be worked into human character? Other races have other gifts; one, the sentiment of beauty; another, the principle of justice; another, the passion for liberty; another, the devotion to ideal truth in science and philosophy. Is it forbidden to make excursions into the outlying literatures of China or of Greece, of Asia or of Persia, and to draw spiritual nourishment from those larger sources, which, after all, belong to human nature? They who can do that are the privileged; they who can do that are the strong. The true Radical, the Radical of the Radicals, sinks his shafts below sect, church, Bible, Old or New; below all partial experience; down into the secret places where man has stored his treasures of thought, and by all that, tries to live.

Orthodoxy is *right thinking;* but who can claim to think rightly? How is one to know that he thinks rightly? It is very plain that nobody thus far has earned a title to monopolize right opinion. To think rightly, is to exhaust thought. No one can be truly orthodox as long as there is knowledge yet to be acquired. Only the divine mind is orthodox, because only the divine mind is omniscient, and being omniscient, entertains no error,

Up to this day there is no human orthodoxy. He is most orthodox who thinks most closely to facts.

We speak of new truth. There is, correctly speaking, no new truth. All truth is old as God himself. There are new interpretations of truth, new guesses at truth, new insights into truth, new readings of truth ; but the Truth is more ancient than antiquity; it is as old as the world ; the last reading only comes nearer the first text. To be orthodox, therefore, we need all the knowledge there is —of literature, science, art. The Radical accepts the last interpretation (so it be a satisfactory one), the last inter-pretation of the oldest truth. Those who accept older in-terpretations are further off from the original sources than he is. The Radical is one who uses the last invented plow for his tillage, because it subsoils most thoroughly. What he wants is the old, original, primeval truth ; the truth that is symbolized in nature, which the Infinite mind, in its first perfect operation, embodied in the uni-verse.

The peculiarity of the Radical, let me say finally, the test of the Radical's genuineness, is not that he holds a certain class of opinions ; it is, that he uses the opinions he entertains. It is not his peculiarity to question and doubt, to cavil and raise issues ; it is not restlessness of mind ; least of all is it flippancy, indifference, looseness or lightness of conviction. Let me declare again, he is not a destroyer. The true Radical is known not by his restless-ness, but by his calmness ; not by his flippancy, but by his seriousness ; not by his indifference, but by his earnest-ness ; not by the lightness of his speech about the great beliefs of mankind, but by the soberness of his speech about them. He is known by his patience, his cheerful-ness, his serenity, his trust ; the singleness of his purpose, the weight of his opinion, his freedom from prejudice, his openness to discovery, his thankfulness for light. He is one who stands deeply rooted and firmly planted. " He stands four square to all the winds that blow." His very name implies that he is rooted and grounded. He *is* rooted and grounded—not in prejudice or tradition, not in dogma or formula, not in sacraments or institutions—he is rooted and grounded in love, that even passes knowledge.

IV.

THE JOY OF A FREE FAITH.

THE theme of this discourse is the joy of a free faith. My thoughts have been turned to this subject by a tone of remark both frequent and confident, which reveals a common persuasion that a free faith is incapable of producing joy. We hear a good deal about the sadness of the "radicals" as they are called, the air of discontent they carry about with them, the melancholy cast of their sentiment, the tone of uneasiness and pain that runs through their writings, the evident depression of their moral state. I do not know that any effort is made to prove this by examples; that would not be easy, for as a class the radicals are remarkably cheerful. But the fact that no attempt is made to prove it, shows how deep the persuasion is. The melancholy of the radicals is taken for granted, as a thing that needs no proof, that is a thing of course, that could not but follow from their beliefs; men, the assumption is, cannot think as they do and not be sad; their world so dark, their God so far off, their Saviour so inaccessible, their destiny so clouded: men must be melancholy without the sunshine.

True, they must; sunshine is the cause of health and life, physical and moral. If this common charge were well founded it would be fatal. Beliefs that do not beget joy in the minds that entertain them are not likely to be true. Joy is the test of sanity. Joy is health; joy is purity; joy is goodness. The joyous man is grateful, innocent, kind. Human nature like animal nature blackens in the gloom. Vice, crime, sin flourish in the shadow. A joyous world would be a perfect world. This is confessed in the anxiety of sects to make it appear that their members alone are happy. The Romanist claims a superiority in this respect above the Protestant, contrasting the cheerfulness of his religion with the austere tenets of Luther and Calvin, his own brightheartedness with the others' painful anxieties. The Churchman remarks scornfully on the grim disposition of the Puritan. The "Evangelical" commiserates the Unitarian, deprived of the celestial solaces and inspirations that come to him through faith in the Redeemer. The Unitarian hears an undertone of complaint and weariness in the speech of the Rationalists, who have cut themselves adrift from the shadowy ark in which he fancies himself to be floating. Possibly the Rationalist pities those who have reduced the articles of faith still lower than he has, and who seem to him to have thrown away the last plank that was bearing them towards heaven. Even Theodore Parker, heartiest of men, professed a deep compassion for those who did not share his faith in the soul's innate assurance of God and immortality. "No rainbow beautifies that cloud; there is thunder in it, not light. Night is behind—without a star." This feeling, of course, is not rational; it is born of prejudice, not of observation. There are sad people in all faiths, and there are joyous people in all faiths; both the joyousness and the sadness proceed perhaps from temperament, and would exist under any forms of belief. The springs of sadness and of gladness are within, deep down, and often hidden, their connection with modes of opinion being concealed entirely. The physicist says that the brightest light as a rule proceeds from the blackest substances; so the most radiant happiness may have its sources, for aught we know, in pools of sentiment that to the ordinary eye look stygian in blackness.

It is not fair to argue from special instances. The poet Cowper was a faithful believer in the evangelical scheme of salvation, and yet was a most unhappy man, his joy-lessness being a cause of anxiety to his friends, and of torment to himself. Ralph Waldo Emerson, the foremost man among American free believers, is one of the most felicitous spirits alive; he lives in the atmosphere of serene ideas, joyous and a perpetual cause of joy. The explanation of the two cases is to be found in the the temperament of the two persons; that of Cowper was morbid and low, with a streak of insanity running through it; that of Emerson is clear and bright, with a natural healthfulness in it that sheds abroad an aroma as from pine trees or newly mown hay. The temperament of Cowper would have taken the sunshine out of the most radiant of faiths; the temperament of Emerson would make flowers bloom from the most wintry ground.

The moral effects of religious beliefs can be judged only from an observation of wide spaces and of continuous years. Generations must be born in them, and must drink them in with the mother's milk. They must form the minds of children, and of childrens' children, being accepted without question, applied without misgiving, expressed in literature, voiced in song, condensed into practical maxims of duty, mixed with the substance of domestic feeling, incorporated with habitual states of mind. When thus lived on and worked over, faiths modify temperament, shape it, induce it. A religion will create its own type of sentiment, as climate creates its own type of animal and plant. All beliefs have their fresh, creative period, and by this they must be judged. When that period is passed, the virtue goes out of them; they create no more; they tend then to uncreate, to disorganize. The relation of the living mind to them being disturbed, there is no more wholesome reciprocity of action, no cordial understanding, no consent of feeling, disposition, or purpose. The reason criticizes, the heart rebels, the conscience doubts and questions, the soul wavers. The faith shows no longer its happy aspect: the reverse side alone appears.

This is the position of the "Evangelical" system in our generation. The ages when people cordially believed it are gone by; the ages when they can be sure of extracting joy from it are rapidly going. Looking over, the other day, the correspondence of Theodore Parker, I was struck by the number of letters addressed to him that expressed gratitude for deliverance from agonies of soul that were produced by the "Evangelical" theology. They were full of groans, some of them bleeding in every line. My own correspondents tell the same story of distress. People of every shade of theological opinion, from Calvinism to Unitarianism, describe themselves as awaking from a dream-haunted sleep, and are as thankful for what is called infidelity, as the victim of nightmare is for the dawn. People I meet among my own acquaintance who are at times brought to the verge of insanity by horrid visions proceeding from their impressions of the ordinary faith of Christendom: they cannot banish them; they cannot forget them; they cannot reason them away; their minds cannot clear themselves of the dogmatical rubbish that clogs all the highways and byways of thought. The people are becoming fewer and ever fewer in number to whom the common faith of Christendom brings joy. There are such, no doubt, both old and young: we may be sure there are; but it is a question whether the joy is as intense or as long-lived as it was in the palmy days of the faith. The genius of the system is on the wane; its creative force is spent; and the ecstacy that accompanied the fresh experience of its truth is sensibly diminished. The rapture of conversion is often followed by disappointment and dejection. The height, if reached, is held but for a moment, then comes a reaction, sometimes into terrible apathy and gloom.

Every faith is joyous in its triumphant days; every faith has its triumphant days, when it is creative, when it stands for light and liberty, when it promises and confers emancipation. What heavens Romanism during the " dark ages " opened to unenlightened masses of mankind in the ancient European world! What liberation from the bondage of the animal nature, from the despotism of institutions, from the crushing dullness of ignorance, stupidity, monotony, vice, violence! The portal of the church must have seemed literally the gate to paradise. The cathedral was a place of enchantment; the music and incense, the pictured madonna, the carved Christ, the emblem of godhead, the symbol of eternity, the chapel, the altar, the lamp of silver and gold, the marble floor, the stone ceiling, the clustered pillars reaching into the shadow, the silent priests in their gorgeous robes, the chanting boys, the mystery of the mass, the crowds of angels, the space filled with fancies of celestial beings, the brotherhood of believers, the communion of saints, the endless vistas into the world to come, charmed and transported the mind. It all meant to the worshipper, freedom ; freedom from doubt and fear, freedom from pain and sorrow. It gave room for faith to soar, for hope to sing, for thought to wander. The oppression that we discover in the system was unfelt; the yoke was easy; the burden was light; the glory alone was visible.

In Luther's day the approaching change was felt. The

heart of the early Protestant swelled with joy at the thought that the spell was broken. He was free from popery and prelacy, from mass and mummery, from priest-craft and ritualism. He could read the Bible with open eyes; he could pray out of his own heart; he could approach his Saviour face to face; he could trust his soul. His emancipated spirit revelled in the delight of unre-stricted faith and adoration. He was a bird loosed from a cage. He was a prisoner released from his dungeon. All he saw was the gladdening light; all he felt was the genial temperature of the day.

To the early Puritan his faith brought joy, deep and serene. To him the austere features did not present them-selves. From him the terrible side that is turned towards us, was hidden. The sweetness alone he knew. He had vistas and openings where to us are only closed doors. Believing himself conceived in sin and shaped in iniquity, a child of wrath by nature, it was unspeakable ecstacy for him to be told that a way was prepared by which he could pass out of his prison-house into the open sunlight of God's favor. Conscious of his own inability to escape from the wrath his nature deserved, could he be grateful enough for the Redeemer who suffered the pains of per-dition in his stead, and made it possible for him to mount to heavenly places by means of a simple act of . faith, which consisted in disavowing the private merit he never possessed, and in loving the greatest of benefactors? The Christ was an awful judge: but first of all he was a gracious Saviour, and he judged none but those he had done his utmost to save; only they who refused his pity incurred his wrath. Was the vicarious atonement an affront to reason? He viewed it as a divine mystery be-fore which he bent in humble awe. The everlasting tor-ments of the damned were awful to contemplate; but the

Redeemer came to rescue mankind from them. In that entrancing belief all painful contemplations were swallowed up. The earnest Puritan could not dwell on thoughts of hell, he saw only heaven. The reflection which tortures us is, that the privilege is not extended to all ; that the divine grace is restricted to a few. " Many are called, but few chosen," says the Holy Book, and the few are foreordained to that felicity from the beginning of the world. But faith saw a way of escape out of this dilemma ; faith saw only the way of escape ; the dilemma did not exist for it. All are chosen who choose to be. Are they few ? That is because few respond to the call. The few might be many, and any individual of the many may be entitled to count himself among the few. It is ground of general rejoicing that the grace is offered to all ; it is ground of special congratulation that each may have the consciousness of being numbered among the " elect." Thus the faith, in any particular case, meant emancipation, and emancipation meant delight.

But the Unitarian has lost the key. He sees only the naked, repulsive dogma, and wonders that human creatures are, or ever were, able to live under it. He rejoices in having cast the burden of fear off. He exults in the idea that he has liberated himself from a cruel bondage, coarse, pitiless, terrifying, the bondage of an iron creed, every article of which was a dogma offensive to reason and hateful to the heart.

Careful reflection makes this evident : that every faith brings joy to the devout believers who interpret it from the inside, that no faith brings joy to the unbelievers who criticize it from the outside. Every faith is a joyous one in its living period, no faith is joyous in its period of decline. And this besides is evident, that freedom and joy are closely associated, that freedom indeed is joy. The freest faith gives most joy. To this conclusion we are brought at length. Let a faith be free, truly free, let it be considered in the light of its freedom, let the element of freedom in it be recognized and felt, and joy will of necessity result, as exhilaration results from a pure atmosphere, as the sweet summer morning bestows sensations of pleasure. If the rational faith be the freest of all, it must be the most joyous of all. Is it the freest of all? I claim that it is.

It is freer than any other from superstition, and that is the soul of all freedom, as superstition is the soul of all bondage. Romanism delivered men from the grosser superstitions of heathenism. Protestantism delivered men from the grosser superstitions of Romanism. The Unitarian movement delivered men from the grosser superstitions of Protestantism. But Rational faith aims at delivering men from all superstition, whatever its name; the superstition of the Church, the superstition of the Bible, the superstition of the dogma, the superstition of the sect, party, organization, order; the superstition of the Romanist, who ascribes supernatural powers to an institution; of the Lutheran and Calvinist, who ascribe supernatural powers to a book; of the Unitarian, who thinks it a matter of vital moment that people should hold to a faint reminiscence of all these.

The Rational believer is happy only when the last fragment of superstition disappears from his mind, and he is free to walk abroad wherever intelligence leads him. In proportion as one is able to do this, is he joyous.

Superstition is reliance for special aid on supernatural powers; it is a sense of dependence on the will of such powers. They may be gods or demi-gods, demons, spirits, angels, imps, beings physical or metaphysical, evil or good, powers of the air, or of the earth; the principle working through them all is the same. The superstitious man is one who imagines that his health and wealth depend, not on his conformity with natural laws and conditions, but on the observance of certain portents or signs on which the favor of the besetting demon hangs. It is doubtful whether any living person is totally, at all moments and in all moods, free from superstition; it can hardly be doubted that the moments when he is free are the happiest.

It is a curious fact that superstition is commonly characterized as dark. Whenever it is recognized it is recognized as dark—all superstitions are confessedly dark except our own—and these last we do not acknowledge. And superstition *is* dark; always dark. Such a thing as a bright and beautiful superstition, such a thing as an innocent superstitution, does not, exactly speaking, exist. The fairy fictions of the nursery are not necessarily superstition. They may be fanciful, and poetic, and nothing more. The child is fond of reading about the fairies, but rarely expects aught from them. If he does, no happiness ever ensues. Be the superintending power ever so kind, be the providence ever so gracious, be the watching spirits ever so loving, the feeling that something must be done to keep the guardian genius in good humor lest evil befal, disables the will and causes anxiety to the heart. Something has been done or left undone, which may put important interests in jeopardy; one can never be quite certain that the gracious powers have been duly propitiated. If one feels that he has not prayed often enough or aright, that he has neglected the observance of a day or the use of a ceremony, that he has fallen short in some point of doctrine, or been careless in the performance of a stated duty, and has thus made himself liable to disaster, however slight the matter may be, however incidental, a shadow falls on the spirit.

There is no serenity except in a sweet strong confidence in the natural integrity of the universe, in the prevalence everywhere of cause and effect, in the tender immutability of law. He alone is happy who believes that nothing happens; that whatever comes, comes through cause and effect, rationally. He alone is joyous who feels glad that it is so, who answers the encompassing forces with meek obedience, asking nothing better than their ordinances appoint. To feel that all is well, though no gift is brought to the unseen, and no propitiation offered—to feel safe, though at home in church time, or in the fields on the Sabbath—to feel safe though the Bible be unread, the communion table unapproached, the creed unrecited, all pious conventionalities disregarded—to feel safe on all days and in all places alike—to be able to read all books, study all knowledge, converse with all persons, entertain all' thoughts—to have no misgivings lest the well-meaning mind be pounced upon unawares from behind some stick or stone —to feel quite at home in what thoughtless people call the outer darkness of unbelief, by whatever ugly name known —to live as in a friendly universe, cheerily, hopefully, knowing that if we ascend up into heaven there is goodness, that if we make our bed in the underworld there is goodness still, that if we take the wings of the morning and dwell in the uttermost parts of the sea, the same goodness leads and supports—this is to be full of joy. And in this way the rational man lives, fitting himself as well as he can into the conditions of the world he is a part of, and trusting the well-knit constitution of things. Should he not therefore be joyous who is a perfect freeman ?

The anxiety of certain liberal people, lest they should not have found the whole truth, lest in some point they should misbelieve, betrays the spirit of superstition in a form perilous through attenuated. The impression that souls are in danger of some calamity in this world or the next unless they have in possession the talisman of a correct faith ; the impression that mistaken opinions in regard to the secret of the universe expose people to malignant influences from some adversary who lurks in error, is one of those subtle illusions which will destroy the peace of even noble minds. How can we avoid mistaken opinions? How can we obtain certainly true ones? What right has any body to think that there are beliefs in which people are necessarily unhappy or unsafe? What right has any body to intimate that his neighbor is on the way to that wilderness where lions are waiting to devour, and no springs are gushing from the ground? We shall not have got rid of superstition till we have got rid of a sorry notion like that, and have become fairly footloose in the realm of mind, not as nomads or roving Bedouins who have no abiding-place, but as citizens of the intellectual world, who are always at home with the spiritual laws. The joy of having this freedom of the universe is something that cannot be described to one that has never experienced it. To have the night as bright as the day, no terrors in the dark, is a privilege which none but the most emancipated minds know, but it is a privilege which the rational faith would gladly bestow on all men.

For this faith releases us completely from the bondage of fear. It does not comprehend fear. What is there to be afraid of, except fear itself? The great fear is the fear of death. What a feature that has been in religion! And religion, that should have taken it away, has intensified it. The natural terror of death is not great. The artificial terror of it is immense. Death is the point upon which the older forms of faith accumulate terrors. Consider the part that death plays in the drama of redemption. What gloomy pageantry the Church of Rome associates with it! What frightful issues Protestantism hangs on its fluttering moments! This most natural arrangement of providence has been seized on by preacher and priest, and worked up into a grotesque importance that completely conceals its original character. The approaches of death are lined with awe and draped with mystery; the circumstances of death are exaggerated into a ghastly importance; the hour of death is watched with painful solicitude: the bearing in death is commented on fearfully. By the bedside stands the priest with chalice and book, prayer and holy water. The ceremonies prepared for the last hour are made to convey the feeling that the great crisis of existence has come, and that the departing soul has struck into the path of its final doom. The old religion did what it could and does what it can to deepen the solemnity and magnify the issues of death. If there were no death the whole system would give way; the church would lose the very ground of its existence; the curtain would fall on the drama of redemption; the whole machinery of salvation would be consigned to the lumber room. Of the people that make death the subject of much thought, the Spiritualists alone take the happy view of it which characterized the earliest Christians, especially the disciples of Paul, who regarded death as a process of transfiguration. The so-called "liberal" sects of Christendom dwell still under the shadow, more or less dense, of the ancient fear. The incidents of death are still in keeping of theology, by which it is regarded as a supernatural, not as a natural fact, and the efforts of divines to keep it within the circle of those associations are incessant.

The rational faith restores death to its legitimate place among the phenomena of nature, and by so doing emanci-

pates mankind from a crushing fear ; it rolls a heavy burden from the mind, reclaims from the dominion of gloom
large tracts of experience, lets in light on sickness, old
age, the weakening and decay of faculty, the departure of
friends, the chamber of decline, the last bed, removes the
hideous spectre from the edge of the grave. Questions
respecting the hereafter it leaves open to science and philosophy, taking them from the exclusive possession of priests
and preachers. It bids theology be silent, and reason
speak. The sense of relief is unspeakable. Existence
recovers its fair proportions. The activities of life come
into play. Industry takes courage, affection blooms, privilege invites, and pleasure smiles. The awful anticipation
is put out of sight, or contemplated with calmness. Life
is free to use up to life's last hour, and the end is thought
of only when it comes.

But no words of description, no words specifying advantages gained, do the least justice to the happy emotions
of this great victory. The joy brims over; the heart is
renewed ; poetry and song express the fresh delight ; the
faces of men and women declare it in their radiant looks ;
family affection feels it ; flowers take the place of the
shroud ; the coffin is a casket ; a thousand signs indicate
the bright change that has come over the moral world.

How can people thus emancipated from fear be charged
with gloom ? Where do they who bring the charge find
their justification ? In their own fears. The rational believers, " red republicans " of religion as they have been
called, are supposed to be in danger from their own freedom in a world infested by wild beasts. But what if they
see in freedom the only chance of escaping from the beasts?
What if the creatures suspected of being wild beasts turn
out to be not wild beasts at all, but useful domestic animals.

4

The rationalists, it is said, still, as of old, are without God in the world. If the allegation were that' they had too much God in the world it would be more intelligible, for this assertion more nearly states the facts in the case. Without God in the world! Can we be in God's world, without God? They only make the accusation who believe that through and through this is not God's world, that vast tracts of the universe are unreclaimed by deity, that God has here and there a stronghold where his children may be safe from robbers; a fortress in Jerusalem, another in Rome, another in Constantinople, another in Westminster, another in Cambridge; a castle called "Church," a castle called "Scripture," a castle called "Articles;" each a walled city, large enough to contain many thousands of souls, but to which the souls must resort from the outer regions of science, philosophy, literature, and art. To those who believe this in any sense, it must seem a sad thing to be wandering at large over the face of the earth, in exile of course, in danger and destitution equally of course.

Theology insists on the minimum of God. It would limit him to times and seasons; it would confine him to points of space, assign to him particular spots on the earth's surface, and forbid his going forth in the world at large. But suppose we substitute for the minimum of God the maximum; suppose, instead of speaking of God as somewhere, we speak of him as everywhere; what then? Must not the joy of his presence be diffused? If we take his spirit from the Bible, and spread it over the human mind; if we take his life from Palestine and distribute it over Europe, England, America; if we destroy the theologian's monopoly of him, and allow the chemist, the naturalist, the economist, the inventor, the artizan, the industrial worker to have their share; if we break up the exclusive proprietorship of the Church, and let civilization enjoy a portion of the advantage that his presence confers; if we dismantle the fortresses of revelation and quarter the armies of the living God about in the homes of mankind, must we not by so doing impart to the many the gladness that was appropriated by the few?

It is the peculiarity of the free faith that it cannot be without God in the world, for it identifies God with order, harmony, and beauty, and these are everywhere, in the world of matter and the world of mind. To perceive this only by glimpses is ecstacy; to have the thought always before one is a perpetual enchantment. The devout believer in the living operations of law, if there be such a man, must be as joyous as the lot of mortals permits. If he be free from bodily ailment, from the pinch of hunger, from the sting of cold; if his physical and mental powers be unimpaired, existence to him cannot be other than a delight. With the conditions I have mentioned he must be free from sorrow. His mind cannot suffer from doubt; he is above fear; he is sure that what befals in the order of providence is well. The link that binds causes and effects together is of pure shining gold. He is unhappy only when, through some infirmity of passion or purpose, he has been unfaithful to the perfect order to which he belongs, and in which he is called to take a rational part. His hours of dejection are those in which he is conscious of being out of harmony with nature; when the harmony is restored by activity, affection, or kindness, it is not in the power of mortal man to disturb his happy calm. His sense of intimacy with the Supreme is unbroken.

I know I am describing something which is far, very far indeed, beyond the range of ordinary experience; but I know that the rational faith tends to bring the experience within reach of every man and woman. There are those of my acquaintance who share it. Of course, outside of my acquaintance there are multitudes who know what it is. As a rule, Radicals are joyous people, joyous, not as children are who live in sensation, but as intelligences are which live in faith. Their joy is unalloyed by misgivings in regard to themselves, and by apprehensions in regard to their neighbors. They are optimists so far as the constitution of nature is concerned. To them the world they live in is the best world possible. Said Theodore Parker in his last sickness: "If not hilarious as when well, I am never sad. In all my illness, and it is now in its third year, I have not had a single sad hour. I have such absolute confidence in the INFINITE LOVE which creates and provides for the world, and each individual in it, that I am sure death is always a blessing, a step forward and upward, to the person who dies." That word is from the heart of the great prophet of free faith in America.

When that faith shall have had time to mature, when it shall have taken possession of the popular mind, so as to be quietly domesticated there, when it shall have tried its efficacy in the department of domestic nurture, when two or three generations of children shall have been reared in it, when it shall have infused a soul into literature, written songs, poems, nursery rhymes, hymns for church and home, its full power as a ministration of joy will be revealed. Then a change will take place in all the habitual feelings of men. New emotions will be excited by the incidents of life. Temperaments will be modified in accordance with the mind's new attitude towards the encompassing world. The ancient gloom will be dispelled. The creature will look into the Creator's face with a smile.

V.

LIVING FAITH.

AMONG the many criticisms that are made on the
Radical Belief, there is one that seems to give a
more hearty satisfaction to the critics than any other, because it touches the most vital part of the matter. The
criticism is that the faith is not a living one. Intellectual
it may be, brilliant, fascinating, plausible, but it possesses
no power of communicating life either to those that hold
it or to those whom they wish to convince. This is the
charge.

This defect is ascribed to various causes. Some say the
Radical Belief is but a heap of denials, and no faith can
live on denials. It has no Trinity, no Incarnation, no
Redeemer, no Vicarious Atonement, no Day of Judgment,
no Perdition, no Salvation for believers; it has no miraculous history, no heaven-sent apostles, no inspired book,
no infallible church, no immutable creed, no special revelations, no saving sacraments, no priesthood or prophecy;
how then can it be living? What has it to live on?
What has it to live for?

Others, who accept the denials of the new faith, and
welcome them, to whom its negative aspect is incidental
to its positive, who are in full sympathy with its ideas of
God, Christ, Christianity, the world present and the world
to come, who see in it the only rational faith, complain,
on their part, of the same thing their adversaries exult in,
namely: that the faith, though it ought to be a living one,

is not. It does not strike root, it does not spread, its boughs are not laden with fruit, it is smitten with the plague of barrenness.

I. That ours is not a living faith is supposed to be proved by its apparent inability to form and establish churches. Every other sect builds costly houses of worship and crowds them with people. Catholicism goes on erecting cathedrals; Protestantism multiplies chapels, organizes religious associations, ordains preachers and pastors. Even Unitarianism has its edifices and its clergy. What institutions of this sort can the Radicals show? Their organizations are soon disorganized, their societies, wanting principles of cohesion, fall to pieces and dissolve. The perpetuity of their churches, which are not churches in any true sense, but congregations, audiences, occasional assemblages, depends on the power of some individual orator to collect about him people enough to afford him support, and to hold them by the spell of his eloquence so long as his popularity lasts; while he lives, perhaps, the society flourishes and looks like an institution. But if he dies, or is taken sick, or loses his voice, or for any reason leaves his place, the association breaks up and the building passes into other hands. The faith cannot get itself planted and instituted; so its foes vociferate—so its friends deplore.

To this proof of lifelessness which has so convincing a look, the Radical serenely replies that, admitting the facts mentioned, he is not in the least disturbed by them. He does not want churches. He does not desire permanent organizations, or closely compacted societies that can live on mechanically, driven by sheer force of momentum, long after the impelling power is withdrawn. These boasted religious institutions show that faith was alive once, not that it is alive now. The object of the new faith is to form associations, however temporary and limited, on the ground of intellectual and spiritual affinities; to make as many centres of fine influence as possible, each to last till its vitality is spent, and no longer. If these centres did not exist, if no sparkling points appeared, no magnetic attractions, no crystallizing processes, then indeed the faith would be lifeless. But so long as these are extant and visible to all men, the faith is doing its characteristic work. The fact that societies vanish is of no significance. The significant fact is that they again and again reappear.

II. But the new faith has no Dogma, it is urged again, and dogma is the foundation of everything. Dogma is the intellectual substance of every faith. To define the dogma and defend it, to expound and propagate it, is the business of the church. This gives the believers their object. But the principle of the Rationalist faith is not vital enough to build a dogma. It has, consequently, no organs devoted to the dissemination of its views; no daily paper, no weekly journal, no monthly magazine. It has attempted these things and failed. Its chief monthly periodical goes out of existence after a short and eventful career. A predecessor sustained a precarious position for barely a twelvemonth; it is a question how long the vehicles now running will continue to move. The faith lacks intellectual no less than organizing faculty. It is deficient in live mind. Having no system of definite thoughts, no coherent formulas of doctrine, it, of course, possesses no electrifying power.

To this statement, which looks grave, the imperturbable Radical quietly makes answer to this effect: that Dogmatism being his chief enemy, he would simply stultify himself by trying to rally people about a dogma. His business is the overthrow of the dogmatic spirit, the abolition of the creed quality, the destruction of those " organs " of faith which revive prejudice and bigotry. He would give faith a natural expression, and let it find its natural channels. If it will not flow in one avenue it will in another. If it collects in pools, lakes, reservoirs, well; equally well if it flows in rivulets. No " organ " can voice it all, or any of it for a long time, or for a great multitude of people, and when one has ceased speaking acceptably it deceases. That our papers and magazines flourish briefly and disappear, is a sign that the living water of this dispensation finds flowing streams more congenial than standing pools.

III. Let this pass, then. A more fatal charge lies against the new faith, and that of a character less easily met. Professing to be progressive and humane, to pray for a kingdom of God in this world, to expect a regenerated social condition instead of a future heaven, it distinguishes itself by no efforts to make real its glorious visions of humanity. It inaugurates no great movements of philanthropy; it institutes no original reform; it sets on foot no crusade against monstrous vices, crimes, and iniquities; it takes the lead in no fresh assaults against the old foes Christianity has been combating for centuries. Where are its grand institutions of beneficence ? Where are the evidences of its interest in the poor, the sick, the afflicted, the abandoned, the disfranchised ? Where are its brotherhoods of self-sacrificing souls ? Where are its sisterhoods of mercy? Where are its hospitals, its asylums, its houses of refuge, its orphans' homes, its retreats for the old, the disabled, the helpless ? The charities of Romanism are known and esteemed of all men. Protestant beneficence gives demonstration of power. The Radical does nothing. He boasts of his humanity, and leaves the humanities to his neighbors. He talks hourly of his interest in social questions, and resigns to his orthodox friend the duty of solving them.

I will not urge the usual considerations by which this accusation is met. I will not cite the examples of eminent beneficence displayed by Radicals; the generosity of this one to the poor; the munificence of that one to the working classes; the devotion of this man's fortune to the cause of popular education, of that one's to the work of aiding homeless women. All these things are done under the inspiration of the old ideas, and have nothing characteristic in design or method. Nor will I do more than allude to the circumstance that among the most advanced and earnest leaders in every grand movement of reform, whether social, financial, commercial, political, or moral, the believers in the new faith will be found toiling and devoting themselves. Statements of this kind do not fairly meet the objection. For these grand movements in humanity—the agitation against war, for example, against intemperance, against licentiousness, against the gambling-hell, against cruelty in prisons and barbarism in legislation—were initiated by men of the old faith. The Radicals found them at work and worked with them. They may have worked with a different interest, under a fresh motive, in an original spirit; but the work was old work, and little has been done to impart to it a new soul, or supply to it new facilities.

Let the truth of the charge be admitted; the new faith cannot compete with the old in what are commonly called "benevolent enterprises." It would not, probably, if it were as rich and capable as the old faith is. Not because the Radicals are stingy, as has been over and over again asserted; but because they *cannot accept the principle on which those enterprises are conducted, and no other principle is yet in working order.* No original work is as yet possible. In the old-fashioned, conventional modes of charity, the new faith has no confidence. It perceives that

4*

they are not rational; it knows that they are not scientific; it strongly suspects that they are not reformatory or regenerating; it is more than half persuaded that they bring serious mischiefs and even permanent evils in their train; its very love of humanity forbids its enlisting itself enthusiastically with their supporters.

At any rate, this species of humane labor is sufficiently well attended to. Both Catholic and Protestant Christendom engage in it with due emulation. There is no dearth of the hospitality which takes from people the responsibility of caring for their sick. There are enough of orphan asylums which snatch children away from the toils and temptations incident to their exposed condition, to make them nuns or monks, or some other quite useless and hopeless thing. There is good supply of " Refuges " and " Homes," that gather in and sink into oblivion many a man and woman and child who should be a help to society and not a burden. Of alms-giving there is a thousand times more than enough, and of pious attempts to draw people into the church by holding before them a soup tureen.

Vast sums of money are given to such charities. Very little of it, probably, is bestowed out of a free heart, from pure love of humanity, with the single desire to improve the social condition of fellow-men, or to diminish mortal suffering. A great deal of it, no doubt, is bestowed in the hope of future recompense. The motto of Protestant charity is: "He that giveth to the poor lendeth to the Lord." The gift is an investment on the very best security. It is a price paid for salvation. It secures a passage to the heavenly courts and a favored place there. The Catholic church obtained its wealth, in a large measure, from persons who wished to secure the safety of their own souls or the souls of their kindred. The Protestant churches obtain the wealth they spend in beneficence by appealing to the love of souls and to the hope of Heaven. How much of the money would be given were this selfish motive taken away, it would be idle to conjecture; probably a very small proportion of it. To say that disinterested beneficence is rare, is to state the case feebly. The beneficence that is satisfied with ordinary dividends, with average returns, with simple interest, is rare. It is the promise of the celestial compound interest that draws the subscriptions to the evangelical stock. This promise the Radical does not consider himself favored with. What he gives he gives from moral conviction or personal feeling, from genuine interest or from genuine principle. It is not an investment, but a contribution; not a treasure laid up in Heaven, but a treasure distributed on Earth.

The old methods of charity, discountenanced by reasonable men, discredited by practical men, denounced by scientific men, are wearing out. But new methods of charity —reasonable, scientific, practical—have not yet been devised. When they are devised we shall see the new faith taking hold, and the old faith dropping off. The new faith will exhibit its charity when it shall find an object that makes to it commanding appeal.

We are brought, then, at once to the question: What is it that constitutes a Living Faith? It is not its theology, its christology, its eschatology, ontology, or pneumatology; it is not the cast of its speculative thought. The Trinitarian hypothesis is no more vital than the Unitarian. The dogma of Christ's divinity is no more vitalizing than the doctrine of his humanity. There is no more quickening power in the idea of God's wrath than in the idea of his love. The most imposing faiths are sometimes the deadest. The most unpretending are sometimes the most alive.

I could tell you the name of a man whose "faith" is so exceeding small that, with the majority of Christians, he passes as a man of no faith whatever. For he not only rejects Christianity under every existing form, and has something approaching to antipathy toward its dogmas and institutions, its usages and its officials; but he will not call himself a believer in God or in Immortality. He is not so much as a Deist, but is what is commonly termed an Atheist. Yet the vitality of this man's—I will not say *spiritual*, I will say *human*—life is wonderful, far surpassing the average measure in those who share every religious help and consolation. Having acquired a competency by his business, he, while comparatively a young man, retired with what he had, fearing lest the absorbing nature of commercial pursuits should weaken his human interests, and the passion to be rich should make him indifferent to the needs of his fellow-men. The loss of two families, the first perishing by drowning before his eyes while he was looking for means of rescue, though they saddened, impoverished, and, for a time, desolated his life, made him neither morose, bitter, nor desperate. He turned himself bravely toward his consolers, seeking solace in his plants and flowers, the relief of friendship, and especially the resources of kindness. His sympathies were his comforters. His interest in humanity was his saviour. Fond of children, he gathered them about him and gave them joy. Two large orphan asylums—one Romanist and one Protestant—stand on ground that he presented for the purpose from his own estate. His services as a public-spirited citizen are generally acknowledged. It is due to his sagacity, judgment, and perseverance that a very beautiful cemetery has been laid out in the city of his residence. No good charity ever appeals to him in vain. His simple habits, unostentatious demeanor, gentle spirit, his truthfulness, friendliness, and entire unworldliness, render him at once honored and beloved.

Here is a thing to be explained. The living force in this rare but by no means singular man was not the infidelity or the atheism ; nor was it any other mode of thinking about religion that had taken the place of these juiceless negations. It was not speculative after any sort. It was the intimate connection he maintained with real interests. He clung to things ; he stuck to plain facts ; he did not wander away from palpable concerns. He had practical purposes which he lived for ; and, living for them, he lived all over.

This is the secret of all vitality. A Greek fable tells of the giant Antæus, who challenged and vanquished all comers till Hercules came. Hercules discovered after some wrestling that Antæus derived all his strength from the ground. Whenever his feet were lifted from the soil, his vigor seemed to desert him ; but the least touch of his foot to the earth imparted to him new life. On making this discovery, the hero, with a vast effort, heaved his antagonist up, and strangled him in a terrible embrace while held in the air.

So faith lives by contact with the ground. The living faiths of the earth have owed, perhaps, the best portion of their power to an immediate, practical purpose that roused and directed their zeal.

What faith has shown more living energy than the faith of the Israelites ? Persecution has not killed it. Scorn has not discouraged it. Exile and dispersion have not scattered or decomposed it. It is flourishing nobly to-day. It builds its temples in the New World as majestic and gorgeous as those erected by the wealthiest Christian sect. It gathers its children, observes its customs, institutes its charities, cares for its poor, prints its journals, enunciates its Law, with a spirit as lofty and a heart as tender as ever. If we ask to what this extraordinary vitality is owing, the answer is : Not to its doctrine of One God, but to an indomitable purpose, ruling and decisive in its early history, active in every episode of its career, sovereign now in its most zealous children, to secure and maintain the position of a peculiar people, called to a high destiny, and to that destiny set apart. To preserve and justify their title to the spiritual command ; to keep the race pure from outward admixture of blood, and from inward apostacy ; to fulfil the national conditions on which the divine favor was pledged, constitutes the deliberate aim and determination of the Jewish people. Should this aim be lost sight of, this determination be relaxed, that moment would probably mark the period of the faith's decline. Its sinews would be cut ; its power of movement would be paralyzed. There is nothing in its ideas that will save it. They will be lost in the ocean of modern thought.

The Mohammedan Faith was a living faith so long as the national spirit animated the Arab races with an ambition to plant their civilization in Europe. The sudden outbreak of Moslem life was prodigious. It was a nation's soul aflame. The religious beliefs were simple and barren in the extreme. They had not inspiration enough in them to stir a tribe from lethargy. It was the determination of the people to make themselves felt in history that made Mohammed's name a name of terror, and set the crescent above the cross.

The Church of Rome has, and always has had in its days of power, a purpose, which is simply its own aggrandisement, the establishment of its rule and authority, the merging of other churches in itself, the gathering of all Christians into its communion. To accomplish this purpose was the ambition of the great popes ; to aid in it the

terrible Order of Jesus was instituted; to this end the
preaching orders were commissioned ; the Holy Inquisi-
tion exerted its pious offices toward this result. This is
what Pius IX. is praying, protesting, calling councils, and
publishing bulls for. The revival of this purpose will explain the revival of energy in the old medieval religion.
The church aims at dominion. It represents a policy, not
a faith; it means statecraft, not religion; its priests are
politicians. The absorption in temporal concerns keeps
the spiritual enthusiasm burning.

Protestantism has likewise an immediate object, which
it never loses sight of. Its endeavor is to *bring souls to
Christ ;* a perfectly definite, tangible, practical thing to
do; a thing that excites ambition, rouses enthusiasm, enlists determination, in truth, calls for all these qualities in
extraordinary measure. The missionary societies labor in
this interest ; the bible and tract societies hold this end in
view ; the charitable societies derive inspiration from this
purpose. Their " faith " does not animate their effort : it
is their effort that animates their faith.

The Society of Friends has exhibited great vitality. If
we inquire into its causes, we shall find them, I think, not
in the beautiful doctrine of the " Inner Light," but in the
stubborn resistance to the spirit of worldliness in its conspicuous forms. It was their battle with formalism, with
the fashions of church and state, with ceremony, hollowness, and pretence, that called out the steadfast courage of
those hearts. Would you find the secret of their power—
read their rules of discipline, laid down as carefully as any
military code, and in the palmy days of the society ob-
served as conscientiously as if they were soldiers in
presence of an enemy. While the discipline was maintained
the sect flourished. But when idleness, frivolity, and fashion came in, and the world spirit made its power felt

among its old assailants, the faith began to decline. It can scarcely be called a living faith now.

If now we instance some Faith which, notwithstanding its pretensions to high spiritual ideas, has never fairly succeeded in earning the title of a living faith—the Socinian or old-fashioned Unitarian—it will appear that its defect consists in the absence of any such purpose as I have described. It has no practical justification for itself. It is not working in the interest of a powerful organization like the Church of Rome. It is not toiling in the endeavor to bring souls to Christ, like the " evangelical " Protestants. It offers no battle to worldliness; flings down no challenge to music, art, literature, the drama; engages in no deadly conflict with formalism, ritualism, or ceremonialism; has, in fact, no well-defined foe. It does not toil to save men from hell, for it believes in no hell of flame and everlasting torment; it does not toil to get men into heaven, for it believes in no such heaven as men can be "got into." The salvation of souls is hardly its object, for it does not put the issue between salvation and damnation with sufficient sharpness to engage the consecration of the will. The social improvement and elevation of men is not its object, for it has no working philosophy of social life. There are ideas enough in it; but it lives in ideas, and like the giant Antæus languishes there. No fine theological shadings, no ingenious biblical interpretations furnish the requisites for contact with a world of realities. Not possessing any ruling impulse to *do* something, it is not happy in the consciousness of *being* something.

The living faith is the faith with a living purpose. What then is our living purpose? What are we aiming at? Let us apply the rule to the new faith. For, bright, intellectual, spirited, and spiritual as this seems to be, it must con·

form to the conditions, or decline. It cannot live on air. Like all the rest it must feel called to a certain work, and the imperative necessity of doing that work must be forced upon it, or the anticipations of those who build on it will be disappointed.

To me, the Radical faith has such a purpose, and on account of it owes all the interest it possesses for me. The purpose is both negative in aspect and positive.

On its negative side, the new faith proposes to itself the sacred duty of making war against the great spiritual powers of Dogmatism and Superstition; regarding these powers by whomsoever wielded, in whatever guise arrayed, as being the foes of all pure religion. These powers, I say —for such they are—powers instituted, organized, expressed in rite, symbol, creed, domiciled in churches, and represented by actual bodies of men. They present a definite object of attack, an object as definite as ever presented itself to an assaulting column. The Hebrew faith never proposed a more distinct end to its prophets, priests, and zealots. The Mohammedan faith had no more palpable intent when it entered on its determined struggle with idolatry. The Catholic faith moved toward no more clearly outlined end. The Protestant faith had in view no more tangible object. An assault on Dogmatism and Superstition is no more visionary or vague than an assault on the foul religions of the Canaanites, or the idolatries of Islam, the heresies of the middle age, or the infidelities of more modern times.

The abolitionist, when he struck at slavery, had no more declared a foe; the temperance men, in their wrestle with the demon of the still, do not confront a more distinctly avowed or defiant adversary. The people who rally to throw off the burdens that oppress the civil and social state of women, are not conscious of being pitted against a more consolidated antagonist. Our enemy is at our doors; he is noisy and violent; the mischief he does is evident to the dullest perception; his baleful influence is visible everywhere. We would keep no terms with him, we would pursue him to his fastnesses, feeling that, in doing so, we are contending for the gravest interests of mankind.

This is the new faith's negative work—its work of destruction; work arduous and long, but extremely needful, demanding effort, patience, faith, courage, sacrifice— but rewarding all these with the conviction that the work is done for humanity, and will endure when the strife shall be ended. Nothing less than a new crusade is called for. If the Radical faith will undertake it, it will have a name and a virtue to live; if it declines to undertake it, no brilliancy of intellect or glow of anticipation will rescue it from death.

The positive aim of the new faith is the creation and consecration of Character. This, too, is a definite, and, it may be said, an original purpose. For, although the old faith respects character, calls for it as the result of religious training and the expression of spiritual experience, it has made it an incidental rather than a primary thing, an evidence of the religious life, not the sum and substance of it. It has given to character an artificial cast, a theological tone, an unnatural twist that answered to the peculiar kind of training the church imposed. The old faith encouraged and cultivated a single type of character, with some degree, not an eminent degree, of success. But in character as a natural, vital development of the man, in plain human character, based on scientific grounds, available for every day uses, good for ordinary life, it had no engrossing interest. It studied neither its elements, its laws, nor its operations. It was more concerned with "graces" than with virtues. And it prized the "graces" for their talismanic potency in opening the gates of heaven to believers, rather than for their wholesome quality in sweetening society.

The new faith concerns itself with the cultivation of simple human goodness as an end sufficient in and of itself. Without reference to beliefs or sacraments, without reference to the rewards of heaven or the punishments of hell, without any particular feeling that goodness is a thing well pleasing in the sight of God, or possesses any character of merit, the new faith emphasizes character in opposition to custom or credence, and whatever else raises a false issue with it; it not only puts character before everything else, it makes it a substitute for everything else, the one indispensable element in experience. And to this end it regards character not as the product of ecclesiastical discipline or theological education, not as a result of "Christian" or other religious tradition and training, but as the consummation of obedience to the plain facts of personal and social life.

Here, too, we have a definite end of attainment. As the Roman Church labors to bring men to Peter, as the Protestant churches toil to bring men to Christ, we endeavor to bring men to themselves. As Romanism aims at making men submissive, as Protestantism aims at making men believing, so we aim at making men self-respecting and true. The Catholic system would break men down; the Protestant system would convert them; we would teach them the laws of rational development. It is a work greatly needing to be done, and requiring the intelligent effort of many people who are united by a common aim and enthusiasm. A religious body that will plant itself on this rock, that will make character the solitary condition of fellowship, the sole test of worth, the single pledge of usefulness, and will make character consist of the simplest human elements, truthfulness, for instance, fairness, honesty, fidelity to things in hand, not in high-flying "graces," or "evangelical" gifts or super-eminent attributes, but in the qualities that meet the exigencies of daily living—a religious body that will do this steadfastly will help to effect a practical revolution in religion. It will inaugurate a new Protestantism. It will precipitate a new departure from the ancient folds.

That there exists any religious body that sees the necessity of this mission and accepts it, that comprehends it and works in it, I do not affirm. I do not declare this to be the actual endeavor, the deliberate, determined endeavor of the rational faith. But something like this should be its endeavor. If the new faith lives, it will be through its fidelity to this charge. The professors of it are, as yet, too much under the influence of their old-time associations; too much implicated in the modes of thinking and feeling that prevail around them; too much in thraldom to the powers that so long ruled their minds, to be fully awake to the demands made on their earnestness. Possibly another generation of men and women, with clearer eyes for actual issues, and braver hearts for radical toil, may have to come up and take charge of the great cause of protest against superstition, and of championship in favor of character. If the living Radical believers are too idle, too faint-hearted or too short-sighted to do it, others will appear in the future who have no such disabilities. The motto of these will be, and the motto will have kindling power over the multitude:

"Down with Superstition; up with Character."

VI.

THE GOSPEL OF TO-DAY.

MY theme is the gospel of to-day—the gospel demanded by to-day, suited to to-day's needs, addressed to to-day's intelligence. The eternal gospel has
its phases, being variously apprehended by the successive
generations of mankind. Truth is one and the same; its
interpretations are many. An early Christian writer
speaks of Jesus Christ as being "the same yesterday,
to-day and forever;" and so doubtless he is in his own
spiritual essence. But the Jesus Christ of the Christian
creeds shifts his position from one end of creation to the
other. He occupies every place between simple humanity
and the Supreme Being. He is mortal man, spiritual
man, ideal man, angel, archangel, emanation from Deity,
Deity itself; being according to one apprehension meaner
than the meanest, according to another, higher than the
highest. Even the Eternal God reveals himself in time,
each eye beholding as much of his face as it can.

No gospel is the same yesterday, to-day, and forever, for
yesterday and to-day are not the same. Every day has its
peculiar need which former days cannot supply or anticipate. To be sure, there are constant needs, such as food,
clothing, shelter, and for these the provisions are constant.
Other needs are occasional, incidental, and though deep,
not perpetual. Human nature has its moods and special
exigencies, which must be met as they arise—the mood of
gladness or of sadness, of penitence or of aspiration, of hu-

miliation or of self-confidence, of depression or of joy ; and the gospel that addresses itself to the mood is the gospel for the day.

The word "gospel" means good news. But what is good news to one man or one age is not necessarily good news to another; it may be bad news, or indifferent news, or no news at all. Jesus brought to his countrymen the message that their Messiah had come to fulfill the promise made to their ancestors through the prophets, that the Messiah's kingdom should be established on the earth, and their dream of social felicity be realized. It was blessed tidings to the Jews, pining in bondage and sick with hope deferred. But it was not a message that the Greeks and Romans and Asiatics cared to hear; it was announcement of no future for them.

Paul brought great news, namely, that the Christ was soon to come, in clouds of glory, to judge the world and save his own. The Christian world was on tip-toe of expectation ; trembling, hoping for the time of its transfiguration ; listening for the trumpets ; watching for the angels who should deliver the faithful from the rule of the oppressor and the misery of a world that seemed on the brink of destruction. But is this good news to us ? Was it good news to the people of the next century ? Do we look for the second coming of Christ ? Do we desire the end of the world ? Would it be a pleasant thought to any considerable number of people now, that they were liable at any moment to put on spiritual bodies and float away in the air ?

Luther's gospel was good news to the hungering souls of his generation ; a veritable "gospel of the day." They wanted to hear that their salvation did not depend on the Church of Rome, the absolution of the priest, the grace of the mass, penance on the knees or with the whip, payment of Peter's pence, daily paternoster and periodical confession. To hear that they might be saved by faith alone in the personal Saviour, and the interior change of the heart under the influence of the Holy Spirit, was something that made their souls leap for joy. It was a proclamation of spiritual freedom, restoring to them their manhood. But the announcement produces no thrill of ecstasy now. The Church of Rome is nothing to us ; we have never been in bondage to it, and never expect to be. We have been spiritual freemen, we and our forefathers for generations. The gospel of Luther is an old and almost forgotten story ; the dust of ages stops the ears that hailed it.

The great teacher gives voice to his time, not to all time. His doctrine is not his own, but the persuasion or the prophecy of his epoch. The Father who sends him is the spirit of his age, which imparts to him its need and its hope. I do not perceive that Jesus brought a new revelation, in the usual sense of the word, or, on his own authority, announced any unknown truth. As he heard, he spoke, and what he heard was the voice from the heart of his people. We find all his thoughts in the religious books of his nation ; sometimes expressed in the very same language he himself used, sometimes in phrases as expressive, though less felicitous than his own. His doctrine, that God is creator, preserver, guide, comforter, immediate presence and providence, pitying father, is enunciated in most touching forms of speech many times over ; it is the burden of prophecy and psalm. His doctrine, that the essence of religion was love to God and man, was as ancient as the literature of his race. That God loved mercy more than sacrifice, that spiritual worth made one greater than the temple and superior to the Sabbath, that the kingdom of heaven was within and not without, a moral, not a political state, were among the first principles of the wisdom he learned as a child. The " Golden Rule " was laid down explicitly by the earliest and latest masters in Hebrew ethics. The substance of the " Sermon on the Mount " may be picked up in different places all along the road of the national progress. The "Beatitudes," less exquisitely phrased than by his poetic lips, gem the pages of sacred song and grace the sentences of proverbial wisdom. Even the " Lord's Prayer " is made up of invocations and petitions that were familiar to the piety of his nation.

Jesus voiced the purer and deeper consciousness of his race, feeling himself surrounded by the spirits of the past ; in his moments of ecstasy, holding spiritual communion with Moses and Elias. His " But I say unto you," was not the claim of a peculiar authority, distinct from that of other teachers, and above them, for he said that he came not to destroy the law and the prophets, but to fulfill them. It was rather the emphatic declaration of the superiority of the spirit to the letter, the claim and right of the soul of the faith to set aside the traditions, forms, and formularies of it. It was not himself he preached, but that which came to him and poured through him.

Paul seemed to be an original teacher, with a gospel all his own ; a distinct and peculiar message, that had never been delivered before. But he took particular pains to say that nothing of the kind was true. The Hebrew scriptures, he said, rightly interpreted, contained all he had to communicate; not in precise words, perhaps, but in symbol and allegory. The first thing Paul did, in addressing a Jewish audience, was to convince them by ingenious exposition of scripture, that his message had been foreshadowed in the beginning, and ought to be received as timely, the appointed word of the hour.

We think of Luther as standing up and delivering a new doctrine on new authority. But he did no such thing. His doctrine was as old, at least, as the New Testament, where it had slumbered for a thousand years, and whence he derived it. He spoke out of the heart of the Christian theology as well as out of his own heart, feeling that his own spiritual experience brought him in closest sympathy with those who most deeply believed and most fervently prayed.

Channing, though pushed out of the churches and forced into a position of isolation and antagonism, preaching what appeared to be a new gospel, never claimed the character of a solitary prophet. He appealed to the New Testament, believed that he had the sympathy of the purest souls in Christendom, and felt that Jesus stood by his side. The Father that sent him was the human nature in whose capacity and dignity he put his trust. He was sure that natural goodness, affection, truth, and justice were on his side, and in that company he could not feel alone.

Theodore Parker, that monumental man who stood like a solitary oak-tree in the middle of a plain—the independent soul, strong of thought and strong of speech, standing up against Bible, church, and creed, casting off his ecclesiastical and doctrinal leanings, throwing down the props of ceremonial, and stepping forth into the open air of thought—nevertheless spake not as of himself, set up to be no originator or discoverer, but pointed to a Father who had sent him. This Father spoke to him in many voices of teacher, philosopher, sage, and saint, bearing witness to the essential needs and the living hopes of humanity. Most clearly and emphatically he addressed him in the profound convictions which he claimed were native to the universal heart, and which gave immediate

5

demonstration of God, immortality, and the moral law. None was ever simpler, humbler, more docile than this sturdy man as he waited on the bidding of the Lord.

No teacher stands outside, independent of all constituency. The most radical teacher has the largest constituency, draws from the deepest well, catches the purest breath in his sail. Mr. Abbot is conscious of walking in a large company, and feels his inadequacy to discharge the message entrusted to him as keenly as ever did an Augustine or a Paul.

The preacher of to-day has a gospel of to-day.

What now is this gospel? First, let us ask, What was the gospel it hopes to supplant? What was the gospel of yesterday and the day before?

The gospel of yesterday proclaimed the glad tidings of deliverance from sin. It addressed man as a sinner, needing supernatural aid and rescue. The alleged fact of sin was the sole occasion of the message. To appreciate the message you must appreciate the occasion—deliverance from sin. Not from ignorance, error, mistake, stupidity, prejudice, immaturity, inexperience, inherited or acquired disability, the effects of an untaught or undisciplined mind; but from an "inward deep disease;" a subtle, malign, inwrought, organic power; a law of corruption and demoralization; a taint in the blood; a traditional malady; an inherited curse, which was incurable except by divine and special aid.

To this little word Paul gave the deadly significance it has borne ever since. Jesus rarely used it, and never in its present theological meaning. It occurs but once in Matthew. It occurs in John but seven times, and only once in a deeper than the usual sense of wrong-doing. In the single epistle to the Romans it recurs more than thirty times, and always loaded with the most terrible significance. It was the key-note of Paul's theology, the soul of his religion. " The bondage of sin," " the law of sin," " the dominion of sin," are phrases often repeated in his letters. He exhausts his remarkable powers of language in describing its irresistible and fatal sway. He ascribes to it physical death, moral disorder, mental decrepitude, and spiritual imbecility. Starting with Adam, it had gone on gaining power from ages ; plunging the races of men into the pit from which they could not rise. It had acquired the force of an elemental law, which took everything under its sway, and drove all the human family before it as the breath of the thunder-storm drives before it the loose straw of the pavement. The risen Christ, risen because sinless, broke the charm, and opened the way by which, through faith in him, the rescued believers might escape from the doom.

In the middle ages, the central thought of theology was the thought of sin. The Church of Rome was an organization for the deliverance of mankind from sin and its consequences. For this the hierarchy was instituted ; for this the priest was consecrated, the altar built, the mass celebrated, the sacrament administered, the rule and ordinance prescribed. Baptism washed out inherited sin ; confirmation imparted strength to overcome actual sin ; communion kept the soul in concurrence with the source of power ; penance chastised sinful desire ; absolution released from the penalties of sin committed ; extreme unction imparted consolation and promise of blessedness to the dying. At every turn the sinner was met by the deliverer. Take the idea of sin away, and you deprive the church of the whole ground of its existence ; you abolish it, or reduce it to a shade that ought to be exorcised.

Protestantism made more poignant and intense the conviction of sin, by making it more personal. Luther and

Calvin dwelt perpetually on the private experience of sin, pressing the matter home to the individual consciousness; driving it in, so to speak, with all their prodigious power of statement, argument and exhortation. What were the Lutheran or the Calvinistic theology, with the total depravity, the vicarious sacrifice, the atonement, the Saviour, intercessor and mediator, justification, sanctification, final rescue and salvation, if this idea of sin were taken away? Evangelical Christianity, as it is called, owes all its vitality to that idea; would be utterly barren and meaningless without it; would, in fact, be sheer nonsense without it.

The liberal sects of Protestantism, Unitarians and Universalists, use the word with such effect as they may in sermon and prayer; fill it out with meaning as well as they can; keep it sounding, at all events, whether emptily or not, well knowing that if they drop it from their theological vocabulary there will be an end of their system. If they cannot say " sin," they cannot say " Christ; " and if they cannot say " Christ," they must hold their peace. The doctrine of sin is indispensable to them, for the only good news they have to bring is that a way of escape from sin is provided.

It is a common persuasion that the consciousness of sin is a deep-seated and indestructible fact in human nature, a fact that we cannot get away from, the existence of which is inexplicable, except on the ground that men are sinners and need salvation. But this is the precise point that I call in question. It is not difficult to account for the so-called " sense of sin," or for the belief that men are sinful creatures. Human experience was not the mother of it, as much as human speculation and sentiment. The speculation began in the East with contemplative men, who strove after states of mind with which the necessities of common life interfered. In their efforts to disengage

themselves from the " bondage of the flesh," as they called
it—that is, from the necessity of providing for their bodily
wants—they contracted a dread and an abhorrence of their
bodily appetites. Their passions became in their eyes evil
and the source of evil. The " animal " nature was at war
with the " spiritual." Their souls were " imprisoned " in
matter, and to effect its deliverance was the wise man's
highest duty. The world was a scene of penance; life a
process of discipline and purification. The sages, in their
writings, dwelt fervently on this aspect of things. Their
litanies were burdens of contrition, supplications to be delivered from the fatal tyranny of the body.

From the East these thoughts traveled Westward. They
filled the air that Paul breathed; they possessed Paul's
mind; they became the cardinal thoughts of his system.
The sense of weakness gave them intensity and sent them
home to the heart. A sense of infirmity is generally
accompanied by a sense of guilt. Helplessness is always
ready to make confession of wickedness. Seasons of depression are seasons of contrition. The times in which
Paul lived were heavy with anxiety and discouragement.
The Hebrew state was on the eve of dissolution; signs and
portents were in the sky; society was disorganizing, and
all knew and felt it; the people groaned under oppressive
rulers; property was unsafe; life was insecure; the country shook with suppressed war; labor was precarious; poverty was frightful; suffering, in every form, was hideous;
the iron tramp of the Roman legions was heard in the distance; the war cloud that was to envelop the nation came
rolling on; the spirit of delusion and fanaticism seized on
the people; madmen saw visions, and enthusiasts dreamed
dreams; melancholy deepened into despair, and despair
rushed into suicide; from no quarter came promise of
help. Then, in their utter bewilderment, the frightened,

frantic people turned their eyes up to heaven, and dropped on their knees groaning and entreating.

Similar outbreaks of passion have occurred more than once in history. At the close of the tenth century a portion of Europe was possessed by the belief that the world was coming to an end in flame. The condition of humanity was most deplorable. The earth seemed ready for burning, and the agony of weakness easily changed into an agony of prayer. In the course of our late civil war, when the Government was apparently brought to bay, when the bloodshed was too appalling to think of, when volunteering ceased, and the draft was resisted, and civil war menaced the North, and the mob spirit began to rise, the panic of penitential fear seized the popular heart, and convulsed it with terrible spasms. Fasts were appointed, crowds flocked to the churches, orthodoxy stirred up its fires, revival preachers plied their whips on the naked, quivering souls, and we heard of nothing but sin and judgment. The tide of public affairs turned, and the sackcloth was put off.

The financial distress of 1857 shook the souls of men even more fiercely. The collapse of credit; the fall of great commercial houses, burying humbler establishments beneath their ruins; the widespread impoverishment, the overwhelming bankruptcy, the general distrust, the crazing helplessness, brought the usual feeling of moral infirmity and spiritual desperation. The professors of the art of agitation produced their instruments of torture once more, and went to work to sting, prick, score and scarify the sensitive conscience of sin. One of the greatest "revivals" of the century took place. The whole land was shaken; the preacher's exhortation was responded to by groans, cries, confessions, that seemed to indicate that the heart of the world was breaking. The return of prosperity and the restoration of commercial credit dispelled the illusion.

The spectres vanished ; the ministers of the revival picked up their tools and disappeared ; the churches were shut, and men recovered their serenity.

The "sense of sin" had another justification in the gigantic immoralities of former times. More than one emperor was a monster of wickedness ; great princes and nobles, even priests, cardinals and popes, illustrated, in obscene and villainous ways, the bestial elements in human nature ; eminent statesmen and philosophers practiced, now and then, vices that would put modern shamelessness to the blush. The powerful tyrannized, the rich plundered, the great outraged justice, the holy violated decency. That at the decline and fall of the Roman Empire a belief in human depravity should have prevailed, is not surprising. A conviction of sin was all but a necessity when the most conspicuous men were the most conspicuous sinners.

Such supports as these had the doctrine of sin—such were its generating causes. But none of these causes exist now with any force. The first certainly does not, for the contemplative life is confined to the very few. It may be said that there is no conscious war between the terrestrial and the celestial life of men. We are quite content with our bodies and their corporeal environment. To be disembodied is not the general desire. Very rarely, indeed, do we find a Plotinus who is ashamed of his flesh.

Nor is our age oppressed with a feeling of helplessness. Far enough from that! If we are oppressed by anything, it is by a feeling of our sufficiency. Small sense of imbecility, the minimum of misgiving, have people who undertake the management of all their own concerns, choose their rulers, make their laws, set up their institutions, prevent famine, beat off plague, stamp out cholera, travel by steam, talk in lightning, and make the forces of nature do

their work. Sense of sin, indeed! It is no easy task to
start a feeble and evanescent feeling of modesty or humility—to make them "realize" the fact that they are something less than omnipotent and omniscient, infallible and
impeccable. The extravagance of their conceit is as huge
as the former extravagance of contrition. Our enthusiasts
talk of reducing everything to actual science, and ensuring
all possible good to everybody. They promise prevention
of disease, indefinite duration of life, perfectly congenial
marriages, assurance of healthy offspring, the extirpation
of hereditary taint, and the redemption of natural existence from all its ills by an easy obedience to known principles of hygiene. We hear of balloon carriages and artificial flying apparatus, by which we shall be enabled to
move like birds through the air. To suggest to such people that they are sinners, has an air of grotesqueness that
borders on absurdity. Their confidence in themselves,
however overweening, has, at least, solid ground enough
to make impossible any general persuasion like that.

The sense of sin is not countenanced now by gigantic
private or social enormities. There are bad men, unprincipled gangs of men, criminals, marauders, and plunderers; but there are no corrupt *orders* or *classes* of men.
There is no wholesale oppression of the weak, no system-
atic grinding of the poor, no general defrauding of the
ignorant, no deliberately organized inhumanities. The
rogues who swindle the public, the plotters and schemers
who corrupt legislatures, are seen and known of all good
men. The public are warned against them, the press
exposes them, opinion denounces them; their proceedings
are noticed, their ways tracked, their plans fathomed, their
motives understood, their character dissected, their doom
foretold. Intemperance and licentiousness are frightful
evils, but less frightful by far than they were, and are

made the mark for general and earnest attack. The virtue of the community is pledged and banded against them. There is conscience enough to put all the most grievous ills away, to banish the rogues, strip the plunderers, dethrone the tyrants of the railway and the "ring," if the way to do it were only discovered, if moral force were but seconded by sagacity. At all events, we feel that our fate is in our own hands; confidence in natural ability is restored; the force of honesty and ordinary virtue is conceded. No one thinks of calling in supernatural aid to break up the "ring" at Albany, or confound the machinations of Fisk and Gould. We ask no intervention of miracle-working saviours to redeem us from intemperance or rescue us from the dominion of the "social vice." If wit, intelligence, prudence, self-love, love of the public good, love of humanity, love of God, will not enable us to redeem ourselves, nothing will.

The consciousness of sin, therefore, is gone; the doctrine of sin is obsolete; the idea of sin has lost its hold on the mind; and with the sense of sin disappears the apparatus for securing salvation from sin. Farewell to incarnate divinity, saviour, intercessor, mediator; farewell to priest and altar; farewell to church and dogma, to revealed theology and sanctifying rite, to formularies of faith and ecclesiastical authorities! *Men are not sinners.* Dolts they may be—blunderers, dunces, simpletons, fools, wrongdoers from ignorance, dullness, inexperience, immaturity, from unbalanced minds, untrained tempers, undeveloped consciences; but sinners, in the old theological or "evangelical" sense of the word, no more. The gospel that announced the glad tidings of salvation finds few hearers among the people of to-day. That message is not listened for. It meets no eager want, and multitudes refuse to go where it is spoken.

5*

Another idea is substituted for the idea of sin--the idea of Rectitude. *The rectitude of human nature;* not its finished perfection, not its complete integrity, but the wholesomeness of its elements and the sacredness of its constitution. Man is not a perfect machine; if he were, he would run more evenly than he does; he would not get out of order or dash off the track. He is an organic being, with powers of expansion and capacities of development; but the law by which he is organized secures all this, if obeyed, not thwarted. He is to take his constitution as it is and make more of it, unfolding its faculties and persuading it to grow in beauty. The "good news" of to-day imports that this growth is possible, that man is not divided against himself, that social interests are not at war, that all the powers are in sympathy and correspondence.

By contrasting in a few particulars, the gospel of yesterday with the gospel of to-day, this essential difference will be made apparent.

The gospel of yesterday announced faith in Christ as its prime postulate; the gospel of to-day announces faith in human nature.

The gospel of yesterday bade sit at Jesus' feet; the gospel of to-day bids stand on our own.

The gospel of yesterday counseled repose on Jesus' bosom; the gospel of to-day exhorts to " rally the good in the depths of yourself."

The gospel of yesterday proclaimed the saving efficacy of the church, as a close corporation, membership in which secured the concurrence of the Holy Ghost : the gospel of to-day proclaims the advent of a free society, membership in which guarantees participation in all the blessings of a common life.

The gospel of yesterday offered salvation through sacraments, prayers, pious exercises, and devout observances; the gospel of to-day offers mental and moral health, through education, culture, enlightenment, and training.

The gospel of yesterday promised saintliness and its reward to those who subdued and suppressed themselves—to the self-renouncing, the self-condemning, the self-crucifying; the gospel of to-day promises wholeness and its rewards to those who enlarge, expand, develop, and perfect themselves—to the noble, the earnest, the aspiring.

The gospel of yesterday praised the beauty of submission : the gospel of to-day sings the benefits of liberty.

The gospel of yesterday set up as a model the converted man: the gospel of to-day erects as its model the natural man.

The gospel of yesterday promised immortality as a boon to believers in the Christ : the gospel of to-day promises immortality as the natural inheritance of rational beings, the extension of rational existence beyond the grave.

The gospel of yesterday opened a vision of happiness in another world : the gospel of to-day opens a vision of happiness here on earth.

These are grave and sharp contrasts, which admit of no reconciliation.

Is it asked on what authority the new gospel is preached ? Not on the authority of instituted church, revealed doctrine, or inspired Bible ; not on the authority of any individual teacher or set of teachers. It claims no miraculous authentication ; it professes not to be the old word under a new interpretation, but is willing to stand on its own merits. That it is in accord with the tendencies of modern thought, in sympathy with current speculation, may be urged as in its favor. But its title to acceptance is based on its reasonableness. *It makes peace between the two worlds, the temporal and the eternal.* The deadly fault of the present systems of religion is their failure to combine with the present systems of politics, reform, trade, education, public activity. The thinkers and the worshippers hold no communion, have no common sympathy, share no interests, mingle in no enterprises. Science and faith are at war. Philosophy and faith are in perpetual disagreement. Reform and religion meditate different achievements and draw in opposite directions. The social economists and the preachers do not understand one another, get in each other's way, cross each other's track, fight each other's proceedings. The two worlds of business and worship do not circle in the same orbit. Men do not trade and pray in the same breath. Commerce with men and commerce with God are appointed for different days. Sense and soul tear one another.

The effect of this is most disastrous. Nothing of moment can be done. No great thing that demands a conspiracy of all the great powers, of thought and feeling, prudence and passion, will and wisdom, knowledge and sentiment, sagacity and aspiration, can be so much as attempted. No cause of political or social reform, no matter of deep human concern in which the interests of thousands are involved, can be carried through even the preliminary stages of discussion. Religious conviction is sure to come in sharp collision with worthy common-sense, and laudable enterprises are thus baffled at the start. On what should be the smoothest road, we go hitching, hobbling, grating along, to the ruin of our machinery and the exasperation of our tempers. Unless this radical evil can be removed, it is difficult to see how society is ever to go on in a career of wholesome improvement. It is impossible to live at the same in New York and in Jerusalem. Human nature has no more ability than it requires for its daily needs, and if the highest order of its energies is shut up in a church and held in reserve for extra-mundane purposes, the amount of disposable force must be seriously abridged.

The gospel of to-day proposes to remedy this defect by abolishing the discord in question, by making it possible to think and pray at the same time, and this it proposes to accomplish by substituting a rational for an irrational principle, and setting both religion and life to a new key. It promises to do this, and, if accepted, will do it. It holds the key of the situation.

Some may ask: Why, if this gospel is truly such a message of gladness, is it not more cordially welcomed? Why is its following so small? Why are its churches so few? Why are its preachers so feeble? We might answer the question by asking another. When was it otherwise? What new gospel was ever welcomed with enthusiasm? Jesus left a handful of disciples. The result of Paul's ardous labor was a group of churches, in all comprising but a few hundreds of people, probably, none of them absolutely solid and settled in his faith. Luther's "good tidings" did not kindle the world. Channing's fell upon dull ears. Parker's met with a heartier response, but even his did not run very swiftly. Too many ears must be unstopped to allow a ready access to new ideas. The more need that they who have heard the new tidings, have received and hailed the message, have been kindled or quieted, stirred or soothed by it, lifted by it to new life, or composed by it to new serenity, should labor to communicate to others the gospel that they are sure the world needs.

VII.

THE GOSPEL OF CHARACTER.

LET our theme be Character: the Gospel of Character. In the book of Micah, an old Testament writing, occurs the familiar passage : " He hath told thee, O man, what is good : and what doth the Lord require of thee but to do justly, love mercy, and walk humbly before thy God?" The New Testament contains many such statements. Jesus says, "Whatsoever things ye would that men should do to you, do ye even so to them, for this is the law and the prophets." Paul writes : " All the law is fulfilled in this one word : thou shalt love thy neighbor as thyself." James declares : " If ye fulfill the royal law according to the Scripture, thou shalt love thy neighbor as thyself, ye do well."

Passing from the Hebrew and Christian writings to the sacred writings of other religions, we find in the Koran, among other great sayings, this : "A single hour of justice is worth seventy years of prayer." We open the " Analects " of Confucius, and light on this passage : " When a man's character is right, the whole empire will turn to him with recognition and submission." Similar declarations of faith may be found in other literatures. I could cite language equally emphatic from the Greek poets, the Roman philosophers, the Eastern sages, the ancient oracles of Persia, India, Egypt, the modern literature of every country and race, the moral essays, treatises, discourses of eminent men of all theological complexions, believers and unbelievers.

The gospel of character is the one universal gospel, proclaimed everywhere in all ages; always in the same spirit, always with essentially the same substance, frequently in the same language. It is the gospel of no church, or sect, or religion, but of humanity. All have a right to preach it; none have the right to claim it as exclusively their own. It is no more Christian than it is Pagan. The atheist promulgates it as earnestly as the theist; the materialist may stand by it as loyally as the spiritualist. It is the voice of experience, the verdict of the moral nature of man.

The first truth of this gospel is that character is the Alpha and the Omega, the first and the last word, the beginning and the end of religion. It is more than altar and sacrifice, more than creed and confession, more than ordinance or custom. Character is substantial and essential. It is good and sufficient of itself. Add to it all the theologies in or out of Christendom, and it will be no greater or worthier. Take from it everything that men in churches call belief, and it will not be diminished in dignity or cheapened in worth. It fulfills all offices. It is courage in danger, fortitude in suffering, patience under calamity, peace in trouble, calmness in agitation, consolation in grief. It answers all questions, solves all problems. It is ready for any emergency. It is prepared to die and glad to live. It has no fear, or distrust, or hopelessness. What it is, is well pleasing in the sight of God and men. It dreads no hell, and it sighs for no heaven; for it cannot fear that which vanishes at its approach; and it cannot long for that which it carries about with it.

The effects that would follow the reception of this gospel of character, the effects that might attend its earnest preaching, may easily be conjectured. Were it possible to suppose that all the preachers in the City of New York might discontinue their weekly thrashing of straw, and devote themselves entirely to unfolding and enforcing this gospel of character, telling men what goodness is, and how they may get it, it would be possible to picture as the result of their efforts a changed condition of society. A new spirit would be breathed into public and private life ; a new tone would be imparted to the sentiments and purposes of men and women ; a new aim for endeavor, a new standard of action, would be immediately proposed. Vice would be discountenanced, crime overawed, wickedness rebuked and stayed. Great evils would sensibly diminish ; politics would be purged of corruption ; governments would become reputable ; commerce would acquire dignity ; trade would be purified ; journalism would cease to be a scandal. The wealthy and influential classes would be thrilled and stirred by a new sense of responsibility ; the unprivileged classes would feel the smart and tingle of a hitherto undiscovered self-respect. A sudden economy of intellectual and moral power would render practicable the concentration of a vast reserve of spiritual force on objects of urgent importance. Jealousies would be laid aside, hatreds abated, divisions abolished, false issues discarded ; and, as a consequence of this, a simultaneous effort would be made to apply the plain principles of the moral law to the work of redeeming the earth.

This being true—and there seems to be no good reason for questioning the truth of it—this gospel of character being so simple, so luminous, so universally recognized, so earnestly advocated, so heartily approved, the neglect of it is the great marvel. If the principles of it are so self-evident, why are they not cordially taken up and

enforced by religious teachers ? Why so much backward-
ness of profession ? Why so much indifference, coldness,
discouragement towards those who transfer their emphasis
from articles of credence to qualities of being ?

The answer is that the gospel of character is not as
unreservedly accepted as we might at first suppose. Character itself is not placed in the position accorded to it by
the great souls of the race. Of course, all good men
believe in goodness ; all worthy men, of whatever religious name, believe in truthfulness, justice, honesty, down-
rightness, and uprightness. But the belief is not primary,
cardinal, or fundamental. It is made conditional on other
beliefs, and therefore secondary. Many things are placed
before it in time and in importance, rites, observances,
traditions, formulas, to which attention is first paid, and
these require so much attention that, before they can be
dispatched, the end and aim of them all, character, has
vanished from view.

Let me, with requisite detail, elaborate and illustrate
my point :

In the first place allow me to advert to a doctrine common to all the " Evangelical " sects, and conspicuous in
their scheme, which seems to preclude entirely the preaching of the gospel of character, and even make character
itself unreal, a shadowy and spectral thing. I mean the
popular doctrine of atonement, reconciliation with God
through the merits of Christ. The doctrine appears in
several different forms; sometimes it is intimated that the
Christ bore the penalty of our sins; sometimes it is implied that through his living and dying, a vast fund of
merit was accumulated sufficient to meet all possible
demands of sinful men. This fund being deposited with
the church, an inexhaustible treasure, may be drawn from
on certain conditions of faith, thus affording any man an

opportunity of paying his debts with another person's money, and cancelling his undischarged obligations with another's conscience. A great deal has been and still is said of the necessity of clinging to the cross, resting on the bosom of the Saviour, flinging one's self unconditionally into the arms of the Redeemer, accepting unreservedly the boon of undeserved grace. We hear the phrase " imputed righteousness," which suggests the idea that goodness may be transferred, carried over like some private possession from one person to another.

What such expressions may mean I do not pretend to understand. To my mind they convey no sense whatever. They are unintelligible. They who use them attach significance to them, no doubt, and significance that is entirely compatible with individual virtue and dignity and worth. But to me these modes of speech hint at ideas that are inconsistent not merely with any gospel of character, but with such a thing as we understand character to be. They forbid the preaching up of character as the all-important, indispensable, radical thing. They forbid any proper analysis of character, any true investigation of its sources or laws, any just appreciation of its elements or conditions. The gospel they imply is a gospel of redemption and atonement, bristling with theological points. The preacher makes it his business to descant on the Trinity, the deity of Christ, the depravity of human nature, the necessity of faith in the atoning sacrifice, the need of supernatural conversion and restoring grace. These preliminary matters occupy so much attention that character is pushed out of sight, almost forgotten, it appears. If regarded as the end of all the believing, prayer, trusting, the end is so far off that it looks shadowy. In any event, character becomes quite a secondary and incidental concern. Not that any cordial believer in the "evangelical" theology despises it, neglects it, sets a mean estimate upon it, or counts it of small moment as a sign or test of the spiritual mind. But the cordial believer does not make it a primary consideration, does not come at it directly, or deal with it as the one absorbing interest.

Does not this whole cast of thought and speech militate against the very idea of building up, training character? The most important element in character—the cardinal element, in fact—is that of *personality*, of individual possession. If anything is our own, character must be. One's virtue cannot be another's. Nobody can be good for his neighbor. What sort of thing is imputed righteousness, transferred sacrifice? Apples tied to the twigs of an apple-tree; flowers glued to a rose-bush. The Romish conception of superfluous worth that is available for those who have no worth of their own, makes all worth a species of paper currency that is good whether the holder have earned it or stolen it. A book pasted full of autumn leaves is not a forest tree.

It is not enough to say that a man's character is his own. A man's character is the man himself. Take away his character and you reduce him to a shade, a simulacrum, a hollow mask or shell. The character is the disciplined thought, feeling, purpose, passion, will of the person. What would he be without it? An image empty of thought, feeling, purpose, passion, or will; no person, that is, at all; a casket, perhaps, of foreign jewels; a receptacle of imported goods; a warehouse of purchased manufactures, but no human being.

In another way the prevalent doctrine of vicarious reconciliation, imputed righteousness, transferred merit, proves fatal to the gospel of character, namely, by substituting a wholly different creation in its place. Character, according to any rational conception of it, consists of the genuine, natural stuff, the very prime material of our common humanity.   It is the last best product of experience and discipline working on the mass that is furnished by temperament, impulse, desire, affection, moral instinct, and resolution.   It assumes the substantial worth of these organic elements; and only on this assumption does the discipline and effort required to bring them into shape possess any moral quality.   But if these elements be, through natural depravity, useless for divine purposes; if the raw material be unfit for the wedding garment; if it must all be condemned as sleazy, rotten refuse, filthy rags, good for the waste-bag, the construction of character becomes quite impossible and inconceivable.   No training will avail where the qualities trained are destitute of capability or soundness.   Discipline is wasted on rubbish. Experience is thrown away on a being whose nature has no consistency or power of healthy progress.   The attributes that are imparted by special grace, as the result of a new heart formed by the supernatural influence of the Holy Ghost, may be very heavenly, but they do not in any sense constitute character.   They come from another than a human source, and are made of other than human material.   They are not the fruit of watching and striving; they have not been earned; they are a gift, not a possession; a boon, not an acquisition; an imparted grace, not a substantial virtue.   They may present something more seraphic and celestial than character, but they do not present character.   They are made not of natural, but of ethereal stuff; they are obtained not by moral, but by miraculous means.

If we are to comprehend character as it is, in its quality, law, sources, developments, we must discard these theological notions, which are potent in raising false issues, interposing veils and obstacles, diverting thought from the practical problems in hand, and putting endeavor on the wrong paths. We must cease to expect from foreign sources what can come from native struggle alone. We must look facts in the face. Until this is done, the strong questions which slip through the theologian's hands will go undealt with, and the urgent business of private and public reform will remain undone.

But there are other obstacles of a different kind which stand in the way of the noble culture of character that the times demand. There are those who reject with even unnecessary emphasis the evangelical doctrine respecting human nature, yet are almost as far as its believers are from a clear apprehension of this new gospel: people who, while admitting that character is the primary and essential thing, confessing its supreme importance, recognizing the fact that it is constituted of natural human stuffs, acknowledging that it is a great achievement of patience, fortitude, courage, faith, and hope, claiming that it is man's duty and privilege to work out this great result for himself—in a word, committing themselves to all the first principles I have laid down, render their whole profession inoperative by insisting that the basis, the only valid basis, of character is the ethical code of the New Testament. Of course, they say, character is the end of all believing ; but there must be believing in order that there may be character, and the object of belief is the New Testament and the words of Jesus. But for them, study of them, devoted contemplation and observance of them, virtue, if not impossible, is very uncertain, precarious, and unsatisfactory. The Sermon on the Mount, illustrated by its author, gives the perfect standard of character, presents the strongest inducements to cultivate character, lays down the rules for training character, prescribes the particular qualities that should predominate in character, and holds up the prize which is to reward its attainment.

So certain are they that this method of cultivating character is the only legitimate one, that they make character secondary to the New Testament. This is my first criticism on their position. The gospel they preach is not the gospel of character but the gospel of belief. They have much to say about the genuineness of the New Testament, the authenticity of its record, the importance of reading it with implicit faith, the surprising grandeur of its moral ideas, the miracle of moral beauty exhibited in Jesus, the need that all should sit at his feet, and look up to him with profoundest reverence. They have much less to say about honesty, veracity, justice, fair dealing between man and man. The numerous preliminaries prevent their getting earnestly at work with men and their affairs. Their problems are all speculative, and semi-theological.

A graver objection to their method is, that it is unscientific. They would ground character on texts instead of facts, on the printed words of a book instead of the actual data of modern experience. None but technical Christians can build on their foundation. The Jew cannot, for he does not believe in Christ; the Turk cannot; the philosopher cannot; the unbeliever of whatever class cannot; humanity in its unchurched, unindoctrinated conidtion cannot. The standard is peculiar; the education is partial; the training is exceptional and eccentric. It is only when we perceive how peculiar, partial, exceptional, and eccentric the whole aim and method are, that we understand the full force of objection to it.

It seems to be forgotten that the Bible is an oriental book reflecting the mind of an oriental people. It seems to be forgotten that Jesus was an oriental, a child of the

East, partaking all the peculiarities that distinguished the eastern type of character. Now, the characteristics of the oriental ethics is PASSIVITY. As a people the orientals are tranquil, sedate, sometimes soft and yielding, sometimes inert, capable of fiery outbreaks of passion, but capable, too, of abject submission. The mild, monotonous climate, the productiveness of the soil, the languid effect of the atmosphere, the uneventfulness of daily existence, the absence of stir and change in the general lot--all conspired to repress their energies, deaden their ambition, and to destroy the impulse as they did the necessity of struggle. Their government being usually despotic, granting no privileges, offering no prizes, guaranteeing no rights, encouraging no liberties, exerted a depressing influence on their aims and purposes. They naturally became acquiescent and content with little; their expectations feeble, their hopes faint, their prospects of an improved condition small, they learned the easy lesson of resignation to the will of Providence, submission to the appointed lot. The vigorous virtues did not take root in their temperament; the vehement desire for personal rights they knew nothing of; the aspiration for liberty, power, privilege, rarely visited their souls. The ethics of civilization, the moral rules of a progressive people, were unknown to them.

The ethics of the New Testament are of this sad complexion. They are the ethics of poverty, weakness, sorrow. They are pitched on a low key, for joyless hearts. They are the ethics of sighing, complaint, and grief. The Beatitudes are pensive. They promise felicity to the miserable; they exalt the timid and the acquiescent. Blessed are the poor in spirit; Blessed are they that mourn; Blessed are the meek; Blessed are the merciful; Blessed are the pure in heart; Blessed are the peacemakers; Blessed are the reviled and persecuted. The religion of Jesus has been called the religion of sorrow. He is the man of sorrows; the meek and lowly; the holy child; the lamb. He invites the weary and heavy laden to his rest. He loves the humble, unambitious mind. His message is to the disappointed, the unprivileged; the burden of the message is, that the Father is their friend.

Special precepts and groups of precepts wear this same expression of gentle self-abnegation and patient submission to fortune. The disciple is admonished to surrender his personal rights and even yield uncomplainingly to wrong. " Agree with thine adversary quickly, while you walk together, lest thine adversary deliver thee to the officer." Compromise is better than controversy. Yield anything rather than contend. " If any man sue thee at the law and take thy coat, let him have thy cloak also." " If a man (a government officer) insist on your going a mile in his service, go two." " Retaliate not on the injurer." " Whosoever shall smite thee on the right cheek, turn to him the other also." Whether absolute passiveness, entire non-resistance be meant or no, such passages discourage resentment, and forbid the exercise of the personal will. To be saintly is to surrender.

The precepts in regard to property and its uses are marked by the same spiritless tone. " Give to him that asketh of thee : and from him that would borrow of thee turn not thou away." " Go, sell what thou hast and give to the poor." " If ye lend to those from ye hope to receive, what merit is there ?" " Do good and lend, hoping for nothing again; that your reward may be great." No mention at all of any rights in property; no intimation that property may have its uses ; no hint that the making of money may be a necessity and even a duty. The destitute are the people to be considered; the privileged are the penniless.

The rule of hospitality is made in favor of those who have nothing. "When thou makest a feast, call not thy friends and rich neighbors, lest they invite thee in turn, and a recompense be made; but call the poor, the lame, the maimed, and the blind." The cardinal principle is, the mortification of taste, the renunciation of grace, culture, refinement, the postponement of all social considerations to the single consideration of making the poor happy.

The one quality eulogized, commended, enjoined, urged without qualification or stint, is the quality of loving-kindness. You are sure to be in the right way if you love enough. Ask no questions; make no comments; offer no criticisms; find no fault; administer no rebuke; plead no excuses; but open hand and heart to all comers, whosoever they may be. Love will justify itself. This is the strain all through. Nowhere will you find similar commendations of equity, veracity, personal honor, or loyalty. We do not hear from the lips of Jesus the stern bidding to tell the truth, to do justice, to be faithful to the work of the hour. He addresses no admonitions to the weak, the miserable, the dejected. Where does he bid the poor to be industrious, provident, thrifty, or self-respecting? Where does he make a point of rousing the wretched to endeavor, or shaming the dependent out of their idleness or despair? Whom does he ever summon to an assertion of rights? Whom does he ever except from the categories of compassion?

The ethics of the New Testament are very beautiful; the character of Jesus is exceedingly lovely; the air of heaven breathes around him; his thoughts are celestial; his words drop from his mouth like gems. We read his delicious rhapsodies with unwearied pleasure; they feed the heart's craving for blessed dreams; they are the ethics of the millennium; the moral laws of a redeemed

6

humanity. They will work admirably when men and women shall be men and women no longer; when passion shall be purified and conscience shall be king; when interests shall no more seem to clash, and relations shall no more be a jangle, and jealousies and hates shall be extinguished, and the long struggle with fortune shall be ended, and we shall all feel like little children in a brighter and nobler Eden.

But this charming code meets with a harsh reception from the temper of our Western world. The modern man finds it quite unfit for a working existence, and while he pays it a sentimental homage on Sundays, on the other days of the week he scarcely recognizes its existence, never its authority. He blesses the peacemakers in church, and the next day takes a contract for supplying arms to a State at war. He hears from the preacher the touching praises of beneficence, and turns a deaf ear to the beggar's cry in the street. He assents to the lessons of brotherly love towards enemies and persecutors, and goes away to commence a long and costly suit for slander, or to expose to disgrace some person who has unintentionally, perhaps, insulted him.

The modern man stands for rights. Rights first, duties afterward, is his maxim. His life is a struggle for power, place, privilege, often for bare subsistence. He must make good his title to labor, to enjoy and use the fruits of his labor, to develop his capacity, to exercise his talent, to throw his influence where it will tell to most advantage. He is responsible for many things; for social morality, for the character of the laws, the spirit and form of institutions, the administration of government. His characteristic is energy. Every strenuous quality is greeted with praise. The passive virtues fall into disfavor. Patience is misunderstood; contentment is disapproved of; acquiescence in the established order is rebuked ; pusillanimity is despised ; humility is, to say the least, not revered ; meekness has a bad name ; resignation is tolerated only in circumstances of despair. The rule is to submit to nothing vexatious, distressing, oppressive, or unjust, but to resist, while strength lasts, the encroachments of evil or mischievous men, of government officials, of legal pressure, of adverse circumstances. Self-assertion becomes at times a sacred duty. Even women must compel themselves to face difficulty, grapple with hardship, resent imposition, repel injustice, and, in the endeavor to obtain what is necessary to their culture and usefulness, assume the disagreeable attitude of claimants and contestants. In the sharp battle for moral existence, even good, kindly, amiable, humane, delicate people must be perpetually on the alert to seize opportunities and secure dues. On no other conditions can modern society exist or modern civilization be carried on.

We do not pretend to obey the precepts of the Sermon on the Mount. It does not occur to us to imitate the example of Jesus in his passive submission to wrong. Who thinks it right or prudent to allow himself to be imposed upon by indolent or insolent people ? Who acts on the principle of compromising issues at any cost ? Who, as a simple matter of wisdom or caution, turns the other cheek to the smiter ? Who, however unrevengeful, placable or generous, deems it best to inflict no harm on the wrong doers, to let criminals escape justice, to allow the enemies of society to go unpunished ? The spirit in our age is willing and more than willing to take the element of vengeance out of the criminal code, but it would erect new moral safeguards against the encroachments of evil.

The New Testament law respecting property is, if possible, still more uncongenial with the modern age.

Property has its rights as well as its duties ; and its duties have regard to the stability and progress of civilization. It is the great instrument in redeeming nature, multiplying arts, projecting inventions. It is too precious to be misused or given away or squandered on incompetent people. Were it held a sacred duty on the part of good men to "put their property in such controllable shape as to make it available for benevolent ends," all the arrangements of the business world would have to be altered in order that it might be discharged. Tools to those who can use them, is our motto. Money to those who have the intelligence to employ it best, to the men of talent and genius, the discoverers, builders, benefactors of the race. It were poor economy to give the hardly earned wealth of a community like ours to the incompetent and imbecile. It were putting ability, sagacity, experience, diligence, to a singular use, if the object of it all were to be the maintenance of the feeble, the stupid, the indolent, the unproductive. Let these by all means have their due share. But to treat them as if they were the sole objects of concern, would be to give them vastly more than their due share. The mischief done to all classes by this species of benevolence is well and bitterly known to all the world. If we sell our goods, we sell them in the best market to those who most want them and can best use them. The poor will derive benefit from the sale in greater opportunities and facility of living, in cheaper food and more lucrative industry. Increasing goods is better kindness than distributing goods. Civilization is a nobler benefactor than charity.

The New Testament rule of hospitality would render cultivated society impossible, for cultivated society is the result of association of cultivated people with one another. An attempt to make such feasts as Jesus recommended, if successful, would lead society downward. But it could not be successful. It would be a silly piece of formal affectation, like the pope's washing of the paupers' feet at Easter time in Rome. None but saints can exercise hospitality on .this gospel plan, and a rule that supposes saintliness in mankind at large is no rule for this world.

The " law of Love," which is the foundation of the New Testament code of ethics, and the essential element in the evangelical stamp of character, is no where recognized as a working principle by the " Christian " people of the Western world. The word is charming ; the sentiment is gracious ; the view is enchanting ; and if visions were principles, and feelings facts, and emotions laws, and sentiments rules of conduct, there would be no difficulty in reproducing in America the type of men and women that the East furnishes. But love is too soft a metal for practical needs. A great deal of alloy must be mingled with it in order that it may do the work of reform and regeneration. All sorts of strong qualities must go with it as guards and guides—knowledge, sagacity, tact, experience, prudence, wisdom, truth. Love does not always work well. None need to look more carefully about them than they who undertake to apply it to the sufferings, sorrows, and ills of men. Who shall say what love requires in any particular case ? the supplicant for it or the bestower of it ? they who feel the need or they who supply the need ? What objects is love designed to serve ? On what conditions is love to be administered ?

We must know whom we are engaged with. The modern man asks questions : Who are you ? What are you ? Whence came you ? What have you done ? What can you do ? What do you mean to do ? It is not enough that you have suffered ; that you are in pain, want, or sorrow ; the question goes deeper : Are you good for anything ? Have you anything to build on ? What are you capable of becoming? What ground is there for believing that compassion, tenderness, patience, forgiveness, pity, will do you anything but harm?

The modern man, the best, the kindest man, asks these questions, prompted to ask them by his humanity; by his anxious desire to do what he can to diminish suffering and relieve want, and reduce the amount of evil about him. Love is not searching enough, or clear enough, or quickening enough. The character that is based on love lacks the substance and cohesiveness which the exigency of life requires.

This want of sympathy between the ethics of the New Testament and the ethics of civilization amounts to a contradiction. Few persons pretend to carry the precepts of the Sermon on the Mount into their business or social relations. There are no practical Christians; Jesus has few imitators. They who make a profession of copying him either go out of the world to do it, or satisfy themselves with professing. The mischief of this state of things is appalling. Earnest, devout, conscientious men are driven out of the world. The rest, seeing how impossible it is for them to conform to the ideal standard, abandon the effort, and fall into the practice of selfishness. The lowest interest becomes their law. They justify themselves in coarse manners and mean pursuits, and an inhuman spirit.

No discipline of character is possible unless character be grounded on the facts of human nature, human experience, and human necessities. The New Testament is a fact in literature; not a fact in life. So little is known about Jesus as a man, living in personal relations with other men, and standing face to face with ordinary circumstances, that his character can hardly be considered a fact in human history. He does not teach us as a person;

he had no home, no child, no wife ; he was without a profession or trade; was neither merchant, politician, journalist, artist, artizan, or man of letters. His attributes are disembodied ; his sentiments are not organized.

Character must rest on facts; but a text is not a fact. Men must be taken as they are, not as they ought to be. We should dream of them as they ought to be, but we must train them on the ground where they live and labor. Before there can be a scientific culture of character, that is, before there can be any culture of character at all, before the qualities that compose character can be determined on and made imperative, there must be a knowledge, not of the New Testament, but of the elements of personal nobleness, and of the issues at stake between man and man.

The investigation of these vital data of character is a work, at present, of some difficulty, hampered as we are by such obstacles as I have described. But enough is known of them to justify us in announcing another principle in the place of that put forth in the New Testament. That principle is JUSTICE. It is the pillar of noble character, resting on primeval rock, the absolute truth. It may be, it will be, it must be, all that wisest love is. It is, in its nature, tender as tenderness, merciful as mercy, pitiful as pity, gentle as gentleness, loving as love. But it is all these because it is more than they all. It has no particular regard for classes, for its regard takes in all classes. It does not enter on a special ministry to the poor, the weak, the afflicted ; for the rich, the strong, the joyous are equal objects of its care. It knows absolutely no distinction of persons, no difference of conditions. It knows human responsibility and duty alone. Its intention is not to soothe distress, but to embolden it; not to support the poor, but to make them self-supporting ; not to feed the

hungry, but to enable them to earn their own bread; not
to console sorrow, but to touch the recuperative energies
that will avail to throw it off. Justice tones up the sentiments, braces the will, and clears the intelligence, for it
judges all by the same standard, and holds all to the same
rule. It emancipates us from the sway of feeling, whose
sentimental rule is so out of place in a world governed by
eternal law.

Justice is both masculine and feminine at once, and the
practice of it is an education in manly and womanly qualities. The ancients painted her in the form of a woman,
and endowed her with masculine virtues. There is a
picture of Jesus in the Wilderness in quest of the lost
sheep. The scene is a sandy waste, with an occasional bit
of rock cropping out from the ground. There is no habi-
tation, there is no forest, there is no shrubbery, save two
or three angry-looking thorn bushes, in one of which a
poor lamb is entangled. In the distance, the clouds of
sand are sweeping along before the wind. In the foreground, the noon-day sun is driving its flaming sword into
the earth. To this place Jesus has come, that he may
save the sheep. His patient arm is outstretched, and
his long, tender fingers penetrate the briars. The great
compassionate eyes melt at sight of the suffering; the
sorrowful, sympathetic face answers the pleading look of
the torn animal. It is very touching, gracious, heavenly.
It is the poetry of tender pity and sacrifice. But as we
look at it, there seems to be a disproportion between
means and ends, a lack of adaptation that takes away from
the picture its artistic charm. All this, we are tempted
to exclaim, for a sheep? Could not the vast intellect that
sits behind the broad brow, the immense kindness that
looks out from the countenance, the prodigious force of
will that is displayed in every line and feature, be better

employed than thus? To devise means of turning the wilderness into a cultivated field or a verdant meadow, on which innocent sheep might browse in peace, were a wiser and a more beneficent deed. Why should the fullness of the heart suspend the action of the brain? Why should excessive compassion push out of the way considerations of equity and economy? Why should not all powers be exercised and all needs consulted?

Justice is guilty of no such error as this. We look at her image as set up by antiquity, and behold a woman's form, stately and graceful in bearing; she stands erect and motionless, seeking none, because she is everywhere, in the wilderness and the city without going thither. Her right hand rests on the hilt of a sword, sharp at both edges, and of keen point, ready to smite transgressors in case of need. Her left hand holds on high the nicely balanced scales, that will weigh characters, actions, motives, with unswerving accuracy; her eyes are bandaged, that she may not see who drops in the weight, whether it be prince or peasant, king or beggar, or what the weight is, whether a crime or a virtue; she blinds herself to all differences in persons, but she herself is not blind; she sees with the inward eye the invisible principles of right and wrong, the impalpable laws of rectitude. These reveal themselves to her in the night. Though they be hidden in secret places she detects them. They disclose themselves to her; they come to her and drop into the scale their own condemnation or praise. She needs not to see what they put in, the scale is held high;—the world sees and judges.

This is the figure the new faith would set up in the highways and byways, as the image of the consoler and saviour. A tract was sent me last week, to one passage in which my particular attention was called. There it was

6*

said that the minister's office was to save souls—not to preach eloquent sermons, or gather large congregations, or collect a large revenue, or get a large salary—but simply to save souls. The silent imputation was, that I was doing all the naughty things aforesaid, and leaving the one indispensable thing undone. But if there be one accusation I feel justified in repelling, it is an accusation like this. Save souls, indeed! From what, if not from false reliances and unsafe refuges, from delusions and sentimentalisms, from the power of phrases and the bondage of traditions, from hypocrisy and cant? He does a good deed who saves a soul from insincerity, unveracity, hollowness, pretence, and sham, and the gospel that saves from this seemingly bottomless hell is no gospel of Trinity, atonement, mediation, justification by a Redeemer's blood—it is the plain gospel of justice and veracity, the gospel of obedience to the natural laws, which are divine commandments; the gospel of mutual obligation, which is the gospel of eternal felicity.

VIII.

THE SCIENTIFIC ASPECT OF PRAYER.

THE subject of this discourse is the Scientific Aspect of Prayer. The Bible doctrine of prayer—there is but one—is simple. It is fully declared in texts like these: "Ask, and it shall be given you;" "All things whatsoever ye ask in prayer, believing, ye shall receive;" "The prayer of faith shall save the sick, and the Lord shall raise him up;" "If two of you shall agree on earth as touching anything they shall ask, it shall be done for them by my Father which is in heaven." There is no variety or qualification. Whatever the request, if proffered in faith by believers in Jehovah or disciples of the Christ, it is granted. The doctrine is borne out by frequent illustrations. "Moses went out of the city of Pharaoh and spread abroad his hands unto the Lord, and the thunder and hail ceased, and the rain was not poured upon the earth." "The Hagarites and all that were with them were delivered into the hands of the Israelites, for they cried to God in the battle and he was entreated by them." "Elias prayed earnestly that it might not rain; and it did not rain for the space of three years and six months;" "And Jabez called on the God of Israel, saying, oh, that thou wouldst bless me indeed, and enlarge my coast and keep me from evil; and God granted him that which he requested." The prayer of Elijah is reported to have brought fire from the Lord that consumed wood, and stones, and dust, and licked up water in a trench. The prayer of Jesus raised Lazarus from the dead. The prayer of the Church opened the doors of Peter's prison. According to the teaching of the Bible, prayer has received every possible form of answer. It has stayed pestilence, abated famine, averted war, arrested the heavenly bodies, made iron float and water burn.

Christendom adopts the belief of the Bible. The doctrine of the Church in every period has been coincident with that of the Scriptures. The same belief is professed now by Romanists and Protestants. Theological books, and books of piety of both schools, abound in stories of literal answer to prayer. The rationalizing evangelist, Horace Bushnell, devotes a chapter of his work on " Nature and the Supernatural," to a discussion of this question, and adduces several instances of answer to prayer in the shape of recovered life and vigor. In England, a sect calling themselves "the peculiar people," are distinguished by their implicit faith in the wonder-working power of prayer. They call in no physician to their sick and use none of the customary precautions against the effect of disease. When the sick die, as they frequently do, they regard the event as of divine appointment. Once or twice the law has interposed, and the " peculiar people " have been called to account by society for tampering thus with human life. Their defense has been the text from James, which they obeyed strictly, and against which, society, assuming the inspiration of the Word had nothing to say. The cases were dismissed by the Court of Justice. To the objection that instances of literal answer to prayers for rain, or health, or safety, or victory, or other outward boons, are infrequent now, it is replied that the infrequency is due to the prevalent skepticism ; that prayers are not offered in faith ; that ours is an unbelieving age, addicted to science and philosophy, which does not, will not, cannot fulfil the conditions on which answer to prayer is promised. Of course people who cannot heartily pray, have no right to complain that God gives them nothing. They who do heartily pray, may still hope to receive.

To test the validity of the common belief, Professor Tyndall proposed this experiment. Let two hospital wards be selected, both equally light, airy, salubrious, both in general respects, equally well cared for. Let the one be set apart for patients who have faith in the healing power of prayer, and whose friends are in the habit of offering prayer in their behalf. In the other, let there be placed people who are not in the habit of praying or being prayed for, but who rely wholly on the natural means of recovery. Let the experiment be carefully watched for five years. The result will show whether and how far prayer may be counted on as a remedial agent. It has been doubted whether Professor Tyndall was serious in the strange plan suggested. If he was not, Mr. Francis Galton, who seconded him, was. The public understood him seriously, and there is no good reason for thinking that the suggestion was made in other than perfectly good faith. Mr. Tyndall is a delicately organized man of sensitive feeling, of imaginative poetic mind, tender and reverent. He is the furthest possible from a Materialist; rather he is an opponent of Materialism; an idealist of a fine intellectual type, a reader of Emerson, and to some extent, of kindred spirit with him. His desire was to establish a fact, nothing more. This is a very important matter. If the popular doctrine is justified by experience, it is well that all men should know it, the sick and the well, patients and physicians, infidels and believers. If, on the other hand the popular doctrine will not stand the test of scientific examination, then equally important results will follow in another direction. Mr. Tyndall probably anticipated no objections to his plan from either quarter; none from the unbelievers, who would doubtless hail such a trial with joy as establishing their faith in the unvarying constancy of nature's law; none from the believers, who would leap to the proof that would in their judgment surely confound the infidel. In a cause so momentous as this, why should not the Lord of the Church make some startling disclosure of his power, as in the days of old when the prophets demanded and received a sign ?

The reception of the proposal was not cordial. The men of science greeted it warmly; the unbelievers professed their sense of its fairness, and their readiness to abide by it; but from the opposite party clamors arose. Some pronounced the plan impious, some impertinent, some heartless, some idle and chimerical ; some declared it a trick on the part of the infidels, a cunning trap laid to bring ridicule on faith. But among the multitude of objections three were valid and unanswerable. It was argued that the experiment would be fruitless of result, because " prayers are not mere utterances in the vocative case of which any specimen is as good as another, but vary in proportion to the depth of intensity of the life thrown into them, so that the very kind of prayers by which Mr. Tyndall would test his case, the formulated prayers for *classes* of persons, are probably those which partake least of the spiritual essence of prayer." This is well put ; prayers aimed at a mark, diplomatic prayers, said for a purpose—prayers of business, as it were, do not fall within the category of availing petitions. Again, it was urged that the primary condition of all prayer is submission to the divine will. The prayer might be refused, not because God could not answer it, but because He did not see fit, in His love and wisdom, to answer it ; so that the failure of the experiment would establish nothing as to the validity or invalidity of the prayer. Another weighty and solid objection ; there is a third party to be consulted— God. In order to render the experiment successful, must not His disposition towards it be ascertained? And who was to obtain that information ? If prayer was a mechanical contrivance that worked like a lever or pulley ; if every earnest intense petitioner were sure of an answer; if there were no reservations on the part of the Father of Creation, the issue might be accepted by both sides, with confidence. But the possibility of such reservation takes all pith out of the negative proof. Again, it was suggested, and fairly too, that the experiment to be successful must conform to conditions of quite impossible delicacy. Suppose that the patients in the praying ward, did show a general advantage over the others in respect of the quickness or completeness of their recovery; it would still remain to be determined how much of this effect was due to prayer, and how much to other agencies, strength of constitution, subtle peculiarities in the disease, the natural enhancement and exhilaration of the animal spirits under the excitement of hope and faith, the increased influence of the mind over the body, which enthusiasm and fanaticism produce. Our instruments are not yet fine enough to detect the hidden causes that conspire to build up or to pull down the human frame. The science of statistics is as yet in its infancy. It deals with blunt facts and crude averages. The only valid induction in a matter like this, must be based on facts collected in fields inaccessible, sifted by methods thus far undiscovered, and collated by a system far more comprehensive than any yet devised. Statistics cannot penetrate the spiritual region of prayer, or define the precise efficacy of prayer, or trace the shadowy boundaries of the mind, or tell what powers hitherto deemed supernatural are stored up within its

lines. In a word, the experiment proposed cannot be conducted to the satisfaction of either party interested. If
no answer came to the supplications of the sufferers or
their friends, the believers in prayer would allege the
want of earnestness in the petitioners, the unwillingness
of the Lord to enter into the plan, or incompatibility with
the divine love and wisdom. If, on the other hand, an
answer came, the unbeliever in prayer would have a right
to say that the result was brought about by other than
supernatural causes. Unless every earnest prayer is likely
to be answered, prayer cannot be adopted by physicians
in the regular treatment of disease. Unless every earnest
prayer be flatly refused, the priests of religion will urge
people to seek refuge during seasons of trouble in supernatural help.

Professor Tyndall's suggestion, therefore, is not likely
to be adopted. It has been valuable, however, as creating
discussion, and as opening once more in a practical manner, a question of the deepest spiritual and temporal
moment, a mere enumeration of the bearings whereof on
human affairs would occupy the full time allowed for a
discourse.

The real question at issue is this : Is God, or is He not,
an individual sentient being, a maker, ruler, administra-
tor, in the ordinary sense of these words ? If He is, the
discussion about prayer is at an end. Prayer is entirely
admissible under that supposition. No one doubted the
literal efficacy of prayer before this belief in the individual creating, ruling, guiding God was doubted. Conceive
of God as an individual being, thinking, forecasting, pro-
posing, planning, governing as the Czar governs Russia,
superintending as an engineer superintends the machinery
of a steamship, or a president the concerns of a railroad
company, directing as Von Moltke directed the movements

of the German army from Berlin, evolving and working out plans as He goes on, holding nations in His hand as the first Napoleon held cabinets and major-generals, feeling personal satisfaction and dissatisfaction with the doings of human creatures ; conceive of God thus, and there is no difficulty in accepting without the least reserve the popular theory of prayer. The whole doctrine follows, for such a being, sitting apart in the focus of the world's whispering gallery, where the faintest sigh reaches His ear, with His hand on the springs that set in motion the enormous machinery of His creation, and effect in obedience to His will all the possible combinations of force, sending electric thrills along the throbbing nerves of law, bringing the currents of power to bear on the most sensitive points, and at His discretion starting fresh centres of energy into life—such a being, I say, omniscient, omnipotent, playing on His universe as a master in music plays on his organ, could, without straining a cord or starting a rivet, snapping a fibre or tangling a thread, respond to the special needs of His children and meet their requests. Why should He not give literal answers to prayers for external things? Why should he not answer prayers for life, success, prosperity, victory, health, and wealth? Not all prayers, for that would be inconsistent with a wise order in the regulation of the world, and with considerate kindness towards people who pray ignorantly and to their hurt; not idle, petulant, or passionate prayers, for they are not entitled to respect ; not the conflicting prayers of men who clamor for opposite things; not the short-sighted, selfish prayers of men who want to engage the heavenly powers in the interest of their petty schemes for place or gain ; but such prayers as voice a human and general need. Such a being might, for instance, refuse petitions for rain hundreds, nay, thousands of times, because

He could not grant to one what would injure another; but can we not imagine a contingency, a case of very protracted and general drought, when, under heavens of brass, on an earth of ashes, men pined and nature fainted, a time when every throbbing brain and every panting heart and every thirsty soul cried out with one great burst of agonized accord for rain, rain, till the multitudinous wishes made the spiritual air quiver ; a time when every living and dying thing should call for one boon ? And why should not such a prayer be respected ? Why should not the atmospheric conditions be supplied and the laws of nature be silently shifted for nature's benefit ?

Or can we not imagine a state of war between two sections or nations, the issue of which involves the gravest concerns of human civilization, the emancipation, we will say, of a whole race, or the overthrow of some dark barbaric despotism, or the destruction of an empire founded on fraud and violence, sustained by chicanery, sensual in its disposition, and demoralizing in its influence ? Can we not imagine such a state, as would render natural and proper the interposition of the world's ruler, in response to such eager solicitation from the nobler combatants as proved that they were heart and soul enlisted in the cause of humanity, and were altogether worthy to be entrusted with civilization's holiest interests ?

Or again, can we not imagine such a God as I have described, and as Christendom believes in, arranging the sanitary agencies with a view to the special benefit of some precious person whose life or safety is unspeakably dear to society ? Can we not think of Him as sending His messengers, air and light, to exhilarate the nervous system, quicken the flow of blood, and all in answer to the intense wish of many who feel that in that life their own deepest interests are bound up ? Such a thing might occur but

seldom; but it might occur, and its occurrence would furnish ground for such interposition as the Christian world
expects in answer to fervent, unselfish prayer. Thus we
should concede at once the whole case, and accept without cavil the arguments of theologians, the testimony of
pious men and women, the solemn averments of those
who declare that within their own experience prayers have
been answered. And why not? Why not consent to
allow the controlling force of prayer as an agency in the
administration of human affairs—an agency not to be confidently reckoned on for special occasions, not an organized agency, but still an agency on which men in solemn
emergencies may rely?

Because, I reply, the conception of God, on which the
whole theory hangs, is one that it is becoming more and
more difficult to hold against the assaults of ripening
knowledge and maturing thought. Men, who, as was the
case of the Bible folks, knew nothing whatever of the
world they lived in, had no proper method of investigation,
never heard of a natural law, never traced the relation of
cause and effect to the most inconsiderable distance, never
traveled, never studied, never explored, held the crudest, the
most child-like beliefs in regard to the commonest phenomena of the natural world, were absolutely without what
we call science or knowledge of anything in heaven or
earth, could easily imagine to themselves a huge being like
a man, presiding over the world of matter and of mind.
As men become acquainted with their globe, with its history, its formation, its elements, to imagine such a being as
ruling over it day by day, forming its floods, scooping out
its sea basins, balancing its continents, mingling its tribes,
administering the economies of its animal and vegetable
kingdoms, working, as by secret wires, the endless complexities of its organization, holding its myriad parts

together and giving a distinct thought to each, becomes exceedingly difficult—so difficult, indeed, that they who apprehend the problem profess themselves unable to form any clear image of the divine mind.   The planet we live on is so full of fibres, its parts are so intertwined, interlinked, interlaced, its elements cross and mingle in such intricate webs, that there is no posterior door or crack by which a foreign will can enter.   It is already a compact creation of mind—a perfect flower of intelligence. ˙

But we are still on the threshold of our difficulty.   This planet is but a speck in the solar system, which is still included in the same network of law that holds the globe together.   And, beyond the solar system, other systems unfold their blazing sheets of glory, till human calculation despairs of conjecturing their limits; and all these systems roll and revolve in obedience to the same rules of order and harmony that preside over the dance of the autumn leaves, when the wind strips them from the trees and whirls them abroad.   The conception of the individual God becomes now absolutely impossible.   All our ideas of mind are confounded.   What sort of intelligence is it that can think in an instant and at once all these myriads of myriads of thoughts, and then has myriads on myriads of thoughts to spare ?   What sort of intelligence is it that, having organized itself in perfect worlds and systems of worlds without number, is able to give special care to every particle, to supplement its own complete expression, to improve its own finished work, to mend, modify, alter, recombine, readjust its own wonderful combinations ?   What sort of an intelligence that, having packed a thousand universes with living purposes, has still more exact and living purposes in store ; having given every conceivable and inconceivable expression to its beneficent intention, has yet whole reservoirs of intention that have not yet been drawn upon ?

But even yet we have not reached the bottom of the abyss of perplexity. For we find that every point of the mental and moral universe is pervaded by compact laws of its own, and is possessed of inveterate habits; is, as it were, a woven web of will, a seamless coat of purpose. Every inch of ground as far as we can fancy, as far as we can dream, as far as we can fling our most audacious conjecture, is filled and preoccupied, crammed with cause and effect, antecedents and consequents, filled till the most ethereal ether is a tissue of gauzy life—a film of feeling so thin that you cannot seize it, so tough that you cannot tear it. The very Fullness is full! The pleroma overflows! What becomes now of the Hebrew Jehovah, of the Christian Father in heaven? Unless this palpitating universe be He, He is past finding out.

Clearly no prayers can be expected to extract another wish or thought or expression of feeling from a Being who is beyond all these lines, and who has put these thrilling worlds between Himself and His creatures, piled these Ossas on these Pelions of intention, and fairly exhausted the possibilities of care in what is already provided. He who begins to see how much he has, cannot in conscience ask for more. To have the smallest appreciation of the wealth of the supply is to see reason sufficient for being dumb.

And so we find what we should expect to find, a decline of prayer with an increase of knowledge. As people understand meteorology and climatology, they perceive the uselessness of prayer for rain. As they understand the strict connection between the harvest and the seasons, they cease to pray for good crops. As they understand the intimate dependence of human health on sanitary precautions, they abate the fervency of their petitions for long and wholesome life. As they understand the necessary affiliation of the physiological and the psychological laws, their prayers for an amiable temper and a kind heart become weak and infrequent.

A visit to the office in Washington, where the clerk of the weather sits with his subordinates about him, catching the whispers of the wind from the four quarters of the heaven, counting the rain-drops that fall on a continent, weighing the atmosphere from sea to sea and from lake to gulf, and making these flying, illusive witnesses tell whether it will be wise for people in New York or San Francisco to take umbrellas down town with them the next day, will satisfy the most devout mind that supplication for a sudden supply or cessation of showers will be ineffectual.

A visit to the Bureau of Vital Statistics, where the currents of disease are traced in their flow over large reaches of territory, and the private correspondence between sanity and sewerage, death and dirt, fever and fetor, cholera and uncleanliness, is established with the nicety of mathematics, will convince the saint that the death-rate is not likely to be modified considerably by the most fervent utterance of desire Godward.

The prayer for fresh accessions of temperance, honesty, peacefulness, sinks into silence before the fact that vices and crimes too obey their laws; that outbreaks of moral distemper accompany changes in the money market; that social morality follows the line of national prosperity which rises and falls with the fluctuations of the seasons; that social disorders have their method; that sins can be reduced to an average; that a skilful actuary will, from given data, compute with much accuracy the probable number of murders and suicides for the next twelvemonth, vice and virtue not being gifts dependent on the favor of a benefactor, but qualities wrought into the texture of the world, to be had by fulfilling the conditions, not otherwise.

The Bible encourages prayer for faith. But we all know that infidelity, like vice, has its causes, which must be removed before it will disappear. The "Age of Reason" in France, with its appalling excesses, was no inspiration of the devil, but an inevitable result of the abominations of the Church, which were again an inevitable result of the abominations of the State, which again were an inevitable result of an ancient but outworn theory of the rights of kings.

Prayer is thus seen to be out of place, because *every possible effect of prayer is guaranteed without it.* Prayer is inoperative, because it is unnecessary. For every prayer that reasonable mortals can make an answer is already provided; answers to prayer being worked into the substance of life. The compact universe, in fact, is an organized response to the supplications of men ; an inexhaustible storehouse of adaptations, the key whereof is placed in every creature's hand. The perfect being could not reply to human beseeching more sufficiently than He has done already. He has even anticipated petition, knowing what things His children had need of before they asked Him, and furnishing them centuries long in advance, with every imaginable means of satisfaction. They fancy their petitions are answered directly by Him when they draw on some hitherto undiscovered treasury, that had always lain hidden at their feet; they fancy that He has just begun to speak because they have just begun to listen.

Does this view of the question seem chilling and repulsive? Then let me, in conclusion, add a few words that may help to remove or correct such an impression. No long argument is required to show that the view taken of prayer and the God of prayer is really more conducive to mental and moral health than the popular view which it displaces.

I. In regard to the material condition of mankind. This depends, all will allow, mainly, if not wholly, on human effort. An indolent society will never be a prosperous one; no estate was ever improved by heedlessness or neglect. Progress in material respects keeps pace with energy, knowledge, purpose, and these increase with the necessity for them. To augment these qualities, therefore, to stimulate the physical, mental and moral activities to their full normal pitch, is a matter of prime importance to civilization. The truth is forced on us by all observation, that the first requisite of improvement is a conviction that man is master of his fate. If he wants a fort he must build a fort. Every social problem brings this truth home to us. It is the incessant cry of merchant, financier, politician, reformer, that matters will be no better till men take the trouble to make them better. Like Cortez, we must burn our vessels behind us, and so shut ourselves up with our work, if we expect to be conquerors.

Now, which belief is most stimulating to activity; the belief that God will answer our prayers, or that we must answer them ourselves? A broad survey of the experience of mankind scarcely leaves room to doubt that the latter faith is the more quickening. Earnest individuals no doubt, feel that their mental and moral energies are quickened and exalted by prayer. But the experience of earnest individuals is not in point here. We are considering the effect of the belief in prayer on the great masses of mankind; and observing these it is evident that people are only too willing to let another do their work, and when that other is the omnipotent God, the complacency with which they will drop their tools is quite intelligible. If in great exigencies, prayer will serve instead of labor, great exigencies will not be provided for, and there will be the most inadequate equipment for the most momentous crises. What would become of medicine if prayer could be relied on to heal the sick? Where would be the Boards of Health if prayer could baffle infectious diseases? Would Social Science have the faintest chance if prayer could alleviate pauperism, promote co-operation, or diminish crime? Should we ever make improvements in naval architecture if prayer would protect us from the perils of the deep? Or keep night watches in behalf of virtue, if prayer would recover the Magdalene, arrest the burglar, or quench the incendiary's spark? Nothing endeavor, nothing have, is the rule of life. For all we get we must pay full price in toil, thought, and care. Our whole power of wishing must go into eyes and ears and finger ends; not an emotion must run to waste. When we see people praying against potato rot and cattle plague, yellow fever and cholera, with their lips instead of their brains, we see an example of that woful misapplication of means to ends, by which the vast misery of the world is accounted for. When we hear them praying against unbelief, infidelity, indifference, worldliness, instead of combating them with knowledge, we see plainly enough why such things prevail. Let men be satisfied to accept the answers already given to those who will take the trouble to look for them in the proper place, and they will be found sufficient.

Civilization, with all its accompaniments, is found to have kept even pace with the decline of prayer; not with the decline of earnestness, ambition, aspiration, longing after higher and better things, hunger and thirst after righteousness, but of *prayer*, which provides what the uneducated suppose, and will always suppose, to be a special dispensation from these purely human qualifications. I am aware that this statement will be gravely questioned; but it will appear I am persuaded on examination, that they who question it are not, as a class, eminent promoters of civilization, or hearty friends of it. They are mainly churchmen, who, if they have an ideal of society in the proper sense of the term, borrow it from the book of Daniel or the Apocalypse. For the establishment of their " kingdom of heaven " they naturally look to prayer, no other sources furnishing the needed supply of power. What they desire and anticipate must come supernaturally, if at all, and their faith in the supernatural will of course correspond to the eagerness of their desire. But they who desire a better physical and social state will find the materials for it not in the outlying spaces of possibility beyond the organized universe, but in the organized universe itself, and in themselves as the crowning portion of it.

II. But this belief, it is urged, falls coldly on the heart ; it chills feeling ; it freezes emotion ; the spiritual nature cannot inhale this rarefied air, but, abandoned in a wilderness of uses, it gasps and dies. Not, I think, when the view of the truth is clear. What the mind needs is balance, poise, serenity, the sense of rest in infinite powers, of repose on divine realities. It is the highest office of prayer to console and tranquilize the mind so that its waves of passion will subside on the bosom of the eternal deep.

The eternal deep is the necessity, not the voice from it. And the eternal deep is not abolished. It is there still, where it was, and more crowded than ever with living forms. Devout persons say : we must have a God to fly to. But is it not as well to have a God who may be reached without flying—who besets us behind and before in life's inexorable conditions, who lays His hand upon us every moment in some nice adaptation to our mortal necessities, whose sensorium is the universe itself ?

An unutterable peace steals over the spirit as one sitting on a rock gazes out on the ocean, listens to the prattle of the sunny wavelets on the beach, to the mellow chant of the breakers on the cliffs, watches the flight of the sea-birds, the silent passing to and fro of ships, the streaks of color on the surface of the expanse, the patient rising and falling of the tide. To look down from a green slope upon a wide landscape with houses and cattle and the varied farm-life is composing to the feelings. A deep, strange, undefinable sense of quiet comes from the feeling of sympathy with such spacious realms of life, the mingled silence and noise, the combination of complete solitude with a vast and active fellowship. We are not addressed, yet a hundred voices seem to be speaking to us. We say nothing, yet are holding inaudible converse with something behind the winged creatures, and the four-footed cattle, and the toiling men. There is an interchange of sentiment. Our petulance and conceit flow out, the vast peace of the whole steals in ; we are comforted unawares, and with calmer spirit return to our duty.

Could we, in the same way, from the hill-top of meditation, or the slope of reverie, look out on the world of divine order and harmony, put ourselves in loving communication with the perfect system of which we form a part, feast on its beauty, admire its grandeur, wonder at its immensity, gather about us thoughts of its beneficence, brace ourselves against its immovable pillars of law, the same effects would ensue, though in much higher degree—calmness and strength would take possession of the breast; there would be no prayer, for the answer would come before the prayer was offered ; the stroke of calamity would be prevented from crushing, the cloud would pass away from the spirit, suffering would lose its sting, sorrow its dumb pain, the will would recover its composure, conscience its serenity, the lurking shapes of fear and sin would vanish.

It is quite possible so to cultivate the habit of meditation that communion with these grand thoughts will be
verily communion with intellectual being—sentiment will
answer sentiment, feeling will respond to feeling, the soul
of order and harmony will melt into the soul of their
worshipper; there will be patience in the slowly-unfold-
ing processes, pity in the gentle forbearing powers, pardon-
ing mercy in the beneficent forces that hide ugliness and
evil away; longing is met and aspiration is encouraged, and
faith reposes trustfully on the bosom of an enworlded
deity. Everything that prayer gives to the pure devotee,
this rapt contemplation gives to the worshipper. He is
made partaker of creation's inmost life. His heart is in
unison with the universal heart.

All prayer resolves itself into one petition: Thy will be
done! They who discover and acknowledge that the world
they live in is the complete embodiment of the perfect
will, are they who most habitually and feelingly offer that
pure petition;—theirs is the living piety, for theirs is the
living God, and the living communion with Him.

IX.

THE NAKED TRUTH.

I TAKE as a text this morning some remarkable words of Paul in his second letter to the Corinthians. Speaking of the spiritual man, he says: "For we know that if our fleshly tabernacle were dissolved we have a divine structure, a house not made with hands, eternal, heavenly. Earnestly we desire to be clothed upon with our heavenly frame, so that being thus clothed we shall not be found naked; we would not be unclothed but clothed upon, that mortality may be swallowed up in life."

There is a common phrase taken originally from Shakespeare — the "Naked Truth." It is used as descriptive of the simple, pure, unadulterated truth, the final absolute truth. The method of arriving at it is to strip off what are called its disguises, whether foul or fair, and get as near as possible to the bare skeleton of literal fact. Analysis is the method; the scalpel is the instrument. The same rule applied to ordinary every-day knowledge would lead to odd results. What if one were to seek the naked truth respecting an apple-tree by digging down into its roots, or of an oak by pulling to pieces an acorn! Suppose that to discover the naked truth respecting a harvest-field, a man of science, instead of visiting the barns where the product is stored, were to pull up the stubble and dissect the underground fibres! To learn the truth about a grapevine, we weigh its clusters and taste their juice; to learn the truth about an orangery, we count and suck the oranges. We speak of the "naked eye." The naked eye is the eye unaided by artificial lenses, the eye unassisted by telescope or microscope, the natural eye. But have not these fine instruments by which the power of the eye is augmented become a part of it? Do they not invest or clothe the organ with new attributes? Do these instruments impoverish the eye or enrich it? Is vision increased by them or diminished? Certainly it is increased; these contrivances supplement the organ, make it more sensitive to the sunbeam, enable it to comply more fully with the laws of light. Fancy the telescope and microscope abolished, and none but "naked" eyes left to mankind, should we be nearer the truth about the eye than we are at present? Would the disappearance of astronomy on the one hand and of physiology on the other, the vanishing of the infinitely great and of the infinitely little, add to our knowledge of the laws of vision? The natural organ is the basis on which the noble science of optics builds. It is most truly itself when it is clothed upon by its heavenly house.

Nature abhors the naked truth and always clothes it when she can. She loves the garment of tender verdure, the investiture of roses and lilies, the splendor of forests. She is fond of presenting herself in state. Where will you find an unclothed rock or stone? Not in forest or field; perhaps in some wilderness of sand, as in Africa or Arabia, where the winds blow the seeds of verdure away, or the scorching sunbeams dry them up. Travellers across our continent describe rocks cut and polished by wind and sand, on whose smooth surfaces the most tenacious plant has no chance to maintain its hold. But wherever else you find a stone, large or small, it is covered with the fine

lace-work of the lichen, which is the beginning of vege-
tation, so fine that only keen eyes can see its tracery; atop
of this is laid the soft mantle of moss, tender and green,
with its pretty flowers and its wonderful imitations of
forest growths; as if this were not enough, thick layers of
soil are added, a still richer clothing for the skeleton;
shrubbery of many kinds makes the concealment more effectual still, and at last the pine, the ash, and the oak,
glorify the whole. The whole is nature's product, and as
a whole it must be studied. To learn the naked truth
about the rock that serves as a base to the forest or the
grain-field, this magnificent mass of integument must be
taken off, the unclothed stone must be disclosed; but to
learn the full truth about the region, every stage of natural
growth must be noted. Nature is impatient of naked-
ness. A great writer standing before a nude statue in the
workshop of a modern sculptor in Rome, expresses the
opinion that the day of such work is gone by. It was well
enough for the Greeks to make nude statues of men and
women, calling them gods and goddesses; the ancient men
of Greece wore little drapery, lived much in the open air,
and were frequently, in the gymnasium or at the public
games, stripped of their garments. But the modern man
is always clothed: his clothes are part of himself; he is
known by his clothes; they express his sense of beauty,
fitness, propriety; they convey his individuality; they
present him; we do not know him without them. The
great painters made much account of the costume of their
subjects, the satin, velvet, fur, even the jewels in ring and
brooch which were sparkles from the inward character.
To learn the naked truth about a man, one would hardly
think it wise to wait till he was dead, and we could obtain
his skeleton; one might wait till he was dead, but in order
to get as far away from the skeleton as possible, in order

to gather up all that had grown about the man in the course of his life, and so to bring out the full personality, the accumulated results of a lifetime are important as exhibitions of character. The exterior clothes the interior.

The point I aim at establishing is this : The naked truth is not the pure truth, but the rudimental truth. Mr. Darwin undertakes to prove that the progenitor of man was the ape. Let us concede the sufficiency of his proof. That, let us admit, is the naked truth respecting the animal we call man. There was a time when his ancestors possessed caudal extremities and perched in trees, travelling over the ground when they had occasion, with bodies prone, and grubbing roots out of the soil. But that was, according to Mr. Darwin, many thousands of years ago. To get at his aboriginal naked progenitor, he digs down through layer on layer of humanity the depth of all those ages, peeling off accretions without number. There at the bottom is the naked truth. But a great many things have happened since then. The ape has become a very different creature, so different that it is only at moments and in rare cases that the consanguinity is suspected between him and the human race. He stands on two feet now, erect, with upright spine and trunk, the spine a column and not a horizontal conduit for transmitting sensations, and that change alone indicates and makes a new creature. Every physical organ, from highest to lowest, acquires a different relative position, and with that, new expansion and increased function ; the arms and hands are freed for use ; the claws become fingers, endowed with nerves of exquisite sensibility. The head is newly poised, and in consequence is rendered capable of new motions. Its shape alters by virtue of its erect position ; the features become handsome ; the countenance, no longer kept down near the earth with back-head upwards but raised to meet the light that streams

from above, falls into harmonious proportions; the brow
expands; the dome of the skull rounds grandly out; the
intellectual part predominates over the animal, and varied
expressions of feeling play over the formerly impassive
and imperturbable surface. The vital centres draw sustenance from fresh sources; the influences of air and light
tell on the frame with greatly augmented force; instead
of crouching low down to the earth, the vital parts hidden
by the mass of the trunk, its eyes searching the ground,
the creature moves through higher strata of atmosphere.
The entire body has an equal chance at the quickening
powers, the eye sweeps the horizon, the uplifted forehead
is bathed in the upper air; the firmament is revealed; the
look pierces the celestial spaces; the all-covering heavens
drop their grandeur upon the creature; the direct ray
strikes the level vision; the brain swells, its substance acquires finer texture, its convolutions multiply; it becomes
an organ of intelligence, sensitive to impressions inconceivably more numerous and inconceivably more delicate
than the maturest ape catches; images are there of objects the chimpanzee can never behold; currents of sensation wind and play which the gorilla is no more aware of
than the Sphynx of Egypt is aware of the breezes that
blow the light sand from its back. In the long process of
centuries, the ape has been clothed upon with many attributes of flesh and blood, every lineament and fibre of
him has been transformed, his very skin has become a
garment so exquisite in quality that it resembles the
original membrane about as nearly as the hair shirt of the
Baptist resembled Paul's spiritual body. To learn the
simple truth about man, all this must be taken into account.
The most perfect specimen of the race tells the purest
truth about the race. The last acquisition contributes to
the last judgment. To know the full truth respecting

7*

man, we should look forward not backward, up not down. It is a matter of prophecy not of tradition.

The materialist comes along; call him Vogt, Moleschott, Büchner, and proposes to tell us the naked truth about the human brain. He discovers there no soul, no intelligence, no mind. He has taken it to pieces and found out what it is made of. Here in brief is the result: eighty parts are water, seven parts are albumen, a little more than five parts are cerebral fat, a little more than five parts are acids, salts and sulphur, the rest is almost equally divided between osmazome and phosphorus. There is the naked truth respecting the human brain, which the poets and theologians speak of in such exalted terms as the "seat of reason," the "dwelling-place of the soul." Yes, that is the *naked* truth, but is it the truth, *robed and adorned?* If you put those same ingredients nicely proportioned and mingled into a silver vase will they perform the functions of a brain, will they throb, tingle and think? will "Hamlets," and "Phædons" and "Principias" exhale from the mixture? will the genius of Rafaelle steam up? will the mental powers of a Bacon become visible, ascending therefrom? Something is added by nature which the chemist leaves out, namely the *secret of combination*, which qualifies the ingredients to discharge their special office. Another thing the philosopher omits to mention, the ages of experience which have deposited the results of cumulative discipline, have discovered the precise proportions in which the animal ingredients are mingled to the best advantage, and have perfected the combinations for their fine uses. The brain is composed of the aforesaid ingredients, *plus* these myriads of ethereal deposits. The education of the brain creates the brain, and the results of education no chemical test will ever discover. To learn those we must take the living organ at the moment of its grandest performance, as illustrated by some Leibnitz or Newton, some Dante, Shakespeare or Gœthe. The *naked* truth about the brain is of the smallest possible value. The truth clothed and adorned is alone significant, and what that may be only the regal intellects will show. That truth the most enthusiastic language is feeble to express. Call it the organ of intelligence, the instrument of genius, the seat of inspiration, the dwelling-place of immortal attributes, and you do not dignify it too much : for all this it is. As the child cannot find the secret of the flower's bloom and fragrance by pulling it to pieces, neither can the chemist find the secret of intelligence by inspecting the contents of a cranium. There must needs be a poet to do justice to the flower; there must needs be an idealist to do justice to a brain.

The argument may be pushed into other spheres with equal pertinency and with greater force. In moral questions the real truth is commonly far away from the naked truth ; the naked truth is but a skeleton. A man lived in Paris whose whole aspect was that of a beggar; he lived in squalor, dressed in rags, ate food that the swine would fain fill their bellies withal ; he spent nothing in pleasure ; he gave nothing in charity; he was known of all men as a disagreeable, sour, crusty creature without natural sympathies or the ordinary traits of humanity : he died, and in looking into his effects a will was discovered bequeathing all he had, a large fortune, the savings of many years, to the founding of a hospital for incurables.

A similar case occurred not long since in New York. The tenant of a back attic room was found dead in a wretched apartment, in circumstances calculated to excite deep commiseration. The floor was uncarpeted, the fuel box was empty, the stove was cold, the window-frames

were broken, and the vacant spaces stuffed with old bits
of cloth or paper, the bed was a heap of rags; the other
inmates of the house knew nothing about the man; they
had seen him stealing in and out, and had supposed him
to be a miser who lived by beggary, and from shame, self-
contempt or misanthropy avoided his fellow-creatures.
But the simple truth about the man was not so easily
reached. That which men saw was literally the naked
truth. The complete truth, robed and adorned, proved to be
that the man lived in his sympathies with the humbler creatures. As the years went by they filled him with pity towards the brute beasts whom he saw daily insulted and
abused in the streets. He lived not for himself but for
them; that they might be happier he was content to be
miserable; in his cold garret he was warmed by the sentiments of his heart; there were kind thoughts in that head
so shaggy and hard; in that withered repulsive bosom tender
feelings had their abode; what Gœthe called the noblest
reverence, reverence for that which is below us, dignified
his soul; he was clothed upon many many times by the
house eternal in the heavens, and so when physically unclothed, he was not found naked. Under his bed was found
enough to gladden the heart of the brave man who makes
the cause of the brute creatures his own. The naked
truth about avarice is often a very different thing from
the real truth.

The principle has moral applications of serious importance. There is an old popular and evil habit of judging
character by picking it to pieces. I am afraid the theologians who had a zeal for the doctrine of natural depravity
started it. Their method was to submit characters to the
action of crucible and retort, to resolve the seeming virtues
and graces into a few very cheap ill-flavored and ill-scented
elements, and to show as the residuum at the bottom of

the crucible an ugly lump of selfishness. The apparent nobleness and saintliness were not discoverable.

Certain minute philosophers, as they seem to me, of the last century, adopted a similar method. Their plan was to strip off what they called the amiable disguises of qualities, the mask of disinterestedness, charitableness, kindness, and show beneath them the play of selfish inclinations. It pleased them to exhibit man at the last analysis as a machine worked by two wires, fear and hope, dread of pain and desire for pleasure. This, said Helvetius and his school, is the simple unvarnished fact.

The gossips, tale-bearers, censorious critics of the community pursue the same evil course. Pouncing upon some well reputed person, they pick at him till they find an infirmity, a foible, fault, some unlovely deed or unlucky step, a blunder perhaps, an ugly speck in the disposition, and setting everything else aside, they hold it up before all eyes, and say: " See here, this is the person you reverence ; this is your saint, your hero, your exemplar. He is no better than he should be." By this rule you may prove any man base. On this estimate no character possesses worth ; for the best inherit vices of the blood, infelicities of structure for which they are not responsible and which they cannot overcome. The question is, have they tried to overcome them, have they overlaid them with any deposits of virtue ?

King David was guilty of very black deeds, lustful and infamous. · There was wild blood in his veins, and power had turned his head. But he confessed his sin, accepted chastisement meekly. He had royal elements in his nature, and he did his best to make them supreme. His acts of penitence and prayer were sincere ; his psalms were an aroma from a great soul, and these after all exhibit the truth concerning the man, not the *naked* truth, but

the truth clothed upon. The instrument by which it is
discovered is sympathy; love alone perceives qualities in
their relations, and every person, the meanest, the guilti-
est, those whose volcanic passions tear the fair surface of
their existence, have their periods of rest when the sunlight and the dew refresh and gladden their being. There
are motives, intentions, memories, hopes, feelings, that
envelop even the worst deeds, and make them other than
they seem.   But this fine investiture is invisible to all
mortal eyes.

The truth I am expounding is so wide that I must push
my exposition further in order to display its bearings. My
friend peels off covering after covering from Christianity,
and having unwrapped and laid by the integuments that
two thousand years have folded about it, shows the small
kernel inside and calls it Christianity. Here you have it,
he says, the real thing as disclosed by the last analysis;
here it is, a faith that Jesus was the Christ. This is
the whole of it; you see how small it is; you perceive
how foreign to our sympathies it is; how little it is
capable of being or doing for us, how small an interest
modern men and women have in it.   All the rest is
aftergrowth.

My friend is quite right; Christianity as a naked new-
born babe was nothing more than this. This was all it
was eighteen hundred years ago; this little seed-corn fit
to feed a squirrel.   But the seed was planted in Palestine,
Asia Minor, Greece, Italy, Germany, Britain. It took
. root, grew and flowered variously according to soil, climate
and nurture.   Eighteen hundred years have elapsed. The
little seed has become a forest; its fleshly tabernacle was
dissolved, and it was clothed upon wonderfully by houses
without number not made by hands. The winds of persecution carried it from Palestine to Europe; it took root

in strange soils; it collected about itself strange influences; its fruit took color and savor from the social world it grew in. The Christ idea that was the primitive germ became transmuted into marvellous shapes suited to the needs of modern people in a world of which the Jews knew nothing; social customs grew about it, laws, institutions, standards of character, modes of life, movements of philanthropy, all characterized by the spirit of the new ages; at length the original germ all but disappears from view in the finer forms of the faith, and what remains is a harvest of moral sentiments, crops of ideas, principles, feelings, that were not contained by any means in the original seed-corn, but which the intellectual light and air of the western world produced as they acted on it. This vast, various, abundant, exuberant product, with its numberless ramifications, its infinite complexities, is Christianity, not a simple thing at all, but a whole world of things, many of which seem scarcely related to one another, worships, reforms, charities, traditions, anticipations, beliefs, piled up layer on layer, spread out wide like the branches of some gigantic tree that has dropped its suckers into the ground till it has become a continent of trees. Theodore Parker said, all sects and churches are required to express Christianity as it exists to-day; and the saying is true, because the leaven of the religion has affected every department of civilization. Indeed there is more in Christianity than all the sects represent. Though Romanism perished, though the Protestant churches disappeared, though the Unitarians and other denominations vanished, there would still be something left, a grace, an aroma, an atmosphere, a spirit and style of being, which men enjoy, feel, live by, but cannot explain.

Once such a thing existed as naked truth, but no such thing as naked truth exists to-day. All truth is clothed and adorned, and when most clothed and adorned is most itself. In times of ignorance people enriched their world with fairies and nymphs, naiads, dryads, spirits of wood and river. But our world is so rich that devices of this kind are not required. The dry bones of fact are covered with the softest verdure, the skeleton rocks are clad with soils, and where once were wildernesses are the habitations of men. They who would find the naked truth now must dig and delve for it.

I pray that in this mass of illustration my point may not be lost sight of. I wish to beget a persuasion that the true way to find truth of any kind is to take it in its most advanced and complete form, and then employ the method of synthesis. Paul says " prove all things," as if that were an undertaking anybody could enter on. But the task of proving or testing the least thing is exceed ingly arduous. It requires all the powers, and tasks all the faculties one has. To find the whole truth respecting a June rose calls into requisition all the resources of modern science, and even with their help the inmost secret will be concealed. The chemist analyses the soil in which it has root ; the naturalist studies its vessels, its stalk, its leaves ; the physicist makes it his business to detect the effects of the sunbeam on its petals ; the physiologist traces the processes of its growth from simple to complex, and at- tempts to show the law by which, in the development of species, it came to be precisely what it is. Finally, the poet takes the flower up into the realm of sentiment, as- sociates it with youth, beauty, purity, love, gives it a place in the world of fancy where it blooms forever.

A prosaic visitor in a picture gallery judged of the paintings on the walls by the extent of canvas they cov- ered, and the amount of pigment that was employed on them. If permitted, he would have found out the naked truth in regard to them with a yard-stick and a penknife. Yet, to penetrate the soul of one of them, how much was required? The eye practiced in lines and colors, acquaintance with the forms of natural objects and the human figure, knowledge of the principles of grouping and perspective, familiarity with the artist's methods, insight into the motives of a piece, the sentiment of beauty, love of the ideal. Leave out any one of these, and the judgment is at fault; combine them all, and no more than justice is done to a master's creation.

Shall we think less of the divine master's creations than of these canvas productions? Will we think to get at the secret of a faith by pulling it to pieces, and not by following the law of its structure? Our modern practice has been in the art of analysis—the art of reducing all things to their elements. It is the scientific method, and the value of it cannot be estimated too highly. To pulverize the solid substances of the earth, to reduce adamant to vapor, and behind the vapor to touch the imponderable forces that perform the work of creation—to grind to powder the solid institutions of men, to resolve establishments into ideas, and behind the mask of usage detect the movements of the bodiless thought that indicates the presence of universal mind, to sift motives and decompose principles till the roots of character are laid bare, is certainly a useful thing to do—all honor to the men that do it! This is to get at the beginning of creation, at the origins of existing things. But it is by the opposite process that we arrive at the glory of creation, and see the consummation of created things. To reduce the diamond to carbon was a contribution to chemical knowledge; but to transform the carbon into diamond was a triumph of creative genius. The dissolution of the fleshly tenement into dust is a feat of daily occurrence; but out of the dust to create a man, is the effort of Omnipotence. Does any one ask which is the nobler?

One may well stand in awe as he thinks of what cheap material the finest things are made, but to preserve the awe, thought must dwell on the fine things, not on the cheap material. A sunset cloud is composed of a wisp of vapor and a sunbeam, but the gorgeous phenomenon attracts all eyes, that watch with emotion the strange phantasmagoria of mountain ranges, castles, cities, grotesque forms of animals, monsters and men, shapes of grazing sheep, camels traveling over wastes of sand, flocks of birds flying in the air. The vision fades but is forever and forever renewed, and as often as it is repeated, the children of men, the glad, the grieving, poets, lovers, mourners, feel the active enchantment in their hearts.

"We are such stuff as dreams are made of," says Prospero, "and our little life is rounded by a sleep." But we are what we are, nevertheless, fearfully and wonderfully made as to our bodies, and miracles of wonder as to our minds. The slenderness of the material does not prejudice the solidity of the result.

Most enduring beliefs of mankind are composed of elements so slight that they almost vanish at a touch. The belief in God, for example, is made of very ethereal stuff, the feeling of awe, the sentiment of veneration, the sense of dependence on higher powers, the emotion of trust, the childlike instinct that leads in search of causes for phenomena; yet the belief has a strength like that of the ancient hills round whose base civilizations appear and disappear, in whose vales hamlets nestle, whose summits watch-towers crown.

An analysis of the faith in immortality makes us wonder how it came into being. Its origins seem not only obscure, but in some respects discreditable, as when one of its roots is seen to be the childish belief in ghosts and spectres. As water-drops compose the rainbow, so do falling tears compose in large part the bow of heavenly promise that spans the abyss of death. It is only while the showers are falling and the sun is low that the arch appears in its beauty.

The world of the hereafter is called into existence by the passionate hopes, longings, demands, anticipations of men and women in their excited hours of bereavement or disappointment. Take these one by one, each by itself, how evanescent, how all but illusory they appear; how wild seems the notion that aught permanent can arise out of them! And yet the faith bears the weight of centuries; great souls find refuge in it; and to multitudes it stands as the one assurance that is certain and immovable. The house not made with hands is the house that is eternal.

Nothing is more solid than character; nothing on the whole is so solid. A great character is the type of the everlasting. It is the crystalization of the qualities that we call divine, immortal—justice, truth, purity, kindness, simplicity, faith. It is the diamond that is hardest of all substances and yet the most dazzlingly beautiful. But what is it made of? Aspirations, purposes, endeavors, good thoughts, just emotions, acts of fidelity which become compacted together, vitalized, organized, till they are proof against all the agencies that would pulverize them or reduce them to vapor.

All fine beliefs grow richer with time, under the successive accumulations of experience that gather upon them. They lose their simplicity, but they gain in luxuriance; they are more complex but more glorious. The belief in God as held by Herbert Spencer or John Tyndall, is to the belief of an ancient Israelite as the heaven of Herschel is to the firmament of Joshua, or a modern city like

London, to Bethlehem. It is too vast to be explored, too complicated to be described. Compare the belief in providence as entertained by the Hebrew prophets, with the belief in providence as held by Theodore Parker or Stuart Mill. They are as unlike as the acorn and the oak ; yet the new belief and the old one are the same, except that some twenty-five hundred years have done their work in depositing knowledge and reflection on the primitive persuasion of mankind.

Place side by side the germinal idea of immortality as described by Lubbock and Tylor with the idea as it lies to-day in the minds of religious people in Christendom. Consider the numerous phases of the faith as it is professed by mankind, from the atheist's conception of immortality in the race, to the spiritualist's familiar thought of the departed as personally alive and near, within reach of communication, and even palpable to touch, from the sentimental dream of Renan, who tenderly addresses the thought of his dead sister, to the sober business-like persuasion of the man of affairs who consults the spirits on matters of finance and politics. The faith that was once a flower is now a forest, solemn with shade, bright with vistas opening right and left to the sunlit world, the refuge of the storm-beaten, the haunt of dreamers.

As faiths thus become rich with time, the minds that are privileged to cherish them ought to expand with satisfaction. The seekers after the naked truth, living under ground among the roots of things, toiling in laboratories, busy at the task of trying all precious substances by fire, resolving the jewels of the world into smoke, the critics whose office it is to reduce things to their rudimentary elements, can hardly be expected to rejoice ardently over their work. They do not see things as they are, but as they were in the beginning ; they see the seed, not the flower ; the sucker, not the fruit ; the germ cell, not the organism ; their gaze is riveted on a point of exceeding smallness ; they have little time or disposition to look around and up. The duty of generalizing must be left to others. They scrutinize, and if at times a feeling comes over them of the poverty and emptiness of the universe, they are not to be blamed, but forgiven and blessed for their needed service.

But they whose faces are not held in this way to the earth, they who can take a broad survey of the world they live in, can catch the odors of its flowers and taste the sweetness of its fruits, can revel in the light of its sunrises and sunsets and enjoy the eternal beauty of its stars, should go about filled with serene thoughts, feeling that now they are the sons of God, content that it doth not yet appear what they shall be, but satisfied that whatever does appear will be more glorious than anything which is.

X.

THE DYING AND THE LIVING GOD.

THE belief in a dying God is the centre of the whole Christian system, as it is also the root of nearly all the ancient religions. The belief, stated in its bare form, is this;—Touched by the unspeakable sorrow of the world, moved by the misery in which the human race lay, shocked by the guiltiness into which his moral creation had fallen, the Almighty left his throne of light, came down from his eternal seat, took upon himself the form of a man, underwent all the sufferings of common humanity, and, at last, after a short career, which was, nevertheless, long enough for him to go through every phase of human experience and life, allowed himself to be put to death as a malefactor by the humiliating punishment of the cross.

This prodigious transaction is held to be justified by the assumed necessity of lifting mankind out of their wretched, sinful state, they being utterly powerless to help themselves, even to raise themselves from the ground, to advance themselves at all in the direction of their own improvement or salvation. Doomed to everlasting death, nothing less than the death of the Everlasting could restore their hope of life.

This is the central belief of the Christian religion, and, as I have said, of all the ancient religions. It is the central belief of the religion of this present time, not by any means remanded to a secondary place in thought. Slightly modified or mitigated it may be in some of its accidents, but at heart it is the same thing at present that it was two, three, four thousand years ago. In the larger number of churches in any of our cities this belief will be preached to-day in the sermons, will saturate the prayers, will breathe through the strains of the organ and the music of the choir, will appear in every emblem that is presented to the eye, will stand before the worshippers' vision carved or emblazoned in the form of cross or cup. It will sigh and wail through the mournful verses of the Episcopal liturgy; it will be the soul of the creed that the people repeat after the priest; it will, in fact, be the pervading idea and sentiment of teaching and worship.

The belief is not confined to Sunday observance or the services of the Church. It is worked into the theories of common life. It comes out in every great crisis of human experience, in each grand event of existence. In the chamber of the dying the priest murmurs it in straining ears. It stands by the grave and rolls over its mould the solemn words of redemption by the blood of the Crucified. Grief confesses the claim and exalts the glory of the dying God. The sorrow-stricken are comforted by the thought that the Lord has died for the sorrowing. The guilty are confronted with the terrible fact that because they were guilty the Infinite Perfection itself had to bow to the bitterness of death.

To us such a belief seems grotesque, and that only. For my own part, I have no words to express the literal absurdity of it. When we think of God as modern men are educated to think of him, as the Infinite, the Eternal, the Unknown, the Unsearchable, the Permanent in the universe, the perfect Wisdom and Truth, the absolute Goodness, the Being in whose hands all these systems of worlds are less than the dust in the balance; when we

think of man and of the little planet that he lives on—
one of the smallest and darkest of all the orbs that God
has created ; when we think of the scale of his troubles,
and cares, and sorrows, of his few battles and faint striv-
ings and evanescent griefs, his superb endowments, his
magnificent apparatus of self-help, his unused powers, and
then picture this great Being as coming down, clothing
himself with flesh, and submitting to be driven about,
beaten and buffeted, scorned, spit upon, and mocked, and
finally nailed to a tree, that these creatures of his may be
redeemed,—why, it is not in the modern understanding to
take in such extravagant incongruities of thought.   The
belief is a poem, an allegory, a parable, a divine romance,
a dream of the soul   It is one of those holy fables of
Providence which, under a grotesque and strange form,
convey, perhaps a shadowy, yet a profound truth.

I do not believe in pouring contempt upon any widespread faith.   Whatever nations of men have believed in
is sacred, even though it be obsolete.   A faith so universal as this, that has prevailed all over Asia, that the Asiatics handed to the Greeks, that the Greeks handed to the
Christians, is a sacred faith ; it means something, and
what it means it is worth while to know.

The belief in a dying God has accomplished three
things.   In the first place, it has imparted to Providence
an attribute of exceeding tenderness.   It has put a tear,
we may say, into the eye of the Omnipotent. It has made
the almighty heart of the world throb and beat with emotions of compassion.   Estimate the power of this if you
can.   When the wise man sits down to teach a child ;
when a man of exalted rank or great power stoops to lift up
from the dust some miserable, obscure, and despised creature ; when a person of eminent character or lofty endowment fights the battle of the scorned and outcast, the very

thought of it touches the heart to the core. But to think that God himself, the Supreme Goodness and Serenity, the Holiness and Peace of the world, actually came down in person, stood by the side of the dying, called back the dead to life, wept over humble graves, took little children in his eternal arms, and comforted wretched mothers for the loss of their darlings, sat in fishing-boats teaching their duty to simple people, the thought of it was 'enough to break the heart of the world, and it did. A great sob of penitential agony went up from those early ages to which this faith was living; a great sob of shame and pity, as if the heart of mankind was breaking. It was too much that all these little ones should be thought of graciously by the Most High. In dark ages, when there was no knowledge, or justice, no general idea of kindness, no conception of Providence, no knowledge of the world, of things, or men, no understanding of human nature or social relations—in those dark ages, truly dark, not only intellectually but spiritually black—in those ages, a faith like this was worth more than all the teaching that could be given by the wisest men. Men are even now reached through their emotions more easily than through their understandings, and a faith like this brought an omnipotent force to bear upon the very tenderest spot in human nature.

Another effect this belief had. It sanctified suffering; it made human sorrow a consecrated thing; it took the pitiful weakness and wretchedness of the world into the sheltering arms of God. The realm of coldness and dreariness was no longer an outside realm; it was annexed to heavenly places, and made a constituent portion of the celestial domain. The sufferers stood nearest to heaven; they were the most loved; theirs was a privileged condition. To be in want, and poverty, and weakness; to be

8

buffeted and despised ; to be persecuted and forsaken ; to
be hated of all men, was to enter into the secret experience of God's own history. By this way mortals found
entrance into bliss. Sorrow no longer implied sin, no
longer shut people out from the Lord ; it was sorrow that
brought people into full communion with the Lord, and
made God verily a Father. The great sorrows of the
world seemed now to have a touching expression in them.
The streams of blood that were shed on holy battle-fields
and scaffolds seemed to pour from the Redeemer's side.
The oceans of tears that innocence shed dropped from
heavenly eyes. The sighs and sobs, the moanings and
wailings of the providentially afflicted, the cries of agony
in sick-rooms, in hospitals, and desolated homes were the
sighs, as it were, of God himself weeping for his little
ones. Yes, those bitterest woes that men bring upon
themselves by their recklessness and guilt—the awful pes-
tilences, the ravaging plagues, the hideous wars, the frightful distempers, that sometimes fairly took possession of
the world and decimated mankind—what were they but
so many expressions of the infinite loving-kindness of
God, that would not allow his people to sink away into
recklessness and ignorance without an effort on his part
to recover them ? Even in the woes that sin brought
down there was something pathetic, pleading, touching ;
and thus all the wretched, and even the family of the
wicked, were brought into the bosom of the Eternal.

Another effect this belief has had. It served as a
refuge from atheism. The atheist says, How will you
account for the wretchedness of the world on the theory
that the world is provided for by a good God ? How can
you explain the existence of want, poverty, suffering,
agony, premature and violent death, broken hearts, crushed
spirits, wasted lives, on the supposition that there is a

thoughtful Deity ?   If God is good, why is not the world
happy ?   If God loves his creatures, why does he leave
them all, without exception, exposed to some kind of des-
olation ?   If God fills his heavens with light, why all this
ignorance ?   If God is compassion, why all this complaint
and bitterness ?   If God loves the world, then the world
should be lovely.   Not so, says this old belief, not so ; it
is *because* God loves the world that the world suffers.   It
is a mis-read legend that Adam and Eve were driven out
of their Eden by an evil spirit.   No evil spirit ever drove
man out of Paradise.   No devil ever broke up that luscious state of moral unconsciousness.

An evil spirit would have kept Eden as it was, an evil
spirit would have multiplied Edens all over the earth, so
that there should be nothing else.   He would have weeded
the ground, never allowing a briar or a thorn to appear.
The days should always be sunny, the heavens always
bright, the airs balmy, the trees fruitful, the ground fer-
tile.   No necessity for labor, if an *evil* spirit was near, no
care, or trouble, or vexation, or annoyance ; no beasts to
be exterminated, no reptiles to be eradicated, no insects
to kill, no violent men to subdue ; nothing but ease and
plenty, and abundance and felicity, in this realm.   An
evil spirit would have made the earth a garden, and there
he would have placed humanity to rot.   That fable was
credited when man had no conception of what manhood
was, or what it was that constituted a *human* creature.
It was the love of God that drove man out of Eden into
the world, where he might know good and evil, where he
should have his destiny fairly set before him, and his fate
in his own hand.   Do you complain because the saints
are persecuted, because the martyrs meet a bitter death,
because the hero must lay down his life for a noble cause,
because the grandest careers come to a premature end,

because the heavenly-minded are destitute and forsaken, because the pure-hearted are scorned, because the "sons of men" have not where to lay their heads? It was God who went through all these things. He accepted suffering. It was He who was poor, and destitute, and forsaken, who had no place where to lay his head. It was He that suffered himself to be spit upon, and buffeted, and scourged, and scorned, and nailed to the tree. It was He who was brought to a premature end after a brief ministry of mercy. Will you say that the kindness of God is an argument against his existence? Will you urge that God is to blame for laying upon his creatures the same experiences that he suffered himself? Will you make the infinite benignity of Heaven an argument against its character? Nay! rather stand confounded before this fact, that Heaven has stooped down and entered into the very secret of suffering, and in entering into it has justified it, explained it, and consecrated it.

This is the hidden meaning of that old belief. Look at it as poetry, and how beautiful it is! Let the imagination take it in, loveliness graces it all over. Let it lie simply in the heart as a sentiment, and it warms the heart to the core. But forget that it is poetry, read it as prose, instead of a parable make it a dogma, and the whole significance of it is changed. Instantly a veil comes over it all, and what was formerly so beautiful, touching, divine, becomes cold, strange, and mischievous.

There are three evils that flow from this belief in a dying God. It is accountable for an enormous amount of sentimentalism, it begets a weak, puny, self-conscious, complaining heart. A dying God, a suffering God!—then what is there worth thinking of but suffering and dying? So men have moaned their sorrows, and told their woes over and over; they have sought sorrow in all places, have gone to Nature for it, have fancied that creation was pitched on a minor key, have detected the sobs of anguish in the falling of waters, the blowing of winds, the rustling foliage of trees, the murmurs of the brooks. Where sorrow existed, they exaggerated it, dwelt upon it, pressed it in, made it more and more an ineradicable part of human experience. Where sorrow did not exist, they imagined it. All people must be sad, was the cherished persuasion. There is sorrow at the heart of everybody. Beware how you trust to joy or to hopefulness, there is a pensive strain in all human experience. So profoundly has this sentiment become impressed upon the heart of Christendom that nothing is accepted as good which has not a tinge of sorrow. Only the virtues that are born of sorrow, it is supposed, are real virtues. Patience, submission, resignation, self-denial, self-renunciation—these are the admitted graces. The pale countenance is the interesting countenance. The downcast eye, full of unshed tears, is the human eye. This tinge of sorrow deepens even to blackness, and blots out the very light of joy. The glory is taken out of nature, the cordiality is taken out of society, the heartiness out of the heart. Here is one evil—that men are made self-pitying, led to call themselves miserable creatures, to say, " How sad we are! how sad our neighbors are! what a wretched world it is! what a vale of sorrow we live in! what a weary time we are all having of it! if there was no other world but this, life would not be worth having!" all morbid, mawkish, and sentimental, all depressing to the springs of health and life.

Another mischief has followed from this belief. It has encouraged not only self-pity, but self-contempt. A dying God—why a dying God? Because men were sunk in iniquity, and could not rescue themselves. But, if God dies because men are wicked, and if the death of God was necessary to rescue men from wickedness, then men must be very wicked indeed. There is no possibility of exaggerating the malignity and depravity of the world. God would not die for a peccadillo; He would not die for a foible or for a fault, for a mistake or for a blunder. God would not come down from Heaven and die simply because men were stupid, or blind, or reckless, or foolish, or passionate; He could only undergo such prodigious experiences because men were utterly depraved; and so they must be. They *must* be, and you must make it out that they are; and if they do not seem to be, you must prove that their seeming does not conform to fact. So, all over Christendom, for two thousand years, men have been peering down into their own consciousness, trying to discover the seeds of evil there, never happy until they did; perfectly happy if they could prove themselves to be good for nothing; entirely content if they could demonstrate beyond question the truth that they were miserable sinners; supremely satisfied if they could comprehend the whole race in the same dismal category. Could anything be more deplorable than that? Could any result of unbelief be more unfortunate? This has been *one* result of the belief in a dying God—that men have disbelieved in their own nature, in the worth of their affections, the integrity of their moral will, the nobleness of their conscience, and the purpose for which they were created. An orthodox preacher once said in my hearing, that men—other men—were born to live; Christ was born that he might die. Was ever a more extravagant statement made than that?

Another mischief has resulted from this belief. It has deprived the world of the benefit of divine inspiration. For it has taken God out of life. The modern world is rendered vacant of divine influence. Men who live, work, purpose, strive, and endeavor here are not blessed in so doing by the divine spirit. That is away in Palestine. God's life culminated in a single hour in the city of Jerusalem. He is shut up in a tomb ; He dwells in the shadow of death; He belongs to the wretched and the sorrowful ; He is the property of the miserable ; He is not for those who are in light and joy, but for those who are in blackness and grief. The consequence has been that to think of God it has been thought necessary to leave nature, life, business, art and literature, science and beauty, and to gather thought around that one hour of crucifixion. Thus, literally, we have been deprived of the magnetic power that comes from a conviction that God is with the world.

Now, over against this belief in a dying God we set the belief in a Living God. A *Living* God. The very phrase has an ocean of light in it. It is full of aspiration. It gives us a sense of buoyancy only to speak the words. At once the universe awakes to joy. Man is a human creature again. He feels the breath of divine energy sweeping through his daily affairs. To come from the belief in a dying God to the belief in a living God is as when one, after wandering for hours in the depths of the earth, say in some mammoth cave, groping about among hidden rocks, creeping along ledges, and crouching in the blackness, scarcely seeing in the distance a little trail of light thrown by the guide's torch, comes out again into the freshness and beauty of the world, to hear the singing birds, to see the green grass, and the trees waving in the wind. It is as when athwart a black cloud a beam of sunlight comes streaming down and gives a glory to the landscape. It is as when after a period of cold easterly storms, during which people have been shut up in their houses, the earth has become saturated with water, the trees have drooped and dripped with wet, and all nature has seemed forlorn, forsaken, drowned, we wake up to find a balmy, sweet dawn. Then the earth itself seems to throb with new life. The birds sing, as if they had learned a new hymn of praise. The drops of rain on the leaves are clusters of diamonds. Man himself goes singing to his work. The windows are thrown up; doors stand wide open; men go out upon their steps to breathe the air; the church spires catch the sunbeams as they pour down from the sky; the fronts of the houses become beautiful in color, and the atmosphere seems oppressed with the task of bearing up to Heaven the grateful feelings of men.

The belief in a living God restores God to the world; makes him a part of it; constitutes him the grand working force in it. It makes him the God of business; the God of recreation; the God of the exchange and the market; the God of the railway and the ship; the God of literature and art, of science and of progress. It puts him down here in the front rank of men. The humanitarian does that service for Jesus when in the place of a dying God he makes him a simple, living soul. Think of Jesus as a dying God, and your thoughts go back mournfully to Calvary; you shed tears; you kneel down in the dust of Gethsemane; you hear his prayer, "Father, thy will, not mine, be done." Your thoughts are drawn away from domestic life, teaching, professions, whatever you may be doing, and are gathered up in a melancholy mood about the suffering King. Take Jesus now into the race; make him a man, a simple, living man; put him here; take him into your shop; meet him on the street; associate him with your labor, with pleasure and care; at once you have the the whole benefit of his being. The full weight of his life is thrown into your scale. His spirit is in your heart. You have the benefit of all that he was, and all that

he knew. The orthodox presses a dying God to his imagination ; the humanitarian has a living God at his side.
There is the difference. The evangelical worships a dying
Christ in his church ; the rationalist goes hand in hand
with a living Jesus to his labor. Just what is done for
the world by substituting a living man for a dying deity,
a living Jesus for a dying Christ, that is done when
we substitute a living for a dying God. We give God
to the world. We make him the life of the world—the
livingest life of the world. We throw the whole momentum of his omnipotence into the scale of our endeavors.

Where will you go to seek the life of the age ? The living age--where is it ? You will not seek it in Wall street
or on Broadway. It is not necessarily commerce, or
finance, or politics, or business. All these things help the
life of the age, but the life of the age is the effort of the
age to create a perfect society. It is the endeavor to overcome evil, to cast out mischief, to reform the wrong, and
relieve the wretchedness of the world. Everything that
does this partakes of the life of the age. Commerce does ;
so does traffic, and invention, and business, and art, and
science, in proportion as they help on this great result.
But the living part of the age is that part of human thought,
purpose and feeling, that goes to make society better.
How will you define a living man ? It is not the man who
is in robust health. He may be very dead indeed. Many
a man is of most rugged health, of blooming complexion,
never tired, sleeps perfectly, always digests his food, and
yet is a living grave. A smart business man is not necessarily a living man. The best part of him may be deceased, in spite of his smartness. His conscience may be
deader than dead, and his soul may never have been alive.
He may be dead and buried. Your bright politician is not
necessarily a living man. Not of necessity does he have

anything to do with living things. He may be a corpse
and the maker of corpses. He may be one of the sextons
of civilization ; one of the grave-diggers of humanity, as
too often he is. A living man is one whose life is in the
effort to make society better; to render the world better
worth living in ; to advance its improvement and help its
progress. A living man is a man who, whatever he does,
whether he be merchant or manufacturer, engineer, trader
or artist, acts, with the purpose through his acting, to
make men kinder, juster, sweeter and fairer than they are
now.

Such is the life of the age, and such is a living man.
Now what is a living God ? It is a God who is living in
this same sense ; a God who is associated with our effort to
make society what it ought to be—just, pure, kind, fair,
and sweet. And it is in vain to think of any other God as
living ; idly do you speak of a God that *did* live. Jehovah's name was I *am ;* not I *was*, not I *shall be*, but I *am*.
God *is*. The living God is the God that *is*. Vainly will
you seek him in the past, you are not in the past ; vainly
will you anticipate finding him in the future, you are not in
the future ; vainly will you think of him as being in Heav-
en, you are not in Heaven ; or in the abyss, you are not in
the abyss. You are here, this moment, on the face of the
globe. Men may say, " lo here, lo there," do not believe
it ; " he is in the desert," follow not after him. Nothing
makes one feel the living God but the sense that one is
himself alive. It is perfectly useless to try to get at a living God except by living ; useless is the wisdom of the
wise ; of no avail the vision of the seraph. The living
God is the God who is living with living men and in a living age. He is with the lawyer who is trying to make
justice the rule of human dealing. He is with the physician who is trying to eradicate the seeds of disease. He

is with the preacher who forgets himself in his truth. He is with the philanthropist who loves his fellow-men better than he loves himself. He is with the reformer who is reforming according to a principle, and not according to a crotchet. He is with the merchant who is opening new avenues of communication between the families of mankind. He is with the trader who is passing round the gifts of providence among all the members of the human race. He is with the artist who reproduces the most perfect beauty. He is with the musician who puts into his song a strain of light and hope. He is with the man of science who is organizing the strong facts of creation. He is with the literary man who is expressing truth in forms of beauty. He is with the conservative who will hold on to all the good there is, and with the radical who will eradicate all the evil. He is with all men, of whatever degree, of whatever station, who are doing something to add a little spark to the blaze which is to consume the rubbish of human experience.

The living God is a human God. Swedenborg says: God is a man, and that man is Christ. We say God is not *a* man, but the *human* in all men. God is the human power, the human element, the element which uplifts, inspires, impels forward to brighter and better futures. Man's justice is God's justice. Man's compassion is God's compassion. Man's kindness is God's kindness. When man forgives, God forgives. When man absolves, God absolves. All God's attributes are human attributes, and they are living as they live in us, not as they live out of us. The very unity of God is one with our unity. Is God one while his family are a thousand? Does not all the recklessness, and hate, and quarrel, and discord of the world break up into pieces our conception of the divine unity? Of course it does; for it suggests a kingdom divided against itself. God lives when man lives. God lives in the human heart; when the heart begins to throb and beat, his heart throbs and beats; and when the human heart dies, then, and then only, God expires.

This is no speculative thing that I have been saying; it is of immense practical moment. If, a few years ago, the Bible could have been set steadily on the side of those who were working in this country for freedom, our war would have been rendered entirely unnecessary ; the mere fact that the Bible, the so-called Word of God, ranked itself with liberty, light, justice, would have thrown the preponderating weight of the religious sentiment into that scale, and would have secured victory. If the Bible could be planted fairly and squarely on the side of those who contend for the social rights and privileges of women, for the improvement of the condition of the working classes, for reform in civil and criminal jurisprudence, these things would be carried, simply because those who put their faith in the Bible, believing it to be the revealed Word of God, would rally to these causes. So, if we could take this great thought of God, fraught as it is with inspiration, full as it is of light and life, of hope and purpose ; if we could, I say, take this thought and associate it with all we believe of truest, all we hope of dearest, all we purpose of best, then all this belief, hope, and purpose would be charged with the very spirit of victory.

Over against one of these beliefs, therefore, I set the other. The one belief looks to the past ; the other has its eye on the future. The one belief cowers before God ; the other stands erect and looks him in the face. The one belief is fighting always with the devil ; the other greets the coming of the angels. The one belief begs its way into Heaven ; the other runs thither with jubilant feet. The one belief shudders in the presence of hell ;

the other smiles in the presence of heaven. The one belief counts over the sins and perplexities, the ills and dis-
advantages of life ; the other counts over its benefits and
benedictions, its privileges and its pleasures. The one belief
is full of awe ; the other is the very incarnation of hope.

A poor woman the other day came to me and said: " I
want you to help us—myself, my husband, and my child."
I asked her what was her need, and she told me their
history. " Are you connected with no church?" I in-
quired. " No." " Have you never been ?" " Yes."
" Where do you belong?" " My husband is a Unitarian
and I am a Catholic." " Will the Catholics do nothing
for you?" " Well, the truth is, neither of us have had
anything to do with religion for a long time. We were
prosperous once, and happy : now we have fallen upon
evil times, and we think of God." Why did they not
think of God in happy times? Why did they not associate God with their felicity, and success, and prosperity ?
Why, when everything went well, was not God hopefulness in their heart, and energy in their will ? It was be-
because he was not, and because in their hopeful and
happy times they were simply selfish, thought only of
themselves, never cared to form fine relationships, or to
make earnest friends, that, therefore, they were left
wretched and dismayed. Must we always be scourged to
the banquet of life? Must we always be dragged into
heaven by the hair of our heads? Will it never be
enough that beauty, and privilege, and opportunity are all
before us, but we must be goaded to them by the fiends ?
Time has been when fear and darkness were the spirits
that saved the world. In the time to come the world will
be saved by light, and joy, and hope.

XI

THE INFERNAL AND THE CELESTIAL LOVE.

He that findeth his life shall lose it, and he that loseth his life for my sake shall find it. Matthew x. 39.

THIS is one of those paradoxes which are familiar in the language of the East, and which Jesus was especially fond of using to impress his thought the deeper upon the minds of his hearers by shocking them into consideration of its meaning. There are two readings of the passage. In the gospel of John the version stands, "He that loveth his life shall lose it, and he that hateth his life in this world, shall keep it unto life eternal." There are two interpretations of the passage :

First—He who exposes himself to danger and to death for my sake shall inherit praise, honor, and emolument, when I come again in my kingdom.

Second—He that lives a life of self-denial in this world shall have his reward in the world to come.

But there is another interpretation that goes deeper than either of these, and in my judgment is much truer. He that denies his lower love shall have the satisfaction of his higher. He that puts away passion shall enjoy principle. He that abandons the life of desire shall enter into the life of spiritual joy.

The life of a man is the love of the man ; the love of the man is his life. The words love and life are closely connected in their root ; and if we substitute in these passages the word love for the word life, a world of meaning is at once unfolded to us that otherwise we miss; because the word love drives the thought inward and keeps it there, while the word life throws the thought outward and leaves it there. We think of life as a thing of duration and extension in space and time. We think of love only as a state or condition of feeling. We speak of present life, past life, future life, of the life here and the life hereafter, of this life and the next life; but of love we only say it is better or it is worse; it is higher or lower; it is on the animal plane or the spiritual plane. In a word, love is a thing of qualities; life is a thing of quantities.

Now, speaking of love, we find that it has a double action; one a self-referring, another social or human, referring to others. The planets are kept in order, you know, by a double force; the centre-seeking, the centripetal force, as it is called, which is always drawing the planet to its central orb; the centrifugal or centre-avoiding force, that drives the globe away from the centre. Either of these forces acting alone would destroy the planet. The centripetal force, acting alone, would, by and by, mass the planets together, and at last absorb them all in the sun. The centrifugal force, acting alone, would scatter them widely apart and fling them into the vast inane, where they would be hopelessly lost; there would be no more solar system. The action of both together keeps the planet in its place, steadily whirling round its centre and fulfilling its part in the divine decrees. So it is with this thing that we call love. At first it is a passion. Man, in one aspect, is a mere organic creature. He is the last development of the material world; a child of the mineral and vegetable; developed out of the ground; a bundle of propensities and instincts. His life is organic and simple, like the life of a tree or a plant. He is a creature of material circumstances and elements. As such he is inevitably self-seeking. Through his five senses man is doing his best all the time to draw in all the world. His eye seeks beauty in every part of the globe; in the ground, in the skies, in the sunlight and the shadow, in the faces of his companions, in the landscape. " His eye dismounts the highest star," as old George Herbert so beautifully says. And, not satisfied with finding beauty everywhere, it must appropriate beauty everywhere. It will draw it in and make it its own. Man catches the sunlight and weaves it into his fine fabrics and tissues, his carpets, his drapery, paints it on the canvas, carves it in the marble statue, insists on having domesticated in his house all the glories of the outer world.

The ear! how it drinks in sounds; how keen it is; how devouring it is! All voices come to it. It will invent instruments to make itself keener. Not satisfied with hearing the sounds in nature, it manufactures instruments for reproducing them. Music is its creature. It builds the organ with its array of golden pipes; it fashions instruments of brass and the stringed instruments; it brings together the orchestras that enchant us with their music.

The sense of smell has narrower range, yet how greedy it is! All odors come to it. It extracts the sweetest scent from the foulest things; it is not content until it puts on our toilet-tables the fragrance of the violet and the odor of the newly-mown hay.

The taste! What a craving creature that is! What an explorer! How it sends its purveyors out into the most distant parts of the creation, dispatches its divers down into the sea, drops its line deep into the ocean, lays snares for the birds of the air. What a plunderer it is of the vegetable and animal kingdom! How it consumes and slays! What devastation it makes everywhere, and what a keen power it has of extracting delicacies from places where nothing seemed to exist! How it divides and subdivides, and combines and compounds, and separates and mingles and mixes! How it uses the subtle element of the fire for its purposes, and what elixirs it extracts thereby; what delicate tinctures and aromas!

The marvels of the *cuisine* are infinite, and man is never satisfied with inventing, discovering, combining, flavoring, and devising new shapes of delicacy. There is no end to it. It goes vastly before human need. We are never content with the things that our senses can bring in to us. The Emperor Vitellius had but one stomach; he could eat no more than the humblest of his guards; yet he spent one million of dollars every week on his table. He did not need it; it was the worse for him; it made him sick; it helped to kill him at last, and it earned for him the nickname of the " hog Vitellius."

Insatiable are these senses of ours. We build cities; we form lines of commerce; we clothe ourselves with silk, and satin, and velvet; we construct vast ships. Yet our ships are only larger baskets; our silk, and satin, and velvet are only a handsomer kind of blanket; our vast commercial cities are but more superb shops and warehouses; our great ports of entry are simply broader doorsteps; and all our vast carrying-trade with fleets of ships is only a more elaborate peddling.

Push the metaphor further. Take the passions. There is the love of power. Can anybody describe its voracity? Did anybody ever have enough of it? Was there ever a man having the most of it who did not want more? The priest is never content with the power he has over human souls. The despot is never satisfied with the power that he has over human relations and conditions. The rich man is never satiated with the power he has over the poor. The tyrant is never weary of grinding. The conqueror is never tired of absorbing. Alexander the Great was not the only man who sighed because there were no more worlds for him to conquer. Every man who has this lust for power sighs for precisely the same thing. Napoleon sighed for it, and the present Napoleon, though a sick man, doomed probably within a few months to die— a man without a dynasty—has such a passionate greed for the power that he has gained that he will not loosen the reins that his hand holds, or give, in conformity with his own promises, the freedom he has pledged to the people. The Pope of Rome, an old man near his grave, at the head of an institution that is doomed by destiny to fall, reaches out both his hands and calls upon the whole civilized world to grant him more power over souls, more power over states. He must regulate public education and control the national and state politics even in America. And the more power a man has the more selfishly he uses it. This passion for power has been the curse of mankind. All the devastating wars have sprung from it; the gigantic slaveries have been of its offspring; it has ravaged peoples; it has exterminated tribes; it has ruined empires; it has blasted states; it has kept the inferior races from developing themselves; it has exterminated children; it has subjugated women; it has gone on pillaging and plundering as if the whole created world was merely its field of ravage. There is an infernal element in this love. We need not speak of a hell hereafter. We need not speak of any demoniac regions on the other side of the grave. Why, but a few years ago we all lived in hell every day that we breathed, and now, hellish beliefs, hellish passions, rule over immense portions of the earth.

The passion for wealth, consider that! There is love

—the love of money. Did anybody ever estimate the power, or capacity, or grasp of that? Did anybody ever have enough, though he had a thousand times more than he could spend on himself, or than his heart prompted him to give away? To get money by fair means if possible, by foul means if necessary, to steal it if it can be had in no other manner; to cheat for it; to pick it out of your neighbor's pocket; to contrive, and plan, and manage, until what belongs to others comes to you; to get it away from the rich and the poor; to make others poor in order that you may have it; to be content that others should continue poor, in abject want, in order that you may enjoy it, is not that the commonest experience of the present, and of the past also? And how the endeavor to keep it, though it be kept for no end whatever, possesses people. The heart grows smaller as the purse grows larger. The conscience dwindles as the dividends increase. The soul goes down into the dust as the fortune mounts up into the air. The more a man has the less he has to give. He will see his poor, old, freezing brother suffer from want and misery, but he has nothing for him. Vainly the widow comes to his door in her need. Vainly the orphans call to him that they may be preserved from ruin. Vainly the poor man, whom fortune has stricken down, pleads for a little relief. Here is an ignorant world asking for means to teach it, a sorrowing world praying for consolation. Here are men of science and knowledge who have discovered the secret of human prosperity, and want but money to set their grand machinery in motion. Vainly do they go to the man who has millions in his pocket. Why, think what happened in Wall street only a few weeks ago! A few men who were enormously rich, fabulously rich, so rich that they had nothing else to do but to get richer, so rich that they wanted all the riches there were, buy up all the gold (why shouldn't they have bought up all the cotton, or the iron, or the wool, or the grain ?) —buy up all the gold and compel men to purchase of them at ruinous prices.   The effect was disastrous.

Two or three weeks ago there came to me a lady, well-nurtured and educated, brought up in luxury, refinement on her face, dignity in her manner, sweetness in her voice ; she said, " Can you do anything to get me a place where I can earn a little money to support myself and my children ?"   " Have you no husband ?" I said.   "Yes, my husband was one of the innocent victims of the gold panic in Wall street, and is a ruined, broken man ; I have two children who must be educated.   I must do something. Can you help me ?"

One week ago to-day I attended the funeral of a man of culture and accomplishment.   He died by a sudden stroke brought on by intense excitement, caused by that same crisis, an innocent victim of it.   It had first broken his mind, then slain his body.   There was his widow left without his support.   There were his three daughters standing on the very threshold of their young life.   And all that was due to nothing else but this infernal love of money.   For this poverty and wretchedness, for this loss of mind and life, those few men were answerable.   Did they care?   Would they care if they knew it?   Probably not ; all they cared for was to amass money, no matter what ruin heaped up the pile.

Take that other love which bears the name of love pre-eminently—that instinctive, passionate love which plays so large a part in the world.   How voracious, how insatiable it is!   What abysses of misery it opens!   What ravages and wrecks it makes!   I need not describe it to you. There is one demonstration of it which, unfortunate-ly, we are never allowed to lose sight of.   This passion has created a class which is, of all classes in society the most pitiable ; a class of women which has always existed, which exists now in undiminished numbers, and, for aught that any of us can see, will continue to exist for generations and generations to come ; a class of women who are the despair of society ; whom we do not know what to do with or what to do for ; whom law and gospel alike stand aghast before ; whom modesty never speaks of and purity never thinks of ; whom holiness looks down upon with horror and pity turns away from in disgust ; whom even mercy hardly dares to compassionate, and philanthrophy is ready to abandon the hope that it can help. The utmost that society, now so many thousand years old, has learned to do for these unfortunates is to draw a line about them, to put them under supervision and control, that the poison of their infection may not eat too deeply into the heart of society. Their life is one game of hypocrisy ; they make believe smile out of a cold and dead heart ; counterfeit raptures that have long been impossible to them ; imitate a love which they do not feel ; pretend to be gay when their soul is full of despair. Women they are, doomed to early blight, decay, and premature death, unpitied, unblest, unwept for, unprayed for. They haunt the night in the cities, proud when they are insulted, and only grateful when their womanhood is scorned ; a class of unfortunates —so unfortunate that every heart bleeds to think of them —victims of this all-devouring passion ; may we not say priestesses, sad priestesses, who sacrifice themselves on this frightful altar ; nay, march into the fire to be burned, that society may be spared the ruin, the devastation, and the shame which this consuming flame would otherwise cause. Is there not an infernal element here ! Is there no hell here ? Walking about in our streets, living in adjacent houses often, a hell so deep, so utter, so black that no poet like Milton has ever been able to paint it, no theologian like Jonathan Edwards has ever been powerful enough to describe it.

This is the infernal love; a love that is altogether exorbitant, that overflows all uses and all needs in every direction. It does not and can not control itself. Unless there were some controlling force, some counteracting feeling, it would bring the race to destruction. But here comes in the merciful provision of Providence. To balance the centripetal power which always seeks self, there is provided the centrifugal force that throws the spirit out among mankind. To counteract the selfish force is the human force. Over against the all-devouring love is the all-embracing and beneficent love of heaven.

What, then, are these forces that I comprehend under the term the celestial love? God has garnered them up in institutions.

The first of these is the institution of marriage; a divine institution grounded in the nature of things, instituted in the laws of human nature, sanctified by all that is purest, sweetest, and best in human life, and demanded by the exigencies of human society. The object of this institution is to hold mankind together. It takes a little group of people, the man, the woman, the brother, the sister, children, and holds them by a bond that can not be dissolved; compels them, as it were, by their love for one another, to deny themselves for the sake of those they live with. The strong must help the weak. The weak may lean on the strong. The wise must teach the foolish. The simple may come for advice and counsel to the wise. The man and the woman complement each other. The great and the little live by mutual support. One common bond exercises such a control over the members of this outer world that whatever difference may exist in age,

taste, culture, disposition, temperament, they are still virtually, to all appearances and to all designs, one person.
This is the intent of marriage, to educate in humanity.
There must be self-denial; patience is imperative. There
is a great deal to bear and forbear, and it is made indispensable. Woe be unto those who would break up or
weaken this institution of God! Woe be unto those who,
in the interest of an animal individualism, would disin-
tegrate this fine communion! Woe be unto those who
preach the gospel of instinct, passion, desire, who proclaim the philosophy of elective affinities, teach the sanc-
tity of impulse, the authority of caprice, and say that what
men have a right to, and all they need to insist on, is
that they shall enjoy themselves, at whatever expense to
society. They who seek to undermine this institution, or
who disseminate views that are fatal to it, think they are re-
moving a superficial disadvantage and sorrow. They are
striving to beget a permanent disadvantage and a sorrow
that the world will never cease deploring. They are
defeating the great providences of God. They are up-
heaving the basis of society. They are doing away with
that fine moral and personal education which is indispensable to the training of men and women in courtesy
and kindness, in free charity and brotherly love. We
know very well and admit very sadly that the system does
not work perfectly. What system does? We know very
well that marriage is often an occasion for tyranny and
selfishness. We know very well that there may be
despotism in the home, with misery, fretting, suffering,
sorrow, more to bear than can be borne, more to forbear
than can be done. We feel all the time how infinitely
far this divine institution is from accomplishing its perfect end. Do we not know that wives are wretched, that
husbands are untrue, that children are neglected, are

spoiled, left without training, in ignorance and willfulness? Do we not know that sorrows are engendered there which nothing apparently can heal? And yet we all know that, if there is any sweetness in human life, it is due in a large measure to this institution of marriage. It is the parent of the best comfort, the sweetest luxury, the most permanent and satisfactory content that the world enjoys. There are homes that are heavens. There is paradise at the feet of mothers and fathers. There is education and training in all nobleness within the four domestic walls, and there is not much of this outside of them. There are examples of dignity and elevation and even saintliness there which stand at the top of all human experience. The mother bending over her sick child to save its life, giving up everything, forsaking the world, watching all night, anxious all day, toiling and anguishing continually that the spark of life may be kept in that little frame—is still the type of the purest disinterestedness that men have imagined. And the picture of a father bearing with his misbehaving son, watching for him, praying for him, thinking of him when he has gone astray, waiting for him to come back, seeing him from afar, running to him, throwing his arms about his neck and kissing the poor prodigal, putting the best ring on his finger, shoes on his feet, fresh garments on his wasted and haggard form, and telling men to kill the fatted calf and feast, because he is returned safe and sound,—why, it is the image of the parental providence itself! Christ could think of nothing more divine than that. When we see parents, as we sometimes do, caring for some poor child to whom they have given birth, and to whom life has been only a weariness and a sorrow, trying to make it easier for him, to smooth his way, to furnish occupation for his hands, to give some pleasure to his heart, to open little glimpses of a better world to his anticipation; when we see how the heart softens and sweetens, how passions become chastened and the mind becomes subdued, how meekness and patience and loveliness steal into the spirit, then we say God bless the institution that can so transfigure weakness, and want, and pain, and sorrow, and can make our poor dependent human nature come so near to heaven even in the hardest experiences of earth!

I know that the discipline of the home is not always wise; that the relation of marriage is sometimes narrowing. The household is limited. It is a small group. It is so in the nature of things. We all know very well that men and women become so interested in their homes, in building up their families, caring for the wants of their own little circle, that they forget the large world outside. Certainly. It must be so. Marriage is not the only institution in the world. It is not the only educator that there is. If Providence had stopped here, we might object that marriage was an insufficient institution. It is. But it is supplemented by another, and this other, the next institution by which God tries to check, control, and educate this selfish, passionate nature of ours, is the institution of Society.

We do not make society. It is not a manufacture. It is not a device of human wit and wisdom. It is not something that we have invented and set going, a machine that we wind up and allow to run. It is an organic creature, the growth of ages. It is a being, indeed, made up of all beings together. It has its roots deep down in the past. Its branches spread wide in the heavens of the future. It is so comprehensive that it embraces every rational creature from the top to the bottom of our life. Who is so great as to transcend it? . Who is so little as to be out of its reach? The greatest depends upon the

9

smallest. There is no emperor, king, or queen, no noble or prince, no magnate, no millionaire, financier, banker, no great genius in literature, no great poet or historian, no intellect however vast, no soul however tender, that is not indebted to the smallest and meanest creature that crawls upon the face of the earth. The emperor on his throne is dependent upon the ditcher, the delver, the drudge, upon the mason, the carpenter, the builder, the farmer who holds the land, the tiller of the ground. There is no queen in her robes of state who is not indebted to the poor sewing woman in her garret, passing her days and nights singing in her heart the dreary song of work. And, again, there is none of these, no poor woman, no sad-eyed, broken-hearted girl, no ditcher, no drudge, no delver, that is not every day dependent upon the great and high ones who sit above. The atmosphere of genius finds its way to them. The soul of goodness reaches down into their darkness, and the spirits that dwell nearest the eternal throne pass their air and sunshine down to these roots that live below the ground.

Let any man try to get away from society if he can. Let any man try to fly in the face of society, and see how instantly he is ground into the dust. Nay, let society try to get rid of any portion of its own organic structure, and then see what ruin and devastation ensue. Society is one living, vital, organic structure, with veins spreading out in every part, with great arteries swelling with red currents of blood. There it is, living and beating with the very spirit of the Eternal in it all the time. It does not do its work perfectly. Its intention is to overcome the selfish desires of men by making them love their neighbor, feel how closely they are bound in with others, help the helpless, teach the simple, lift up those who are cast down, serve those who are above them, offer their tribute to the noble and the good, make their contribution to the intellectual, the moral, or the material wealth of mankind. That is the purpose of it—a purpose to educate men, to discipline them, to subdue their weaknesses, their levity, and their foolishness. It does not do it. Society is full of anarchy. It is full of wretched spirits who wish to tear it in pieces. Nay, the very structure of society, the very fact that it is so closely woven together, gives the opportunity that rude, lawless, and violent spirits need to make their own advantages out of their fellow-men. On this very account the tyrant is able to spread his dominion so widely. On this very account the despot is able to shake the earth as he does. Because the web is so fine, a violent finger will tear it to pieces. But then, much that is noblest in us owes its training to this very structure of society. The patriot is its offspring. The philanthropist is its child. The worthy citizen is its common creature, and the men who labor that the world may be better—the reformers who are ready to lay down their lives for the good of their fellow-men—are born out of this respect for fellow-men. Just as often as anarchy rises and tries to tear the social fabric in pieces, the fine web forms again, and the great work goes slowly on.

A few days ago a man died in London who illustrated simply and beautifully this truth. He was not born to wealth, or comfort, or luxury, or high estate. He made his way upward by his own efforts. He was a lonely man, unmarried, with never wife or children, with few near kindred; he worked by himself, and by his patient working amassed an enormous fortune. Many, in his case, thus alone, self-sufficient and self-dependent, would have been satisfied to live alone and to exalt themselves at the expense of others. They would have become hoarders of wealth—what we call misers. They would have contracted themselves more and more, forgetting neighbors, oblivious of human obligations, and doing nothing of that duty which is incumbent upon every man and woman who lives in the modern world. But this man remembered that he was but one member of the family of mankind. He remembered that he had a duty to perform and a debt to discharge. He knew that his wealth came from the labors of the working class, and he tried to give back to the working class a portion of the benefit that they had conferred upon him, by building, in the heart of London, more comfortable homes for them to live in. America, by continuing to be America, to reward his faith in her had poured enormous wealth into his lap; having the wealth, he remembered America in her time of need, and poured it back into her bosom, that America might be richer, that her untaught millions might be taught, and that a better civilization might be started and established in the southern land. Say what you may about the wisdom of his charities and the success of his benificences, we can not forget that he accepted and fulfilled this mission, that the mere fact of his being a member of society overcame his selfishness, drew him out of his loneliness, warmed his heart, enlarged his sympathies, strengthened the bonds that bound him to his fellow-men; and now his memory is in all minds, his name is spoken in humble gratitude by the lowliest and the loftiest lips. A Queen sheds tears as he dies. His statue stands in bronze in the great city of London; carved out of grateful memories and pure affections his statue stands in the niche which every good heart has for those who love their fellow-men.

One thought more is necessary to complete what I have to say. The education of the family is limited. So is that of the State. In both there is room for great selfishness, for tyranny, despotism, and violence. Another edu-

cator is needed.   Men must learn to love each other, not
as members of the same household, of the same town,
city, tribe, state, or nation, but as members of the same
great *human* family.   This love alone can be purely disinterested.   The family love is selfish within its limits.
Social love is within its limits selfish.   We know well
how in the State the politician may produce disorganiza-
tion ; how in society those who hate one another or who
mean to plunder one another have abundant opportunity.
Selfishness is not eradicated by these institutions, and so
God plants another.   It is the Church.   The church represents fellowship on the simple ground of humanity ; the
Church is not American or French, Roman or English,
it is simply the *Church.*   It is not for the poor or the
rich, for the wise or the simple, for the great or the small ;
it is for everybody.   The Church knows no differences
between men, but only one fundamental resemblance.   It
speaks of the one God and Father of all ; of the Christ
who is the brother, the friend, the sympathizer, the servant of all ; of the common lot, the common origin, the
common destiny, the common birth, the common heaven,
the common need, the common suffering, the common
sorrow, the common consolation and redemption.   The
Church speaks simply of man—not of man and woman,
but of man—mankind.   Its symbol is the communion.
Think of the first communion supper.   Think of those
twelve men ˙ seated around a table with their Master.
There was John, the intense, passionate, morbid enthusi-
ast and seer.   There was Peter, the organizer, the practical man, the man of simple common-sense, whose name
is associated with the Church of Rome.   There was James,
the ritualist, the formalist, the priest of the early church,
the man who wore the priestly robes and went through
the form of granting absolution to the people, the man

who stood for ordinances and sacraments. There was Judas, the business man, who carried the bag. Then there was Matthew, and the rest of the disciples who left no mark whatever in history—simple men, stupid, ignorant, who had no comprehension of their Master whatever, and who were ready to run away when danger came. There they all sat, and among them the great Christ, sweet, serene, and benign, breaking his bread for all of them to eat, giving the cup that he tasted to all of them to drink, blessing them all alike, pronouncing upon all his peace. The symbol is never realized, never fulfilled. Can we ever dare to hope it will be fulfilled? The Church has never done its duty. It has never tried fully to do its duty. In fact, by generating an aristocracy of its own, an aristocracy of believers, a family of the elect, a select class of the devout, it has done what it could to break up the human family. And yet, here and there, in little spots about in different parts of the world, you will find these simple, scattered groups of men and women meeting together without distinction of lot or of person, and bound together by a love so simple, sweet, tender, and strong that all the hostility of the world can not drive them asunder. Imperfect as the work of the Church has been, it has still held up its sign, the sign of the communion, the sign of the cross, the sign of the dove. Still it has spoken of the great All-Father; still of the Christ, the one Brother of all; still of the great Heaven that opens to all the immortal destiny.

Slow and long and weary is the process of educating man out of his selfishness—hard and laborious beyond our telling or conceiving. But it is done—feebly, imperfectly, gradually, by slow and tedious stages. The time will come when each one of these divine institutions will fulfill its end more gloriously than it has yet, and, as it does, each will prepare its way for the next, until at last we shall have on the earth a *society*—a society of men and women who are brothers and sisters, mutually dependent and mutually faithful, mutually loving, serving, and blessing; then the prayer of Jesus will be answered : " May thy kingdom come, may thy will be done on Earth as it is in Heaven."

XII

THE IMMORTALITIES OF MAN.

This mortal must put on immortality.—1 Cor. xv. 53.

OF all the great religious ideas, none has been so un-worthily treated as the idea of immortality. Of all its grand legends, none has been so meanly interpreted by Christendom as the resurrection. It is popularly re-garded as a matter of bones and blood. It is read as the story of a mortal who renewed his mortality, rather than of a mortal who put immortality on. The point of sig-nificance in it, indeed the solid proof of it, is made to consist in the ability of the risen man to eat " a piece of broiled fish and an honeycomb."

Fairly considered, the New Testament does not record the physical resurrection of Jesus as a body, but his spirit-ual resurrection as a power of life in the soul. Thus Paul —the first witness and the great preacher of the resurrec-tion—taught it. But even supposing the corporeal resur-rection of Jesus to be recorded and to be true, that was not of the first importance. More than one resurrection of nobler import has Jesus had in history. There was a resurrection in thought, when, rising in the mind of Chris-tendom, he stood a being of light, glorifying the barren spaces of speculation as the central figure in a new the-ology. Another resurrection he experienced in Art, when, as a new ideal of spiritual beauty, he enchanted the souls of Raffaelle and Titian and Da Vinci, and through them fascinated the modern world. Again he rose as the image of moral perfection, showing the heavenliness of purity, patience, peace, humility, aspiration, to the children of a coarse and cruel age. And yet once more, as a vision of tenderness, pity, compassion, and utter kindness, as the spiritual brother of mankind, he came out from the grave of a kindless past, and showed men how they should live with one another. A great soul has many immortalities; they increase in grandeur as its history unfolds and the spheres of power open before it. The corruptible puts on more than one form of incorruption, and the mortal robes itself in resurrection garments of many hues.

When often asked if I believe in the immortality of the soul, I am tempted to reply: " It is precisely in that I do believe. It is the sum of all my convictions. Believing that, it is hardly necessary to say what else I cling to. I believe not so much in the soul's immortality as in the soul's immortalities." The difficulty of talking on this subject arises from its depth and extent. We hardly know where to begin; we never know where to end. There is so much to say, that it sometimes seems best to say nothing, lest one should be misapprehended. But I will try to say something intelligible on this great theme, about which so much that is unintelligible has been said, and which yet is unexhausted. Let us consider three or four of the ways in which our mortal puts on immortality.

I. In the first place, there is a sense in which the body is immortal. Not the ancient, orthodox, and generally approved sense; that is abandoned by thinking men. The doctrine of the Church has always been that, at the last day, the identical bodies of men and women shall be raised for judgment. Augustine said: " Every man's body, howsoever dispersed, shall be restored perfect in the

9*

resurrection, complete in quantity and quality. The hairs that have been cut off, the nails that have been clipped, shall return; not in such quantities as to produce deformity, but in substance as they grew." Dr. Gardiner Spring, but lately deceased, wrote: "Whether buried in the earth, or floating in the sea, or consumed by the flames, or enriching the battle-field, or evaporate in the atmosphere, all, from Adam to the latest born, shall wend their way to the great arena of the judgment. Every perished bone and every secret particle of dust shall obey the summons and come forth." One Church Father held that the teeth were providentially made eternal, to serve as the seeds of the resurrection. Others opined that the resurrection body would be in the shape of a ball, like the head of a cherub. According to an old rabbinical tradition, a small, almond-shaped bone, called the *ossiculum luz*, formed the nucleus round which the organic elements would gather, or the germ from which they would be developed in the resurrection. This bone, they fancied, was indestructible; no pounding on anvils with steel hammers, no burning in fiery furnaces, no soaking in powerful solvents, threatened it with demolition or touched it with decay. It was incorruptible and immortal. Modern speculation has entertained a similar fancy.

The author of a curious book, called "The Physical Theory of Another Life," imagines that the body may contain some imperishable particle in which the soul has its seat—a particle imponderable and imperceptible, which, when the gross elements of the body decompose, assumes a higher life and evolves a nobler organization. Leigh Hunt, in his charming book, "The Religion of the Heart," indulges some such dream. "Physiologists tell us," he says, "that the vital knot of the nerves is no bigger than a pin's head. Who shall say of what size is the knot of the knot,—the life and soul of the life itself, that which receives all our sensations, and acts upon them and thinks ? "

Modern chemistry, which is supreme in the realm of matter, which resolves the subtle air into its constituent elements and takes the light to pieces, brushes such notions away as idle fancies. Nothing ethereal eludes its grasp. The "spiritual body" it cannot see must be attenuated indeed! Chemistry says: Not thus is the body immortal, but rather in a fashion conceived by most men to be fatal to the very idea of its immortality. It is decomposed; it passes into the elements; it dissolves and escapes in air; it mingles with the productive agencies of the ground, and reappears in leaves and plants. It is glorified in the grass that is green on the grave, and the wild flowers that make living the meadow. The soft garments of the spring are the resurrection robes of thousands of mortal forms. Science preaches eloquently the persistency, the indestructibility of force. Our bodies are magazines of power; and when the "silver cord is loosed" that binds the frame together, the emancipated force takes other shape, flows in new directions, and performs fresh work. The death of the body is its transformation; the dissolution of the body is its discharge to new offices. It escapes from vault and coffin; it baffles the worm, and, without displacing stone or sod, becomes ethereal, and floats away.

The belief, if it be nothing more, is tranquillizing and pleasant. It may make no one more thoughtful or regardful of the body that is reserved for such fine transfigurations; it may teach none to respect the frame so sweetly predestined: but it should have power to disarm the grave of its merely loathsome terrors; it should, to some degree, purify the charnel-house, expelling the phantoms of mould

and rot, and placing white angels in the spot where the
dead body had lain. This idea of fleshly immortality should
relieve us of our disgusts, and make us think more amia-
bly, if it cannot make us think more lovingly, of Death—
the angel that can spiritualize our much-abused and often
grievously insulted dust. The first step towards gaining
a complete victory over death will be to think more sweetly
of its processes. If with our clod it deals so tenderly, the
dealing will surely be no less tender with what we respect
more. Superstition demands the resurrection of the corporeal man, that he may appear in very person to be
judged and punished. Reason prefers to think of the
corporeal man's dissolution as the release of the body from
its duty. It is consoled and elevated by the thought that
Nature loves the particles of even the vilest body, and
when its temporary possessor has done brutalizing it, will
kindly change it into forms of loveliness all her own.

II. A nobler immortality is that we have in the memory
of those that love us. It is more than figuratively true
that we live in one another. With very many the inward being consists more in others' lives than in their own.
If there be a human creature who is wholly unloved; who
has no affections, or possesses no power of gaining affections; who touches his neighbors as one particle of sand
touches another, at the hard surface, never blending or
mingling : if there be a human creature whom no wife
clings to, no brother or sister cherishes, no child reveres or
blesses, no friend confides in, no neighbor looks up to with
admiration or reposes on with trust—such a creature knows
nothing of the immortality I speak of. But few, if any,
are as unfortunate as this, and none need be. Organic
ties bind most of us to more persons than one; and if
organic ties do not, ties of mutual service, of sympathy
and tenderness, do. It is seldom, indeed, that one dies

leaving none bereaved. Seldom, indeed, does one die and not leave himself behind, a power of sadness or gladness in other hearts for years—a presence visible to the mind's eye, tangible to the heart's feeling, absent never by day, and often disturbing sleep by dreams—a presence that cannot be banished ; for it is part and portion of the mind itself, that we would not banish if we could for worlds.

If the child of few years, the infant of few months, have no other immortality, it has a very dear and blessed one in the heavenly heart of its mother—an immortality of light ineffable, to which comes no shadow, in which is no doubt or fear or imperfection—an immortality that deepens in grace and glory as long as her consciousness endures. The baby taken from her arms is transfigured in her bosom. Seeing it no more, no more holding it in her lap, she talks with it and smiles with it, sits with it in the nursery, rambles with it over the fields, prattles foolish fancies to it, drops asleep with it nestling in her breast, and wakes to see its little face looking down upon her. It was *flesh* of her flesh, and bone of her bone ; it *is* thought of her thought, feeling of her feeling, and life of her life. Before it left her womb, it stirred unutterable longings, opened new fountains of hope, whispered bright promises of happiness ; no sooner did it appear, than a new world within her was ready to welcome it—a world that the expectation of the new-comer had prepared. From week to week, through the period of its dependence on her, the stranger had been enlarging, uplifting, softening and enriching her nature, making her a sweeter and better woman ; and each new thought or feeling is associated, is identified, with the image of the young Messiah, who preached the kingdom of heaven, and brought it. When he goes away, is all that lost ? No, indeed, it remains ; the child remains—always to her thought a child, though her thought becomes feeble and her memory of many another pleasant thing fails.

An old man, a physician, who called himself an Atheist, lost his son—his only boy—a youth of fine character and promise. To the question whether he believed him to be still living, he replied : " Yes, in me ; in my heart he lives ; and as long as I have thought and feeling, he will have thought and feeling in me. When I cease to be conscious, he will die." To few people, perhaps, will the thought of such an immortality be satisfying, but to none should it be unimpressive. It suggests a life after death that, though impersonal, is genuine and real, the hope whereof should be stimulating. To live in another, in several others pos- sibly—to live as a precious memory, a pleasant thought, a kindling anticipation, a sweet solace, an example of good- ness, a help to virtue,—is surely to live a very real exist- ence, far more real than most people dream of when they dream of heaven. To live so is worth praying for and work- ing for. This kind of life may be more effectual than the life in the body was. The dead mother often sways her child more than the living mother did ; the imagination, quickened by sorrow, working mightily to fix impressions which the actual word or look could not secure. To be allowed to live thus in her child's future, the mother would gladly relinquish her hope of an everlasting future for her- self. This immortality, at all events, may be assured : those who love us will remember us—alas ! when we wish they might forget. That which has, for better or worse, become an organic portion of being cannot be obliterated. Whether its quality there be the quality of the angel or the fiend—whether our immortality in the hearts of those who love us be an immortality of bane or bliss—it is inev- itable. Though the bane or the bliss be ours in anticipation only, though we neither suffer the one nor delight in the other, the anticipation of it alone should make us lead nobler lives. If the prospect of misery or happiness for ourselves hereafter is enough to sober or inspire us, how much more should we be sobered and inspired by the thought that when we are gone, we may be the cause of life-long misery or happiness to those that love us better than we ever loved ourselves !

III. A grander kind of immortality yet—grander, though less affecting—is that we have in humanity. We live in humanity; we are vitally connected with it as members. The human race is an organic being, that lives and grows from age to age, animated by one spirit, actuated by one power. "No one liveth to himself, and no man dieth to himself." Standing midway between those that have gone before and those that are to follow after him, he receives and transmits the qualities that build up the social world. Existence is a process of receiving and giving. In us live the fathers ; in the children we shall live forever—every atom of our nature being taken up, absorbed, worked over, as material for the coming man. As Lessing puts it: "The immortality of souls is indissolubly associated with the development of the race. We who live are not only the offspring of those who have lived before us, we are really of their substance ; and it is thus that we are immortals, living forever."

This idea has, for thousands of years, been rooted in the world. Traces of it are found in the ancient religions. It was hinted at in the Egyptian doctrine of transmigration ; it was conveyed in the Indian doctrine of absorption ; the Chinese acknowledged it in their worship of ancestors. The ancient Hebrews, previous to the captivity, seem to have known no other doctrine of immortality than this. The dying Hebrew was said to be " gathered to his fathers ; "

and, as he passed away, the thought last in his mind was of the posterity in whom he should continue to live. The Hebrew's prayer was for long life and for children and grandchildren—generations who should transmit his virtues, and call him blessed. His kingdom of heaven was on earth; his dream of eternity was the glorious future of his race.

Gleams of the same belief shine through Pythagoras and Plato and other sages of the old world. This is the belief of the Positivists of our own time. They cherish no hope of private immortality; that they describe as the fond anticipation of egotistical minds. They have much to say about living again in those that shall succeed them —about making a contribution to the happiness of their posterity—adding something to the capacity, skill or virtue of the coming time—leaving behind works that may follow them; as they have entered into the labors of others, they would make it worth while for others to enter into theirs, consoled by the knowledge that no fragment of living bread will be wasted, that no accent of the Holy Ghost will be lost.

The great master of this school declares that for every true man there are two forms of existence; the one temporal and conscious, the other unconscious but eternal; the one involving the presence of a body which perishes, the other involving the action only of intellect and heart which cannot die—the latter alone worthy to be called that noble immortality of the soul after which the best aspire. To his female companion—who complains that such an immortality appals her, by giving to her a sense of insignificance that reduces her to nothing, and who begs to have revived in her a feeling of her own individual existence—the master replies, that the Great Being, Humanity, cannot act except through individual agents;

the collective life is but the result of the free concurrence of the efforts of simple individuals; all are nothing without each one, and each one, while embodied and conscious, may feel himself to be an indispensable part of the living whole; each is predestinated, and each is useful; each has a message, because each is sent. In the same strain another writer of great power: " Whatever happiness we derive from pure regard to our fellow-beings, and from satisfaction in the general welfare, will cling to us as long as we are capable of entertaining it; and whatever deeds we do, not ' in the flesh,' for the gratification of self, but 'in the spirit,' for the love of God and mankind, we may know to be as immortal in their nature as God and mankind are immortal."

There is the conception—it must be confessed, a very impressive one to the calm, brave mind. For thirty years this gospel of immortality has been eloquently preached, not without effect. It has taken strong hold, not on the intellectual and passionless only, but on the working-people of intelligence in Europe, who have thrown off Christianity and discarded faith in a personal God. It is a belief that deserves consideration and respect from all who consider the claims of truth, and from all who respect the serious convictions of earnest men. If it is not to be lightly accepted, it is not to be lightly ridiculed, for it contains the elements of great power.

The heartiest objection to it is, perhaps, its heartiest recommendation. *It effectually destroys egotism*, that taint in the common belief; it gives no encouragement to the selfish wish for a happiness purely personal; grants no indulgence to the longing for a heaven of idle rest or unearned recreation; rebukes the rash claim for private and unmerited rewards; says to men, avaricious of crowns and thrones in the hereafter, what Jesus said to the ambitious youths who asked for seats at the right hand and left hand of his throne: " What you ask is not mine to give." If pure disinterestedness be noble, then this doctrine has a character of supreme nobility ; for it requires the renunciation of every interested or covetous passion ; it bids men labor for what they shall never share, and fight for what they shall never enjoy. To any but the earnest, loving and self-sacrificing it is cold and dreary ; but to these it is inspiring and grand.

The doctrine is human, purely human—human in its very texture. It rests on the fact of human fellowship ; it derives its vitality from the power of the sympathetic feelings : love—deep, unselfish, consecrating love, for human beings as such, for human beings, unrelated, unknown, unborn—is its animating principle ; the love of duty is its strength ; the faithful ministry of mutual service is its living pledge and bond. It is nothing without others, many others, all others ; its grandeur consists in the solemn perpetuity of that eternal Being called Man, whose existence rolls on through the ages, gathering might as it rolls, swelled by the great and little tributaries— the rivers and rivulets, the brooks and tiny brooklets, that add their rushing volumes or their trickling drops as it pours along.

The doctrine is spiritual. Rightly apprehended, it is the only purely spiritual doctrine that is entertained ; for it puts out of sight altogether, and utterly abolishes, the consideration of " mine " and "thine." The spiritual fact is the faculty of living in ideas, truths, laws ; the spiritual glory is the glory that comes of so living ; the spiritual being is the being who lives " not for himself alone," not for his private enjoyment or satisfaction or development, but for that which is a great deal more than himself, for that which is not phenomenal and passing, but stable and permanent, which will live when he is no more, the glory whereof he can increase and in a measure create, though in it he is absorbed. Lucifer forfeited his spirituality by setting up for himself. His brethren preserved theirs by their meek surrender to the perfect Will. As the spirituality of God consists, not in his being bodiless, but in his being self-renouncing—as a God who made the end of the universe to be his own glory would be precisely the reverse of spiritual—so is he the seeker of a spiritual immortality who desires to live in others' future more than in his own.

The doctrine has its fine inspiration too. The first aspect of it sends a chill to the heart. The ordinary man or woman feels annihilated by it. What is the ocean's debt to the drop of water? What is the sun's debt to a candle? What effect has a summer shower to sweeten the bitterness of an Atlantic or Pacific sea? How shall the planet feel the leverage of my little finger? What contribution is my faint breathing to the mighty blasts of truth and conscience that must blow the vessel of humanity onward? This doctrine of immortality in the race may answer for a Buddha or a Moses, a Jesus or a Paul; it may satisfy a Pythagoras, a Socrates, a Plato; the Augustines and Luthers, the Xaviers, St. Bernards and Fenelons may rejoice in it; Dante and Milton, Shakespeare and Lessing, may press it to their bosoms; Mozart and Beethoven, Handel and Mendelssohn, may wish nothing better; Leibnitz and Bacon, Newton and Galileo, may dwell on it with rapture; it may fill the dream of Raffaelle, Angelo, Da Vinci; for their great lives poured into the ocean of humanity as the waters of the Mississippi pour into the Gulf, as the waters of the Orinoco pour into the Atlantic, heaving up the level of the sea, and thrusting its purple current miles from the shore. They who are conscious of vast power can rejoice in great influence: but those who are conscious only of great weakness can promise themselves no such recognition, and must droop for lack of inducement.

If recognition were demanded, if an immortality of fame were the immortality coveted, this objection would be fatal, for the famous are the few. The mass are soon forgotten, living but a little while in the memory of their friends. But fame does not always follow influence. Many a great benefactor is scarcely remembered even by name. Many are quite unknown. The mass of mankind make humanity, not the few; the multitude of the lowly and worthy decide what the future of society shall be. He who contributes a life of simple truth, sets an example of daily honesty, makes a happy home, trains his children well, is a loyal friend and a good citizen, practices the greatest duties in the smallest way—does more to augment the sum of moral power in the world than any artist, however admirable, any poet, however sublime, or any genius, however inventive. The doctrine of immortality in the race is peculiarly encouraging to the humble, earnest toilers, the unprivileged and ungifted; for their contributions are just what they choose to make them, and what they add is that which is most indispensable to the common good. We are not surprised, therefore, to learn that this doctrine is especially popular among the artisans, who know that all they can contribute is industry, patience, fidelity, intelligent skill, temperance, prudence, economy, but who know, as none others do, that these qualities are precisely what humanity needs in its struggle for life.

IV. I have spoken at some length on this view of the immortal life, because it is unfamiliar, and because it is misunderstood. I have spoken earnestly because I could not speak at length; the words had to be vivid because they had to be few. But I leave it, now, to say something on that other form of immortality—the personal, individual immortality—which is the hope of so many millions of mankind, which is, in fact, the only form of immortality by most people thought worth considering. The belief in conscious immortality has a strong hold on the human race. It is ancient, though there were times when it did not exist. It is widely spread, though there have been people who did not entertain it. All men do not believe it, and cannot. All do not desire it, life not being so rich to all that they would continue it if they could. All do not hope for it; for there are those who think the hope audacious and extravagant. All dare not claim it, there being not a few modest souls who cannot think themselves or their neighbors worthy of so inestimable a privilege as that of renewed existence. This life, they say, is more than we can manage; it would be worse than rash to demand another and a longer one. Such will actually resist the arguments that are urged in favor of their falling heirs to such an overwhelming estate.

But such considerations do not affect greatly the moral consciousness of mankind. Most men—all men, at some periods—live in their feelings; and their feelings all twine round this column of personal immortality, as the vine clings to its upright trellis. The instinctive love of life abhors death, protests against dissolution, insists on continuance. Living man cannot think annihilation; he can only think life. Thinking man cannot conceive of thought as ceasing, and in the activity of his mind finds prophecy of endless intellectual progress. Loving man cannot bring himself to believe that the objects of his affection are gone from him forever, or that he shall ever lack objects to love. The deathlessness of the beloved seems to be an axiom to the heart. Earnest, aspiring man, feels certain that he shall be allowed time to fulfill his dream and attain his perfection. Then, too, we are persons : each one of us says *I;* and, when he says it, feels himself to be an indestructible monad, a separate entity, a solid thing, that he remembers as having persisted through a changeable past, that he is sure persists now, and that he cannot persuade himself will cease to persist through any changes that may befall. All this is instinctive. Reasoning has little or nothing to do with the assurance. In fact, the more we reason about it, the weaker it is. "The only occasions," says a sincere writer, "on which a shade of doubt has passed over my conviction of a future existence, has been when I have rashly endeavored to make out a case, to give a reason for the faith that is in me, to assign ostensible and logical grounds for my belief. At such times a chill dismay has often struck into my heart, and a fluctuating darkness has lowered down upon my creed, to be dissipated only when I had left inference and induction far behind, and once more suffered the soul to take counsel with itself."

The strength of the faith lies in these elemental feelings, in what Theodore Parker calls the "consciousness of immortality." The so-called "proofs" derive all their force from these persuasions. The "evidences" are pretexts, apologies, excuses; the "arguments" are illustrations; they convince none but the already convinced. Christians appeal to the resurrection of Christ. But Paul, the original preacher of the resurrection, writes : "If there be no resurrection of the dead, then is Christ not risen." None but believers in immortality will believe that Christ rose. The belief evidences the evidence ; the fact follows the faith it could not create.

Now, it is not to be denied that in these modern times the belief has been wearing away. Men are not ruled by feeling, as they were. Ours is an age of research and reflection with the few; of absorbing practical activity with the many. Science, a new prophet, lifts up a loud and importunate voice. Chemistry has raised a host of doubts in regard to the existence of an intelligence or soul separate from organization; and there are philosophers who boldly assert that mind is the product of organization. Historical study has shown the groundlessness of the ecclesiastical traditions of the resurrection. Criticism takes away the risen form of Jesus. Temporal activities and worldly interests undermine the foundations and impair the substance of ideal hopes. The devotion to earthly affairs disinclines— yes, disables—the mind, so that it cannot feel at home amid unsubstantial things. The release from the rule of priest and church brings emancipation from the old authorities which upheld the dogma, and the liberated, rebellious people find that they have thrown away the supports they had rested on, and have no independent supports of their own. They have never believed the doctrine for themselves, but have taken it on trust from their religious teachers. They have ceased to take things on trust from their teachers; consequently they have no assurance, and their faith leaves them. They never did truly believe the truth on its merits; now they cannot even say they believe. They never had a personal conviction; now they cannot pretend to have one.

There is a profound skepticism on this subject in our modern society. Of scientific men, some openly avow unbelief in the future life; some decline to say anything about it, as not coming within their province; and some accept without question the dogma of the Church which claims a revelation from God, and the miraculous energy of the Holy Ghost to quicken its own dead. Worldly men, whether of business or pleasure, are thinking of other things, and give the matter little attention. Their faculty of apprehension acts feebly on these sublimated themes, and the great anticipation fades away from their minds. A few hardy philosophers deny immortality to the common herd, who can neither deserve it nor use it, and claim it for the morally great and good, who, having appreciated this life, may advance a respectable title to another.

Thus the popular faith goes on crumbling in pieces. Old arguments are overthrown, or fall by their own weight. The many believe by force of having believed; the few, who are noble and spiritual, believe on grounds purely moral, listening to the prophecy of their higher, rational nature. Some of the more intellectual put the matter aside as of no pressing concern, and say that they are prepared for either result—immortality or annihilation. They are willing to trust the Power that made them. Sure that what is best for them will befall, they await, unanxious, the solution of the mystery. Says Emerson: " Of immortality the soul, when well employed, is incurious. It is so well that it is sure it will be well. It asks no question of the Supreme Power. Immortality will come to such as are fit for it; and he who would be a great soul in the future, must be a great soul now."

The advent of Spiritualism saved the popular belief in immortality from the danger, if not of total, yet of partial eclipse. To the multitude of mankind Spiritualism brought a new revelation; and the eagerness with which it was welcomed, showed the need of it that was felt. Hundreds of thousands—nay, millions, in America and in Europe, in sober England and mercurial France—hailed the promise of communication with rapture. People of every degree and class—the instructed and the uninstructed, toilers and thinkers, mechanics and mathematicians, merchants and men of letters, tradesfolk and philosophers, physicians, lawyers, professors, judges, divines—investigated and embraced it. It met the crying demand for palpable evidence, for substantial and incontrovertible facts. It challenged the experimental method of modern science : it courted skepticism ; it offered proof for tradition, law for miracle, the confirmation of the senses for the dogma of faith. It came to the doubting disciple and said : "Reach hither thy fingers, and behold my hand ; reach forth thy hand, and thrust it into my side, and be not faithless but believing." The Baron de Guldenstubbé, of Paris, attests that more than fifty persons—among whom were barons, princes, counts, colonels, physicians, men of culture, and artists of renown—witnessed again and again the astounding phenomenon of direct communication by writing from invisible beings.

That a belief thus attested and published should have spread like a new gospel of the kingdom, is not wonderful. It would have been wonderful had it not. It was what the world was waiting for. It came as answer to a passionate prayer ; it was the bringing of life and immortality to light that desponding mankind groaned for. The shadowy realm came into view ; the gloomy barriers of the sepulchre disappeared ; the dividing flood was dried up ; voices were heard from the Silent Land ; the bleak waste of the Beyond was lively with happy forms ; dirges changed into songs ; the raiment of mourning fell off. The heart reached out its eager hands once more, and was thankful to embrace something more substantial than a shade. The " family in heaven and earth " was reunited.

That to multitudes Spiritualism has been an unspeakable solace, an unmixed boon and blessing, it is impossible for me to doubt. I have seen the sweet, humanizing effects of it too many times not to be persuaded of them. I have seen it reviving hearts and refreshing homes. How far its benefits have been qualified by the beliefs that have been associated with it, I do not feel called on to determine. Mr. A. J. Davis, a high authority, declares in effect that Spiritualism has abandoned its true mission. Instead of persuading the unbelieving world of the existence of departed spirits, it turns to the spirits and calls on them for oracles and information. It sets up the trance speaker in place of the rational teacher; substitutes the *séance* for the church; drops the old revelation through prophets and apostles, only to promulgate a new one through *mediums ;* discards the literature of Christendom for the " inspirations " of illiterate men and women; and in exchange for the ancient religions of mankind, erects a new religion on ghostly foundations. The mission of Spiritualism, according to Mr. Davis, is to convince people of their immortality. With that its duty began, and when that is done its duty will end. If it would accomplish the purpose for which it was sent into the world, it must retrace its mistaken steps. If it fails to do so, it will not only forsake its calling, but will fasten on the world another superstition in place of the superstitions it is outgrowing, and will alienate from it both men and angels.

To the weighty criticism of Mr. Davis, I, who am but a thoughtful looker-on, shall presume to add nothing. My purpose has been to show some of the many doorways into the immortal life. The mortal certainty does put on immortality. In many forms we surely live again, live eternally and for ever. We cannot die if we would. Death has no dominion over us. We may live in the future as we will, cherishing the hope that most inspires. If we crave personal immortality, the greatest minds and the best hearts of the race countenance our belief in it. If we are unable to entertain that expectation, there remains the other—an immortality of wholesome influence in the race. If that seems cold, vague and bewildering, the knowledge that we may live in the hearts and souls of those who love us, offers a kindling anticipation and a tender promise. From one of these convictions—why not from all?—we can obtain the strength and the consolation we need; can be lifted out of despondency, and saved from the folly of sordid or shameful life. The faith that most dignifies and consoles is the best. That is the noblest conception of immortality that most gloriously animates and irradiates our dust.

XIII

THE VICTORY OVER DEATH.

"The last enemy that shall be destroyed is death."—1 COR. xv. 26

TO the large majority of mankind, whether reflecting or unreflecting, this description of death as the great enemy will seem to be literally true. It is the enemy of whatever in existence is friendliest—of pleasure, of happiness, joy, satisfaction, mirth, affection, success, prosperity, greatness. An old covered bridge at Lucerne, in Switzerland, is decorated with a series of twenty-four pictures, entitled, "The Dance of Death," representing the "king of terrors" as surprising people in their blissful moments. The lover, the lord, the fine lady, the courtier, the prince, the merchant, the reveler, the soldier, each at the most critical moment, is arrested and hurried away from the place of honor or the scene of delight. It was a favorite theme in the Middle Ages. Painter, poet and satirist celebrated this "dance of death" with the grim humor that was characteristic of the superstitious time. Religion kept such scenes faithfully before the people's mind, and the people welcomed them with the ghastly satisfaction which images of horror ever excite.

The dread of death is universal and instinctive; and yet how many rush into its arms! Suicide is a most impressive fact in this connection. The disappointed lover, the discouraged adventurer, the suspected clerk, the child wounded in its self-love or fearful of punishment, faces the great enemy and invites his blow. Every now and then the community is shocked by suicides so unprovoked and so frequent, as almost to persuade us that the natural fear of death is passing away.

The inconsistency is easily explained. Lord Bacon says there is no passion that will not overmaster the terror of death. For passion is thoughtless; occupied wholly with an immediate suffering, it makes no estimate of any other kind of pain; absorbed in an instantaneous sorrow, it takes no other sorrow into account. The mind entertains but one passion at a time, whether it be joy or fear. But men are not always or generally under the influence of passion. Ordinary life is calm, calculating, considerate, and it is to ordinary life that death is terrible.

It is the thought of death that is terrible, not death. Death is gentle, peaceful, painless; instead of bringing suffering, it brings an end of suffering. It is misery's cure. Where death is, agony is not. The processes of death are all friendly. The near aspect of death is gracious.

There is a picture somewhere of a frightful face, livid and ghastly, which the beholder gazes on with horror, and would turn away from, but for a hideous fascination that not only rivets his attention, but draws him closer to it. On approaching the picture the hideousness disappears, and when directly confronted it is not any more seen; the face is the face of an angel. It is a picture of death, and the object of the artist was to impress the idea that the terror of death is in apprehension. Theodore Parker, whose observation of death was very large, has said that he never saw a person of any belief, condition, or experience unwilling to die when the time came; and my own more limited observation confirms the truth of the remark. Death is an ordinance of nature, and like every ordinance of nature is directed by beneficent laws to beneficent ends. What must be, is made welcome. Necessity is beautiful.

But no sweetness of death sweetens the apprehension of death. That, save to the philosophic or enfeebled mind, is seldom otherwise than fearful. Few can contemplate calmly their own dissolution; few look quietly forward to the termination of their friend's existence. To thousands, life is simply an effort to escape from death, to avert or defer the evil hour. Disease loses half its terrors for us when we feel sure it will not prove fatal. Years of sickness, of weakness, of agony, are welcomed in preference to death. Old people who have nothing left either to do or to enjoy, shrink from the thought of dissolution. The sentiment which Shakespeare puts into the mouth of Claudio, in "Measure for Measure," expresses the common feeling of the average of mankind:

> "The weariest and most loathed worldly life
> That age, ache, penury and imprisonment
> Can lay on nature, is a paradise
> To what we fear of death."

The terror is older than the records of mankind, and it has a solemn character that associates it with doom. There is a mystery about death. It seizes on the imagination. Its silence, its secrecy, its unavoidableness, its impartiality, its pitilessness, the absence in it of anything like moral emotion, its refusal to be questioned, the grim irony of its whole procedure, invest it with an awe that is oppressive. There seems to be something behind it; some vast power, conscious yet insensible, endowed with will, but wilful; a gloomy power that nothing can break. All mysteries are summed up in that of death.

" From the globe of black day to the summit of Venus,
    I traversed all the difficulties of the world ;
    Every tie which was fastened around me by deceit and illusion
    Was loosened, except that of death."

This impression of death must have been made late in the experience of the human mind. Ages must have elapsed before it was indelibly stamped there, for it implies the growth of reflection. If we can imagine the time when the human race was hardly distinguishable from the brute creation, we shall perceive that no terror of death could have existed. Man probably had at this epoch no more thought of death than the beast had. Not till he had separated himself by development from the animal creation, and in some respects ranged himself under different laws, could death have seemed a singular or startling event ; and even then the state of violence, warfare and perpetual confusion that prevailed everywhere, must have made all reflection on death impossible.

The usual accompaniments of death concealed its character. Individual men died by the bite of the serpent, the claws of the lion, the hug of the bear, the spring of the panther, the tread of the huge beast, the fall of rocks, the overflow of the flood, the enemy's club or spear. Hunger, thirst, cold, carried them off ; war and famine swept them away by hundreds ; but there was always a visible cause, palpable, usually violent, commonly sudden, and the effect was connected strictly with the cause. Death was associated with a shock of some kind. There were innumerable isolated facts of death, but there was no law or inevitable sequence of death. Death without a weapon that accounted for it was probably unthought of. Of course there were deaths without violence. Women and children died ; but at that period, and for ages on ages after, women and children were of no account. Old men

died ; but not many men lived to be old, and the few who
did were not worth considering. Their death was probably hastened by the violent act of their own people, who
felt that they were a useless incumbrance. Strong men
alone were considered necessary to the stability of the
tribe. Their lives alone were significant ; their fate alone
was interesting.

Not until hunting and war had to some extent ceased
to be the universal pursuits, and something resembling a
condition of peace had begun—not until existence had
fallen into fixed conditions of regular habits, could anything like a sober appreciation of the phenomenon of
death have become possible. Then, at a period in the career of man comparatively recent, centuries on centuries
after the epoch just described, the fact may have broken
on the human mind that death was an event of universal
and inevitable occurrence ; that it came to all alike—came
at all times, under all circumstances, to men, women and
children—came without noise, without weapon or bloodshed—came when no enemy was near, when the wild beast
was driven far off, when the elements were quiet, when
the flood kept its natural channel. Then, for the first
time, the conviction began to gain strength that there was
a POWER OF DEATH. Not yet, however, were these uninstructed people able to conceive of what we call the law
or ordinance of death ; not yet were they able to think of
death without a death bringer, an enemy who killed with
malicious intent. There was no more a visible foe, no
more a distinct foe in each particular instance ; the slayer
was invisible ; moreover, there was but one universal
slayer, one enemy for all mankind, one subtle, diabolical
adversary, who dwelt in the mysterious chambers of the
air, and, invulnerable, unassailable, shot his vengeful arrows into human hearts. Who was this awful avenger?

Who was this remorseless slayer? Why did he slay?
Why did he hate? What had the race done to him that
he should massacre them one by one, never sparing an individual for any cause whatsoever? Could he not be dis-
armed, placated, bought off by gifts? Was no rescue, no
respite possible?

Then we may suppose began the earliest efforts at
emancipation from the dreadful curse. The priest arose,
charged with the duty of making intercession with the
awful destroyer. Altars were built, fires were kindled,
sacrificial knives took the blood of innocent beasts, a perpetual smoke carried aloft to the dwelling place of the
frightful king the gloomy prayers of the crouching multitudes; sorcerers practiced charms, soothsayers muttered
incantations, jugglers practiced magical arts; the whole
apparatus of superstition was called into play to rid the
race of its curse, and procure remission from the destroyer.
Religion scarcely had a purpose distinct from that of
evading the necessity of death.

By the side of the priest stood the physician, with his
herbs and philters, his potations and talismans, trying to
heal the wounds the priest tried to prevent. The priest
and physician were brothers, as they always should be.
Their officers were alike; their purpose was always the
same; they waged the same warfare, in the same interest,
if not with the same weapons or on the same field. Their
common enemy was death, the enemy of the race. Each
to some extent shared the duties of the other. Both were
sacred persons, holy and honored, set apart, maintained at
public cost, endowed with special privileges. The priest
was a physician, the physician was a priest. The priest
had the gift of healing by his touch; the physician had
the gift of expelling evil spirits. Neither could do his
full work without aid from the other. Approaching the

same problem from different sides, they frequently met for exchange of counsel and co-operation of endeavor. At first the priest overtopped the physician, as the office of placating the slayer was more essential than the office of warding off the deadly arrows which still, sooner or later, reached their mark. Gradually the physician acquired equal eminence with the priest, for the priest's intercession was obviously futile. The slayer did not relent; no answer came to the supplication; the darts fell as thickly as ever and were as fatal. Death was unavoidable; but it might be postponed, it might be alleviated, its agony might be mitigated. Men bless the good physician, and well they may. His is still a sacred calling; his is the order of the Holy Ghost. He belongs to an ancient and noble fraternity, a brotherhood which, in all times and places, has been in league against death. Grouped in many schools, practicing many methods, pursuing many lines of study, distinguished by many titles, wearing many badges, equipped with a great variety of arms, they all march under a single banner, the banner on which is inscribed the name of the Prince of Life. Every honest physician is a soldier trained for this great war. His weapons are the plants, the herbs, the minerals; air, light, water, electricity, every remedial force in nature; the vital powers of the frame, the laws of healthful living. With his cunning instruments he repairs injury, cuts away the diseased parts of the body, mends bruises, heals wounds. Faithfully he keeps his post, standing between the living and the doom that threatens life. It is his mission to introduce life safely into the world, to protect it, to come to its rescue when assailed, to mitigate its pains, to ease its conditions, to nurture its powers, to prolong its term. He snatches the little children from the clutches of the dark angel, and gives them back to their mothers; he restores parents to their distressed children; he gives sleep to the restless; he keeps the family circle together; he is the preserver of beauty, and strength, and virtue. But for him the power of death would indeed be felt to be a curse; death would be the great enemy. But the physician gains no victory over death. He baffles it, checks it, arrests it, puts it off, disarms it of its agony, compels it to wait more convenient seasons, makes it respect conditions; but he gains no victory over it. Death, in spite of him, comes to all at last. None escape; none ever will escape. The physician cannot save himself or those dearer to him than himself. It is touching to see how powerless he is to strike the destroyer down. When the fatal hour comes, he that has rescued hundreds cannot rescue his wife, his child; he who has prevented hundreds from falling into the grave, stands by helplessly and sees his only darling slip over the edge and disappear. All the medical science of the century avails nothing to save the best man of the century when his hour arrives; nor can we imagine the time as ever coming when it will.

It is this law, this power, decree, doom of death, that so impresses the imagination of the world. Paul felt this; it was never absent from his mind; it seems to have been the one frightful fact to him in all the universe; it tinged all his thought; it is the key to the secret chambers of his speculation. The simple historical fact, that "death reigned from Adam to Moses, even over them that had not sinned as Adam did," was a fact of tremendous significance in his view. He speaks of the "law of death," of "the ministration of death," of "death as passing on all men." The unavoidableness, the irresistibleness of the experience overwhelmed him. Death to him was not a fact merely; it was a fact with a terrible power behind it; it was a doom, a curse, a penalty. Paul always associates death with sin. Sin is the cause of death. But for sin there would have been no death; for " Sin came into the world and death by sin, and so death passed upon all men, because all had sinned." " The sting of death is sin." The law of death and the law of sin are the same. Sin was the mysterious destroyer. Break his dominion, and death is abolished.

Here comes in the Redeemer's office. He came to break the power of sin, and thus strike a blow at the heart of death. The Christ of Paul was above everything else the sinless man. This was his peculiarity. In this lay his redeeming power. What he may have been as teacher, revealer of truth, reformer, exemplar of righteousness, was of quite secondary import. It was as the sinless man that he saved—saved from death, which was the great salvation. " The first man was of the earth earthy; the second man was the Lord from Heaven." " The first Adam was a living soul, a vital principle; the last Adam was a quickening spirit." " As in Adam all die, even so in Christ shall all be made alive." " As by one man sin entered into the world, and death by sin, and so death passed on all men, because all have sinned; so the grace of God, and the gracious gift through one man, hath abounded unto many." " The law of life in Christ Jesus hath made me free from the law of sin and death." The resurrection of Christ was thus a logical necessity. We may almost say it was a foregone conclusion. In advance of proof, perhaps in advance of trustworthy evidence, it might have been assumed on the strength of the conviction that the Christ was sinless. At all events, the least hint, the faintest rumor, the slightest tradition of a resurrection, would have been sufficient for the apostle's ardent logic. If others believed it on any ground whatever, Paul was ready to accept an opinion that jumped so exactly with his hope.

The sinless man could not die. Christ was sinless, therefore the grave did not hold him. The preaching of the resurrection was, therefore, the great business; that was the heart of the gospel; everything else proceeded from that. The sinless Christ institutes an order of sinless men; the risen Christ establishes a line of risen men. "Now is Christ risen from the dead, and become the first-fruits of them that slept." "Every man in his own order, Christ the first-fruits, afterwards they that are Christ's at his coming." "The sting of death is sin, but thanks be to God who has given us the victory through our Lord Jesus Christ." "If the Spirit of Him that raised up Jesus from the dead dwell in you, He that raised up Christ from the dead shall also quicken *your mortal bodies* by His Spirit that dwelleth within you."

This language is to be read literally. Paul meant exactly what he said, nothing more and nothing less. He meant that believers in Christ were not to die any more; that physical death was for them abolished. If any had already died, they would rise in bodies of light on the morning when the Lord should descend from heaven with a shout and the trumpet's sound; the others would not die at all. "Behold, I show you a mystery; we shall not all sleep the sleep of death, but we shall all be changed, in a moment, in the twinkling of an eye. The trumpet shall sound, and the dead shall be raised incorruptible, and we shall be changed. These corruptible bodies shall put on incorruption, these mortal forms shall put on immortality;" and when all this occurs, "death will be swallowed up in victory." In anticipation of this wonderful transformation, this dropping off of the material covering and unfolding of immaterial forms, the apostle breaks out into rapturous peans of joy; he cannot contain his transport. "O death," he cries, "where is thy sting! O grave,

where is thy victory!" Henceforth none need die; all
may be transfigured. The earth need never again be
opened to receive a lifeless body; the carnal part was to
pass away like an exhalation, and be no more seen. For
a little while the rapture lasted; for a very few years the
small company of men and women who cherished the
apostle's faith, lived as if death had literally "no dominion
over them." Death to them was not

> " So much even as the lifting of a latch ;
>   Only a step into the open air,
>   Out of a tent already luminous,
>   With light that shone through its transparent walls."

The dream did not last long. The laws of nature soon
dispelled the illusion. One by one the company of believers fell asleep; the apostles themselves died and were
buried like the rest; no trumpet sounded, no Lord appeared, no grave gave up its tenant, no forms of light
gleamed in the air. Faith in Christ had no virtue to alter
the physiological conditions of being, to adjust the relations between the human body and its environment, to
prevent the occurrence of accident, to arrest the action of
hereditary disease, to avert the consequences of impru-
dence, ignorance, folly, to render harmless the sudden
blow, the pestilence, the fever, weakening of the blood,
paralysis of the nerves. The constitution of things remained as it had been from the beginning, and gave no
sign of interruption. Death was as inexorable, as impar-
tial, as remorseless as ever; it spared the believer as little
as the unbeliever; it respected the saint no more than the
sinner.

Victory over death, then, was not to be hoped for.
The only victory that might perhaps be achieved, was
victory over the fear of death. To dethrone the king
being impossible, the only feasible attempt was to deprive

him of his terrors. This the church undertook. There
was the sepulchre; but a doorway could be opened out of
it. The dark river still rushed on; but lights could be
set on the further shore. The believer must see corruption, but need not remain in it. Faith in Christ could not
save from death, that was certain; but it could save from
the bitterness of death. The death-bed of the believer
was declared to be soft and downy, his last hours peaceful,
his departure a sweet release, his unconsciousness a pleasant sleep, his final thoughts and experiences happy. Angel
faces were imagined in his chamber; glimpses of the risen
Lord, such as were granted to the early saints, were
promised. Of the "agony, the shroud, the pall, the
breathless darkness and the narrow house," nothing was
said. The teaching was all of the spiritual form that
could not perish—of the risen Saviour, of the waiting
angels, of the "green fields beyond the swelling flood,"
and sunny mansions, and deathless songs, and fadeless
flowers, of crowns and snow-white garments. Nothing
was omitted that might help to make complete the victory
over the ancient terror. The church, through all its
voices, gave lessons of cheer: flutes and dulcimers were
sweet substitutes for the clangor of the last trump.

With a hope like this, Christendom ought to stand on
jubilant feet and welcome death with smiles. It should
count the fear of death a shame and a sin; it should pronounce the natural terror of dissolution an infidelity. Not
once in a year should its Easter day be celebrated; every
day of death should be a glorious Easter; every grave
should be a gateway; every funeral mound a mount
of ascension; a festive hour should be the hour of transfiguration, and it should be greeted with murmurs of
thanksgiving and hymns of praise, by people with radiant
faces and shining robes. The hour of death should be

greeted more joyously than the hour of birth, as the hour
that ushers the immortal being into a cloudless, tearless
world.   And so it would be but for one drawback, one
fatal qualification, less serious to the devout unquestioning
member of the Roman church than to the thoughtful believers of Protestant communions, whose faith is a private
conviction resting on personal experience.   The Romanist
reposes in the assurance of the church; the Protestant
must have the assurance of his heart; for him, therefore,
the qualification I speak of is of the gravest consequence.

The victory was promised to believers only ; to all others
death remained terrible as before, nay, a thousand times
more terrible.   To the unbeliever it was represented as
the awful power that dragged him before his judge for
sentence.   "Afterwards they that are Christ's," said
Paul.   His hope was for none besides.   "When thou
hadst overcome the sharpness of death, thou didst open
the gates of heaven *to all believers,*" said the ancient Te
Deum.   Death to the unbeliever was painted in the most
hideous colors.   To him the last hours were hours of physical and mental agony ; doubt and dread took hold on
him; his bed was a bed of coals; no visions of beauty
dawned on his sight, but ghastly shapes haunted his fancy ;
his chamber was infested with evil spirits, demons glared
at him in the night, imps of hell grinned and gibbered by
his pillow ; he tasted in advance the bitterness of perdition.   It was taken for granted that the death of the unbeliever was horrible; no evidence to the contrary was
admitted.   Priests took the liberty of declaring, against
all proof, that infidels like Voltaire, Rousseau, Paine,
suffered in dying the torments of the damned.   They
knew it ; they could not have died in peace ; all appearances to the contrary must be regarded as deceptive.

Whatever the by-standers may have seen and heard was delusion. The unbelieving heart in its inmost recesses must have known its own condition, must have felt the tooth of the devouring worm.

But who can be sure that he is one of the true believers? There is the terrible question that constantly recurs to reflecting minds, and that makes the apprehension of death more bitter within Christendom than it ever was without. To the natural dread of dissolution is added the unspeakable dread of that which may come after dissolution—the fear of perdition for one's friends, if not for one's-self. The thought of death has been made appalling beyond description by this dreadful uncertainty— an uncertainty which weighed most cruelly upon the most conscientious, and most frightfully tormented those who had the best right to peace. Horrible misgivings gathered about the bed-side of the so-called believer. The priest sat by close, trying to extract comforting admissions from the weak, distracted mind—questioning, cross-questioning, taking down words, noting expressions, watching the changing lights in the eye, hanging on the faintest breath, doing all in his power to insure a triumphant passage through the dark valley. The most miserable death-beds have been the death-beds of the saints, whose hearts were tenderest. The callous suffered nothing. The believers had misgivings; the unbelievers went their way untroubled. Few men ever feared the thought of death as the believing, devoted, excellent Cowper did, and his experience was by no means a peculiar one. Certainly no "infidel" we know of has suffered so. The "qualification" preyed on Cowper's heart. This is the reason why the victory was not won. It was impossible to tell who deserved it, and the fear that one might not deserve it added to the ancient enemy a sting, the poison whereof was deadly and could not be extracted.

Happily, this cause of defeat is now in great measure removed. The "liberal believers" have modified and in some respects completely changed the conditions of successful battle with this formidable foe. The technical belief in Christ is not by them demanded. Immortality is declared to be the common inheritance of mankind, the general privilege of human nature. By virtue of his intelligence, his affection, his moral will, the power of his personality, man is pronounced invulnerable to death. It is contended that being continues precisely as it was before; that individuality persists, that consciousness is uninterrupted, that love easily overleaps the dividing space between one sphere of existence and another; that, in fact, no dividing space exists; that death is but a change of form, affecting outward conditions merely—a change which, so far from being a shock, a convulsion, is a process in the orderly growth of the spiritual being. The terrors of the world beyond are also abolished, the abyss of hell is covered up, the vengeful demons have disappeared, the flames are quenched, the instruments of torture are laid by, the burning sandy wastes are reclaimed and converted into delicious gardens. Where the devils lurked, the angels wander; where the damned writhed in agony, the children play; the heavenly Jerusalem covers the whole plain of the hereafter.

To all who believe thus—and the number of them is increasing day by day—death is virtually abolished. The grave is filled up and planted with flowers; the hour of departure is the hour of release, the hour of new birth, hour of freedom, of expansion, of joy, hour of answer to life's question, of reward for life's labor, of fruition to life's hope, of achievement to life's endeavor, of deliverance from life's burden and sorrow. To these the old conflict is over, never to be renewed.

> " This is the bud of being, the dim dawn,
> The twilight of our day, the vestibule.
> Life's theatre as yet is shut, and Death,
> Strong Death, alone can heave the massy bar,
> And make us embryos of existence free."

All this time physiology has been busy undermining the foundations of the old fear. With its fine instrument, science, with its unerring method, it has made its careful approaches and drawn its firm parallels, till at length the citadel has been forced to surrender. Reason tells us that death is an ordinance of nature, an institution of the organic world, a provision of Providence; inevitable because beneficent; inevitable as the development of life on the planet is inevitable; admirable as the order of the world is admirable. It has its place along with those indispensable agencies of progress which cannot be altered without unsettling the fundamental plan of creation; it has its mission by the side of the benignant powers that bring creation to its perfection.

When the force that lies concealed in the germ-cell of the human organization is spent, death removes the frame, now serviceable no longer, to the vast laboratory where nature converts the worn-out material of the universe into forms of new use and beauty. The cast-off garments reappear in the beauteous vesture of tree and grass, and flower, and yellow harvest; not an atom of refuse but has its lovely resurrection. When the last scene of existence is ready to close and the play is over, death gives the signal and lets the curtain fall. But for him the tiresome acts would drag on, scene after scene, when the meaning was exhausted; but for him feebleness would continue its useless being, drooping, complaining, whining, wearing out strength and cheerfulness—a burden to itself, an incumbrance to others, a dead weight on all. He dismisses the tired actors and actresses to their rest. Tithonus, beloved of Eos, the dawn, obtained from the gods the boon of immortality on earth; but the foolish boy forgot to ask for the accompanying gift of perpetual youth. His organization wasted and wore out while his years ran on. His immortality was an endless misery. He was, by his own prayer, condemned to the horror of being unable to die.

When space is needed for the new generations that come crowding on, death gently clears the way for them. One generation goes that another may come. The bright, strong children appear, line on line, rank on rank, and enter on their heritage. They bring new eyes for the landscape, new ears for the music, new hands for the work. They break upon the scene with shouts of joy; they swarm over the welcoming earth; they try their bright minds on the old questions; they press their brave hearts against the old experiences. The departure of the old makes their advent possible, gives them room and opportunity. We smile on death when we greet these with smiles; we drop tears of tenderness on the grave when we drop tears of gratitude on the cradle in which these are rocked. The earth is not big enough for all at once.

> " All things that we love and cherish,
>   Like ourselves, must fade and perish;
>   Such is our rude mortal lot,
>   *Love itself would, did they not.*"

It is death that flings open the hospitable doors and bids the crowd of new-comers to the feast of life. That so many laugh and sing; that so many eat the ambrosia of life, and sip its nectar; that, after thousands and tens of thousands of years, the beauty of the world is still new, the order of the world still enchanting, the routine of the world still interesting, the joy of the world still intoxicating, the problem of the world still inviting, the work of the world still engaging; that the experiences of life, though millions of times repeated, do not lose their zest— all this we owe to the benignant ministry of death.

But for death, no gain, no improvement, no endeavor, no progress, no fresh intelligence, no renewed will. For the new search there must be new curiosity; for the new curiosity, new impulse; for the new impulse, new organization. Humanity rolls on in successive waves, one swiftly following another, each pushing further than the last. No single generation secretes the force that is available for all time; it is given in portions to every age in turn. Death marks the pulsations of the heart-beats.

The law of death is thus a law of progress. The beauty of the world demands death for its appreciation; the resources of the world demand death for their development; the beneficence of the world demands death, that it may be shared; the glory of the world demands death, that the myriads of mankind may behold it with freshly wondering eye; the intellectual and moral grandeurs of the world demand death, that they may be perfectly understood; earth and heaven alike demand death. It is the child of the perfect wisdom and the primeval love.

To mortals, death still has its agonies and terrors; but the time will come when the advent of death will be as sweet as its intention. The time is coming when the conditions of life will be better comprehended, and the laws of life be more implicitly obeyed; when children will be more healthfully born and more wisely nurtured, when physical excesses will be diminished, when the secrets of organization will be discovered, and remedies be multiplied for human ills, and rules of prevention be adopted, and liabilities of accident be reduced in number by carefulness, and peace be made between the organization and its environment, and hereditary taints be worked out of the blood.   Then the last enemy will indeed be destroyed; death will be a sleep ; man will

> " So live that when the summons comes to join
>   The innumerable caravan that moves
>   To that mysterious realm where each shall take
>   His chamber in the silent halls of death,
>   He'll go, not like the quarry slave at night,
>   Scourged, to his dungeon, but, sustained and soothed
>   By an unfaltering trust, approach his grave
>   Like one who wraps the drapery of his couch
>   About him, and lies down to pleasant dreams."

Milton Keynes UK
Ingram Content Group UK Ltd.
UKHW010027300124
436936UK00003B/66